MW01093577

THE OTHER FAMILY

THEO BAXTER

INKUBATOR
BOOKS

Published by Inkubator Books
www.inkubatorbooks.com

ISBN (eBook): 978-1-83756-502-3
ISBN (Paperback): 978-1-83756-503-0
ISBN (Hardback): 978-1-83756-504-7

CONTENT WARNING

This book contains scenes that may depict, mention or discuss: pedophilia, sexual abuse and suicide.

1

SAMANTHA

Not again...

Tears were choking me because of how hard I'd cried, but I still mustered the strength to beg, "Please, Dad, don't do this. I need you."

I was standing by the door of his bedroom, frozen in place. He was sitting on his bed. An empty bottle of whiskey sat by his left thigh, and a gun was pressed against his right temple.

I'd come to ask him if he wanted something for lunch since I hadn't seen him the whole morning, but I'd caught him trying to kill himself again.

"You'll be better off without me," he slurred. It was obvious he was intoxicated and in the midst of one of his episodes.

I didn't know what was actually wrong with him because I couldn't ask. He got angry if I tried to bring it up, but from what I could gather from the internet, he was either depressed or crazy. I couldn't blame him if he was feeling sad. I was also struggling with Mom dying, although it was over two years ago that we'd lost her. It was hard to continue life without her.

There was one problem with the theory that he was acting out of grief. He had been like this while Mom was alive as well; it was simply that she knew how to handle him better.

I didn't. *He's going to kill himself.*

"How can you say that?" I cried out. "You're the only family I have."

"I'm nothing. I'm worthless. I need to die. So all of this" – he tapped the gun against his temple – "will stop."

"Are you really going to leave me all alone?" I demanded. "You can't do that to me. I won't make it without you."

Where my father was concerned, I wasn't above using any means necessary to stop him from harming himself. Unfortunately, we had been through all of this before.

He started to cry. "I'm sorry for being like this, Sam. I know you'll be better off without me. I'm just a burden." Once again, he tapped his temple as though trying to repel things from his head.

I knew he wasn't to blame for what he was doing. Whatever affliction he had made him act like that and say those things. I wasn't trained to deal with this. I was just a fifteen-year-old girl who was scared of losing her father. And I most definitely blamed him for drinking instead of asking for help. His mental state always took a turn for the worse when he drank this much.

"No, I won't allow you to do this to yourself, to do this to me." I was adamant. "I need you. I need you to be here for me. I need you to parent me, take care of me."

That only made him close his eyes and cry harder, and the gun wavered.

I used that moment of distraction to take a couple of steps toward him. My goal was to try to take that gun away from him. Since he was fit, a bit grizzled, I knew that would be possible only if he let me.

"You can't leave me, Dad. I haven't finished my training. There's so much you still have to teach me." I took another step forward. "Who will protect me if you abandon me now? What's going to happen to me when you leave me all alone?"

That made him open his eyes, as I was standing in front of him.

"I'm sorry, Sam," he choked out.

"I know, Dad." Very slowly I put my hand over his hand. I could feel the heaviness of the gun underneath his fingers. "Give me the gun, Dad. You're not dying today. You're not giving up," I said softly.

He looked at me, without saying anything, and I knew this was my moment. I wouldn't get another chance because he could quickly bounce back and then spiral even harder, so I had to act while he was calm.

He allowed me to move the gun away, and I sighed with relief. *Another crisis averted.*

Suddenly, my phone started ringing, violently breaking the silence.

My dad's hand jerked uncontrollably, and the gun went off. Sudden sounds were one of his triggers.

The bang was so loud in such a small space that my ears started hurting immediately. I hissed. The slide deeply cut my palm. Blood started pouring out of the cut, but I still held on to the gun. I couldn't lose it now.

The bullet caused only the slightest damage apart from my hand. The slug ended up lodged in the wall.

Refocusing on Dad, I saw that his eyes were completely wide, almost wild. Apparently, what just happened had snapped him out of his state, and now he was horrified that the gun had gone off so close to me, so close to really hurting me. No matter what, he was always very careful when I was around guns.

"Oh my God, Sam, are you hurt?" he asked. "Are you in pain?"

He tried to look at it, but I wouldn't let him. I had to take care of the gun first. I also wanted to snap at him. Of course I was hurt. And I was furious that he'd once again put me in this situation.

Why can't I be a normal teenager, dealing with teenage stuff, not preventing my father from committing suicide every Saturday?

But as well as the anger, I was also still terrified, adrenaline coursing through my veins because of how close he'd come to killing himself.

In the past I'd managed to stop him by simply catching him wanting to do it. Ashamed, he would stop, promise he would never do it again. However, things definitely changed over time, and it was becoming harder and harder to stop him. *I got lucky.* What if next time I ran out of luck?

I used my other hand to finally grab the gun from his hand. I felt much better once it was completely in my possession.

"Let's get that cleaned up," he said, springing into action, reaching for my injured hand, which was still bleeding at a steady rate. Now that the danger had passed, so to speak, I could definitely feel how much it was hurting me.

"I got it," I replied, moving away from him. I ignored the pained expression on his face. He'd brought it on himself as far as I was concerned. *Acting like a crazy person, wanting to kill himself, leaving me all alone,* I thought and found myself getting riled up all over again.

After wiping the blood from the gun with the hem of my shirt, I removed the bullets, then put the gun in the safe and closed it. Unfortunately, I knew that wasn't secure enough considering we both knew the code, which was Mom's birthday. Sadly, I had no idea how to change it. I opened a dresser drawer and placed the bullets inside.

With that settled, I took care of my hand. It was a pretty deep cut, but luckily, it wasn't my dominant hand, so I could manage. Once I cleaned it up and stopped the bleeding, I bandaged it up.

Dad followed me around the house. "I'm so sorry, Sam. I didn't mean for this to happen."

I had turned away from him, removing the first-aid kit from the kitchen table, and I closed my eyes for a bit. That was what he always said. Right before promising that he would never do something like this again. And then he would eventually break that promise.

"I know you are, Dad," I said, continuing with my work. Knowing he felt wrecked and gutted after each episode only made matters worse, not better.

Shortly after that, we heard a car approaching, which wasn't a frequent occurrence, so we went out to investigate. It was a police car. I cursed silently, too late realizing I'd left the house wearing a bloodied shirt. There was no point going back to change. I was sure the officers had a clear view of it.

And I didn't have to wonder why the police were

knocking on our door. Our newest neighbor, Jack, had to have called the cops on us. He'd probably heard the gunshot.

I cursed some more as two police officers exited the car.

The deputies greeted us in that professional, yet cautious kind of way.

My father greeted them before turning to me. "Samantha, you can go back in the house. I'll handle this."

I stayed put. I wasn't leaving him alone after what had just happened.

"What can I do for you, Officers?" my father asked, not even trying to mask the disdain in his voice.

Dad didn't have what one would call a good experience with law enforcement. He was of a mind that they usually caused more damage than good.

Mom had died in a traffic accident when a drunk driver hit her, but the police still tried to find ways to pin it on Dad. They were unsuccessful, of course, since he didn't have anything to do with it. And that wasn't the only example, so I learned to be wary as well. It was always prudent to be careful around people who wore badges and guns.

"We got a call suggesting shots were fired at this address."

"It was one shot," my father corrected. "It was an accident. It misfired while I was cleaning it."

I winced inwardly. I really wished he'd have used a different lie because he didn't look like he was capable of doing anything at that moment, let alone cleaning firearms.

"The new neighbor overreacted perhaps. He's not accustomed to our ways. It was an accident as my dad said." I backed him up just to be on the safe side.

The deputies refocused on me, and I put my injured

hand behind my back. Unfortunately, there was nothing I could do with my bloody shirt.

"What happened to you?" one of them asked.

I gritted my teeth. "I cut my hand washing the dishes."

The lies are piling up.

The other deputy smirked. "You're both pretty clumsy today."

I'd been afraid they might not believe us. All the same, I stood my ground and ignored his comment as though not bothered by it.

"Well, if that's all, I won't keep you here any longer," my father said, clearly trying to get rid of them.

"Do you mind if we look around? Just to do our due diligence," the same deputy said.

Dad nodded, although it was obvious how displeased he was.

I opened the front door and gestured inside, too late realizing I'd used my injured hand. I wanted them out of our house, away from our property as fast as possible. I didn't want them snooping around because if they saw something they didn't like, then my father would be in trouble. He was having enough troubles in his life.

"Tell me, Mr. Cotton, what do you do for a living?" the first deputy asked.

"I'm retired," my father explained. "Military."

He'd tried to get a proper job after retiring, but he couldn't keep one even if his life depended on it. His health prevented him from operating like a normal human being. So most days he worked as a mechanic.

As we all chatted like we were friends, they snooped around, and I knew what they were seeing. At times I was pretty ashamed of how I lived. The house was a mess.

I did my best to clean, but it wasn't always easy. Ever since Mom died, Dad had started behaving strangely, differently, and slowly I realized he was turning into a hoarder. There was drama each time I tried to throw something out, so I gave up. And now, with the police milling about, I wished I had tried harder. I didn't want them to get the wrong impression of us.

Then again, all the empty whiskey bottles and rifles scattered around didn't help. I mentally groaned that I hadn't had the time to hide them.

Dad had built a special cabinet where we were meant to keep all of the guns, but he liked to have them out, at the ready, just in case.

Maybe this will work in our favor, I thought. This way it really looked like Dad was cleaning his guns.

"Do you have permits for this arsenal?" one of the deputies asked.

"Yes, of course. They're in that cabinet," he said and pointed.

The deputy allowed him to go and get them before handing them to him. The deputy skimmed through all the papers before looking at his partner. I didn't like that look one bit.

"We would like you to come with us to the station, simply to clarify all of this."

"Why would I do that? I didn't do anything wrong," my father rebelled. "I already explained what happened. It was an accident. And you can see all my permits and licenses are up to date," he continued, starting to get agitated.

As they started to argue, I slipped out of the house and ran to our other neighbor's house. I wanted to see Billy, not the asshole who called the police on us. Billy Meeks was Dad's best friend. If anyone could help us get out of this mess, it was him. He was level-headed and smart.

I rushed inside without knocking. I found Billy in the living room, watching TV. He turned in his wheelchair. "What's happened, Sam?"

"The cops are at our place, and they want to take Dad away," I said, a bit out of breath.

"Because of the shot that was fired?" he guessed.

I nodded.

"Let's go," he said.

We returned to my house just in time to see Dad being taken away in handcuffs.

"I didn't do anything," Dad protested, defending himself.

"Why are you taking him away?" Billy demanded.

"For disturbing the peace," one of the cops replied.

That was such a bullshit charge, and we were all aware of it.

"You should come with us, too," the other deputy said to me.

"She's staying here with me and my wife." Billy was adamant. "And I'll follow you, so don't worry about anything," he added to my father.

That calmed him down a little.

"I'm sorry, Sam," Dad said.

I knew he wasn't apologizing for this mess, but for what he'd tried to do earlier.

"I'll be all right, Dad."

Hearing that, he calmed down a little more and allowed those bullies to push him into the police car.

Once again, I started crying. I was overwhelmed by a

great sadness. Sadness for what was happening to my father, for how those men were treating him as though he were a criminal.

And sadness because I had a feeling this was far from over.

2

SAMANTHA

Billy, his wife, Emily, and I sat around the table in their kitchen as Billy told us what had happened at the police station.

Dad had gotten so angry and agitated at being there, away from his home, from me, that he caused a scene. Instead of locking him up, the sheriff did something even more devious. He called the doctors, and they decided to put my dad on a psychiatric hold. They also filed a report to Child Protection Services.

As Billy spoke, I couldn't stop biting my nails. I was extremely worried about Dad. I was also worried about myself. I had no idea what would happen to me. I didn't want to be taken away. CPS could do that, at least temporarily, because Billy wasn't a relative.

At the same time, part of me was relieved Dad was in the hospital, because that meant he wouldn't be able to hurt himself. He wouldn't be able to drink alcohol either, and who knew, perhaps this would be the wake-up call he needed to turn things around and get better. At least that was the hope.

"I know this is a lot to take in." Billy's voice snapped me from my thoughts. "How are you doing, Sam?"

"I'm fine," I said without thinking, which was my typical knee-jerk response to such a question.

Show no weakness; show no fear, Dad always said during our training sessions, and that stuck with me in other aspects of life as well. Life was a battlefield, after all.

"You can be honest with us, honey," Emily said, patting my hand. "We love you and your dad as though you're family."

And to be truthful, the sentiments were completely mutual. It was just that I wasn't used to talking about my feelings. I only used to do that with Mom, and when she died, I simply shut down. I tried to not only stop talking about feelings but also to refuse to have them at all. Life was easier that way. But right now? The walls I'd built inside myself were definitely tumbling down.

I sighed. "I hate they took Dad away and locked him up in a crazy house."

I was angry. I had half a mind to go to Jack's house and egg it because his stupidity was what caused this mess in the first place. If he hadn't overreacted and called the cops over nothing, then none of this would have happened.

"But?" Billy urged.

"I know I can't complain about it, knowing that's probably what he needs at the moment, to stay alive," I confessed. A tear fell down my cheek, and I quickly wiped it off.

Emily squeezed my hand in silent support, and I squeezed it back. I appreciated having them in my life. I wouldn't know what to do if I was alone.

"What happened today, Sam?" Billy asked.

I remained quiet. I didn't want to tell them Dad had tried to kill himself again. I felt ashamed.

"When I heard the shot, I figured you were practicing, like usual," he added.

I shook my head. "I don't know what happened. Last night everything was perfect. We cooked together, he made me laugh with some stories from his youth, but then this morning he wouldn't come out of his room. Something must have triggered him because the next thing I knew, he was sitting in the bedroom with his favorite gun pressed against his head."

"Oh, honey," Emily said, getting up so she could hug me.

"Was he drinking?" Billy asked.

I nodded.

He cursed, shaking his head.

"No girl needs to see her father in such a state," Emily said, releasing me.

"True," Billy grumbled.

"I just wish I knew what happened. Did I do something to upset him?" I said, expressing my concern.

"This isn't your fault, Sam." Billy's voice was firm. "Your father fights a lot of demons."

"I try to understand, but I don't. He doesn't want to talk about it, and it makes me so frustrated, so confused."

"It's not simply one thing," Billy said. "Remember, we were professional soldiers for twenty years, a career most of our brothers don't live to achieve. However" – he paused, then looked at Emily as if for permission, and at her nod, he continued – "I think I know when and how it all started."

"What happened?" I probed, eager to hear something, anything, about Dad and the troubles that plagued him.

During his episodes, he would scream all kinds of things, like *there's so much blood, take her away, save her, no, not her.* I never understood what any of it meant.

"Our unit was called to provide security for a humanitarian group that was bringing medical supplies to the war zone," Billy said, his tone serious and reflective. "We came to this village, only to realize we were too late. The insurgents already went through it. They'd killed the entire village. Not just men, but women and children as well."

Oh my God, that's horrible.

"Your dad searched each house thoroughly, hoping he would find someone who'd survived. That was when he stumbled onto the nursery where all the children had been executed."

I gasped. Although I tried, I couldn't stop my brain from picturing that scene. Immediately, I was so heartbroken that the people I loved had to see something like that, that they had no choice but to go through it.

Billy continued, "We were all pretty shaken by that sight, by the savagery of it all. Your father really took it to heart because at the time your mother was pregnant with you. Something changed in him that day, and he made it his life's mission to find those responsible and kill them. And each time he failed, each time he reached a dead end, it chipped away a piece of his heart."

"That's horrible," I managed to say, although I was still reeling from shock. I was so sorry that those people, those children had died so brutally, and that Billy and Dad had to carry this awful guilt for not being able to help them.

"It was. And the worst part is that things like that are still happening to this very day."

I felt a surge of gratitude toward Billy. This revelation

helped me understand Dad and his struggles a little better. It was obvious that he was still traumatized by what he'd seen. He drank excessively, he had nightmares, and he'd even tried to kill himself a few times.

But there was one thing that still eluded me. "Why did Dad never seek treatment if what happened to you all bothered him that much?"

"You have to understand, Sam, we were raised in a different time. It was considered a weakness to ask for help. It was something to be ashamed of, and in our world of the military, you were ostracized if you ever admitted mental health problems."

"Well, now he will have to admit them," I said, making a face. He was in the hospital now, so he would get help whether he liked it or not.

"Perhaps this arrest could be good for him," Billy agreed, although he still looked a bit uncomfortable.

It was on the tip of my tongue to ask him how come he was so put together while my father was so messed up, but I didn't. Part of me was afraid I wouldn't like the answer; the other part didn't want to be disrespectful. That would be prying, and I shouldn't pry, considering Billy hadn't volunteered any personal information.

"It can't get any worse," I replied with a small shrug. As far as I was concerned, Dad had hit rock bottom, and if he needed doctors to push him back up, then so be it.

I yawned. I hadn't realized how tired I was.

"I'll prepare the couch for you," Emily said, getting up.

"That's okay. I can sleep in my own bed," I said, not wanting to trouble her.

Billy raised an eyebrow. "Actually, the sheriff's department has your house under investigation. You can't go home until they're done."

After everything, I couldn't even go home. All my things, my clothes and my books, were in my room. How was I going to live without them?

"Don't worry, honey, you can stay with us as long as it takes," Emily reassured me, misunderstanding the horrified expression on my face.

"I'm not worried about that," I blurted before I could stop myself, and that was true. Although it was a huge inconvenience, it wasn't at the top of my list of things to stress about.

"Then what are you worried about?" Billy asked, picking up on the subtleties in my voice.

"I'm worried about speaking to the police and the social workers." I knew I'd be questioned by all of them, that was how the system worked, and I didn't want to get Dad in trouble.

"We have your back," Billy reassured me.

"Thanks," I said, remembering my manners.

"Can I ask you something else?" Billy said cautiously after Emily left the room to sort me out a bed.

I braced myself but nodded.

"How do you feel with him gone?"

I sighed. "I really don't know," I said honestly. On one hand, I was terrified the doctors would lock him up for good, and I didn't want to lose him. On the other, he wasn't well, so maybe he should be locked up until he got better.

Since Mom died, he hadn't been up to the task of being a father, or anything else for that matter. The only time he showed any interest or enthusiasm was during my training.

The worst part was that I knew he was doing his best to

prepare me to survive in this harsh world that would only get harsher in the future, but the most selfish part of me felt tired of everything. Of feeling like this. I wanted to be someplace quiet and healthy for a change.

I wished I were simply the kid, and he were the parent, because since Mom died, the roles definitely felt reversed. And as much as I loved him, I couldn't continue taking care of him, being the grown-up around here, because burning the candle at both ends would kill me.

I really miss Mom.

"Do you think you would benefit if you went to see a therapist?" Billy asked.

I was surprised at his question, because Billy was like Dad in many ways. He didn't trust the police or the government either. So talking with a stranger, someone who wasn't part of the family, about the deepest most intimate parts of one's life was a huge no-no for him as well.

All the same, I gave it some thought. And I had to admit, if only to myself, how scared I was. I was my father's daughter, after all, and I had been taught from an early age that I could only rely on a small group of people in this life.

"I'm not sure," I replied eventually, hoping he wouldn't press.

As though he could read my mind, Billy nodded. "No pressure, honey. I just want you to know that it's an option if you see fit," he said kindly.

Emily returned. "You're not alone, sweetheart," she said, giving me another warm hug. "We're here, and we'll sort this mess out together."

I had to fight back tears because that was exactly how I'd felt since they took Dad away, as though I'd been left completely alone, without a certain course of action to take.

But now, knowing I wouldn't have to deal with it on my own helped a lot.

"Thank you, guys, I really appreciate it."

"Don't mention it. That's what family's for."

"The couch is ready," Emily said. "You can go to sleep now if you want to."

I nodded, wishing them goodnight.

Despite their kind words, I was still worried. I tossed and turned all night on that squashy couch; I couldn't sleep a wink, thinking about my impending doom.

What if they don't let Dad out? What if I say the wrong thing to a social worker and they take me away from him? I stopped myself there. I couldn't even think about something so horrific.

They had to let him go. He had to return home. He had to.

3

JESSE

A fucking useless piece of shit with a scrambled brain. That was all I was.

At times it was really hard to focus. It was even harder stopping all the horrible images and catastrophic thoughts that were penetrating my mind.

At times it was so difficult navigating through it all that I felt like I was drowning.

At times there was nothing but darkness around me, and the only light I could find was at the end of the barrel of a gun.

Shit.

I couldn't believe I almost blew my brains out in front of Sam. As though that kid hadn't been through enough already. If I had actually managed to go through with it, Katarina would've never forgiven me. She would haunt me forever in the afterlife for traumatizing our baby girl.

Hurting Sam was the last thing I wanted to do, yet I kept doing it. I was a total piece of shit. But luckily, I had no time for self-pity at the moment.

Although I hadn't committed any crime, the police were treating me as though I were a criminal. I knew they felt threatened by me, by what I believed. However, that wasn't my problem. Under the law they swore to uphold and protect, there were no differences between us. I was just another citizen – paying my taxes and staying out of trouble.

Unfortunately, that wasn't enough. Since I refused to conform, be like all the rest of the sheep, I was deemed a troublemaker.

And mentioning I was a war veteran only made matters worse, because that made me a troublemaker with skills. As far as the rest of humanity was concerned, we were nothing but a bunch of basket cases once we returned from war.

People liked to think they were grateful for all we did, for the fact we fought in wars to ensure their peace and stability. But as I'd learned all too well, that only applied if we had the decency to die in said wars. If we survived and returned home, we stopped being heroes. We became men who should be avoided, ostracized, and pitied.

Not that people were completely wrong. It's true, we *should* be feared because being up close to so much evil and being confronted with the worst parts of humanity definitely did something to a person, it damaged the soul, and that was something none of us could ever recover from.

The police teamed up against me, trying to destroy me, although I never did anything to any of them. Billy did his best to bring some reason to the situation, to help out. Sadly, it was too late. They had already decided I needed to be locked up. However, to my utmost horror, I didn't end up in jail.

I was taken to a psychiatric facility.

I was locked up in a loony bin for seventy-two hours for

observation because they deemed me a threat, a menace to society and to myself.

They had every right to lock me up, although I hated it. It was what I deserved for being so weak, succumbing to my darkness, and almost killing myself in front of Sam. How could I even think of putting her through something like that? She deserved better.

I knew I was far from perfect. All the same, Sam was my daughter, and nobody could love her, protect her, take care of her as well as I could. I'd promised Katarina I would protect our daughter with my life.

Are you sure you're the best for her?

I banished that last thought.

I hoped I hadn't scared Sam too much. She was a tough kid; I was aware of that. I was so proud of the person she was becoming; however, I was terrified that my madness would rub off on her. That it would damage her beyond repair.

I'll find a way to make it up to her.

For that to happen, I had to get out of this place. After the seventy-two-hour period, they had no right to keep me if everything was all right with me. That was a big if. I had to convince a bunch of doctors I was okay. *Piece of cake.*

So instead of acting out, succumbing to the rage I was feeling, or dwelling on the fact I'd almost killed myself, I did everything that was asked of me. I ate, drank, and slept normally, or at least pretended to sleep when the lights went off.

I didn't mention my suicidal tendencies, PTSD, anxiety, and nightmares. Instead, I did my best to mask my sickness because I knew that if I showed them the real me, they would keep me there indefinitely, and that was something I couldn't allow. I had to return home to Sam. That was all that mattered to me.

Although part of me recognized that this was probably the place I belonged, the rest fought like hell to get out because my daughter needed me. I did my best, but still there was a moment when I came pretty close to losing my temper.

It happened when the shrink mentioned Katarina. All he did was ask if I felt guilty that she died, and that triggered me.

I wasn't with her in the car that day. I wasn't the drunk asshole who slammed into her car, pushing her off the road. I was the drunk asshole who stayed home, feeling sorry for myself, as usual, which meant Katarina had to pick Sam up from school.

So, yeah, I did blame myself for her death because if I hadn't been drunk, if I'd gone instead of her, then she might still be alive. Of course I didn't share any of that with the shrink. I simply shook my head because, no, I didn't blame myself for what happened to her, I lied.

They tried to drug me on top of everything else, so each time they gave me tranquilizers, I spat them out when nobody was looking.

I was aware the doctors knew something was wrong with me despite my best efforts to convince them otherwise. They tried to force me to speak about my traumas, but I remained tight-lipped and faked ignorance. I couldn't let anyone in on the stuff inside my head. I would never have been able to return to Sam if they'd known how broken I was.

Every time one of the doctors came to check on me, I would ask about Sam. I was desperate to speak with her – to hear her voice, find out how she was doing. At last, given that

I'd acted like an exemplary patient, I was allowed to phone her.

Unfortunately, that phone call was brief, and there was someone standing over my shoulder throughout the entire conversation, which meant I had to choose my words with care. All the same, it was so good to hear her voice. I reassured her I was completely fine and promised I would be home soon.

I spent a remarkably boring weekend in the hospital. There was nothing for me to do but think about my life and all the wrong decisions I'd made that had led me down this path.

I have to stop drinking. I knew that. But drinking was the only way I knew how to silence the voices in my head and banish the images plaguing me.

All the same, it was more than obvious I had to make some changes in my life. Like I said, Sam deserved better. I had to fix my head somehow. I had no idea how, but I was determined.

I recognized the irony of the situation, being surrounded by doctors who could help me, but I couldn't relent. I would deal with this on my own.

Once the seventy-two hours passed, they had to let me go. I gave them no reason to keep me there.

One of the attendants urged me to accept a referral to a therapist.

My first instinct was to flat-out refuse it, but perhaps that was what I needed. At the same time, the notion of speaking to a stranger about my demons made my skin crawl.

Nonetheless, I accepted the offered card. I told myself I did it simply to humor him.

But I didn't throw it away.

4

SAMANTHA

As I feared, I wasn't only questioned by the sheriff, but by child protective services as well.

This wasn't my first rodeo with them. Living the way we did, being labeled as survivalists, doomsday nutcases, meant that social workers would come around from time to time. They tried, but they never managed to take me away from my parents in the past.

Mom and Dad had trained me how to handle government people, but it was still nerve-racking because I constantly worried that I would say the wrong thing. I didn't want to get Dad in even more trouble than he already was.

This time, not only was I questioned, but I was stuck at Billy's house. Billy and Emily were great people, and they went out of their way to make me feel comfortable and welcome, but it still irritated me that I couldn't go back to my house just because the sheriff wanted to snoop around.

I snuck inside to grab some of my things, but I ended up stumbling into a bunch of cops milling around.

"What are you doing here, kid?" a deputy asked. He had a beer gut so big I was sure he couldn't tie his own shoelaces.

"I live here," I snapped.

"You can't be here," he snapped back.

"I need some clean clothes and books for school."

"This place is off-limits. Sorry." It was more than obvious he wasn't sorry at all.

Cursing under my breath, I returned to Billy and Emily's and marched into the living room.

"What happened, Sam?" Emily asked.

I shook my head, trying to dispel the curse-laden exclamations that I couldn't say out loud. "They wouldn't let me get my stuff. Why won't they just leave us alone?"

It wasn't like we were doing anything wrong, yet they treated us as though we were criminals. It was so unfair.

"Society doesn't like those who are different from them," Emily said. "Those who dare to divert from the norm have always been feared and persecuted."

That didn't make me feel better. I didn't want to be feared and persecuted just because I believed in slightly different things than everyone else.

I was a normal girl, who most of the time did normal things. I went to school, tried my best to learn and get good grades, and I hung out with my friends. Unfortunately, I was labeled as different and weird.

"I just want to be left alone to live my life," I stressed. Was that really too much to ask?

Why couldn't my parents be normal or something? *Even being Amish would be better than this.* I instantly felt ashamed of having such thoughts. I was proud my parents had such strong beliefs, that they saw through the propaganda, saw society's decline and recognized all the dangers and found a solution in order to protect our family, to protect me.

"Don't worry, honey. They'll be out of our hair soon enough," Billy said, trying to comfort me.

"How can you be so sure?" I challenged.

"Because they'll have to leave once they find nothing."

I gave him a look. "I think they've already found plenty." They'd found the fallout shelter, the guns, and the training field Dad and I used every day to hone our skills.

Billy chuckled. "Point well taken, but having those things isn't illegal. All the guns are registered, licensed, and everything was built under strict codes."

"Are you sure?" I asked. It wasn't that I didn't trust Dad. It was simply that I knew how easily he got distracted by his demons. So there was a chance he'd made a mistake somewhere along the way even if he wasn't aware of it.

"I'm one hundred percent sure because I helped acquire it all. I helped him build the shelter and the firing range," Billy insisted.

It was good to hear that. All the same, that didn't mean we were out of the woods yet. The police wanted Dad gone, for whatever reason, and I feared they would find a way despite him being innocent. Dad had told me stories from various societies throughout history and what the cops of the time did, so I knew it wasn't beneath them to plant evidence to get what they wanted.

While I was fuming, a phone started ringing.

Billy called out to me a few moments later.

I went to the kitchen to see what he wanted. "Yes?"

He held up the phone. "It's your dad."

I rushed to answer. "Dad?"

"Hi, Sam," he greeted me. He sounded well, like himself, if a little sad.

"Are you all right?"

"I'm out of the hospital," he reassured me.

"They let you go?" I couldn't hide the surprise in my voice. I'd had my doubts that they would. Although I was happy he was free, I was also slightly nervous although I couldn't explain why.

"They had to," he replied simply.

"Where are you?" I asked.

"I checked myself into a motel for a few days," he explained. "I think that's for the best."

I frowned. "Why? Come home."

I didn't like the idea of him being completely alone in some motel. What if something triggered him and he had a bad episode? *What if he tries to harm himself?*

"I'm drying out from all the booze, Sam. I promise I won't let myself get like that ever again," he added.

I remained silent for a few moments. That put tears in my eyes, and I turned away so Billy wouldn't see me crying. "You've said that before, you know." It was true, and I couldn't help challenging him.

"I know. I know. This time is different. This whole thing has really knocked some sense into me."

"You know, you're such an asshole for scaring me like that," I told him, unable to stop myself. I had so much bottled up inside me that something had to break.

I heard Billy chuckling behind me, but I ignored him. I wasn't trying to be humorous. It really scared me, seeing how close Dad got to actually dying. I would never forgive myself if I didn't manage to save him. And I resented him for putting me in that position.

"I deserved that," Dad muttered, and it was obvious how much my words hurt him.

It seemed he was now prepared to own up to his mistakes instead of getting all defensive and angry. I took that as a good sign.

"I'm sorry for everything, Sam," he continued. "I'm sorry for scaring you, for hurting you. I know I haven't been at my best since your mother died."

I closed my eyes for a moment. It was true that he had spiraled out of control after Mom died, but his issues hadn't started then. He had been battling this since I could remember. I feared if he didn't do anything about it, we would end up in that same spot, the exact same situation as the other day.

"How's your hand?" he asked.

I looked at my palm. I took the bandage off. Although it was healing, the wound still looked red and angry. It was a reminder of what happened the other day. As though I needed one.

"I don't care about my hand, Dad; it's fine. *I'm* fine," I reassured him. I'd hurt myself plenty while training. I could handle a minor wound like this, and he knew that. Despite everything, I knew I couldn't allow the guilt to eat him alive because that could lead him down a very dangerous path. And I needed him better, not worse.

"However, I do care that you tried to kill yourself again," I added, deciding to be completely honest. In the past, after his episodes, I pretended none of it happened, eager to move on. Since then, I realized that sweeping the problem under the rug solved nothing. He needed to be confronted; he needed to know how much some of the things he did were hurting me.

"I'm sorry," he repeated meekly.

"I can't keep going through that with you. I just can't," I said, shaking my head although he couldn't see me.

"I know, I know, and I'll do whatever it takes to not put you through that ever again."

I didn't like how he phrased his commitment to me. It didn't sound like he was promising he'd never do it again. To me it sounded like he would just make sure I wasn't around when he did it. Then again, perhaps I was reading too much into mere words.

"Good," I said, hoping I was wrong about how it sounded.

"I'll do better, you'll see," he replied.

I sighed with relief. "I love you, Dad," I said as tears pooled in my eyes.

"I love you too, kid, with all my heart."

I knew he did. And he was a pretty terrific Dad apart from his episodes, which made me sad. He was so broken, and I felt powerless because I had no idea how to help him, fix him, save him. Then again, if Mom never managed to do it, what chance did I have? I was only a kid.

We hung up after that.

Without saying anything to Billy, I went to the living room and lay down.

I couldn't stop thinking about Dad. Although he'd said all the right things, I was still really worried. I knew he wanted to be better. I knew he never wanted to go through something like that again. I knew he never wanted to put me through it either.

Nevertheless, wishes alone weren't enough. Empty promises weren't enough to prevent him from getting triggered again. The right words wouldn't stop him having another episode.

Will he be able to sober up this time around? Will it make any difference? I wondered.

I realized I wasn't about to hold my breath, and that made me almost sadder than I've ever been...

5

SAMANTHA

Dad called Billy to let us know he was all right, still off the booze, and I had to admit, I felt ashamed for doubting him. It was obvious how much he was trying to be better. So that this time around he could stay clean and sane. My dad was stronger than our misfortunes, stronger than all his demons. Things would be different this time, I dared to hope.

He wasn't pleased when he learned he couldn't return home. I could hear him raging over the phone as he spoke with Billy. However, I found that to be a perfectly normal response to injustice.

Billy asked Dad to drop by the house for a barbecue. Barbecue and beer were magic words that always cheered Dad up, so he agreed. I made sure Emily bought that alcohol-free stuff for Dad. I didn't want him tempted in any way.

I felt nervous while I waited for him to arrive. And I couldn't understand why. It wasn't like I hadn't seen him in ages. Only a few days had passed since his episode. I was sure he hadn't changed that much. He would still be the same old Dad. It was just that I needed to see him to confirm that.

I looked down the road, expecting to see him. And then I remembered that his truck was still parked in our yard. They'd taken him away in the police car, so I had no idea how he planned on coming back. It wasn't like we had a bus stop in front of our house.

As I was sitting there wondering why I hadn't thought of that before, a red pickup that had definitely seen better days stopped in front of Billy's house.

My dad got out of the truck, thanking the driver for the ride before it moved along.

"Dad," I yelled, rushing toward him.

He smiled, opening his arms.

I jumped into his embrace, hugging him tightly. I wasn't even aware how much pressure and stress I'd been feeling up until that moment when it all suddenly went away.

"I missed you, kiddo."

"I missed you too," I mumbled since my face was pressed into his body. His smell was comforting.

"I was so worried," I said, pulling my head ever so slowly upward so I could look up at him.

"I'm back," he reassured me, "and everything's gonna be all right now."

I really wished I could believe that. I wanted to believe that with all my heart. It was just that the social worker was still pestering me, and the police officers were refusing to leave us alone.

Then again, perhaps they would all back away now when they saw my father walking about, fully functioning.

"Can you tell the sheriff to get the hell out of our house?" I asked hopefully.

"I planned on having that chat with him as soon as possible," Dad grumbled.

I saw a glint of something dark and menacing in his eyes for the briefest of moments, and I hoped Dad wouldn't lose his temper. That wouldn't work in our favor.

"Let's go to the back," I urged him. "Billy and Emily are waiting for us there."

I knew the only reason they hadn't come to the front to greet Dad was because they wanted to give us some privacy to greet one another.

"I'm starving," Dad complained in a teasing tone, but then he winced when he saw my bandaged palm.

I cursed inwardly. It didn't even hurt anymore. It was just that Emily put some salve on it so it would heal quicker, and that needed to be protected.

"I'm so sorry for hurting you, Sam," he said, taking my hand and kissing the bandaged palm.

"I'm fine, Dad," I said quickly to reassure him. "And I'll continue to be fine as long as you don't try to hurt yourself again."

He looked away. This wasn't easy on him, I knew that. Then again, it was no picnic for me either.

"I'll do better," he said with conviction as he looked me in the eyes. "I'll do a lot better from now on, and I'll never put either one of us in such a position again."

I believed him. I said as much. "Let's go eat now," I added.

He simply nodded.

Billy and Emily greeted Dad as soon as we came to the back of the house. I always liked to watch Dad interact with Billy; it was obvious they had been friends for a long time.

"Where's that food you promised me?" Dad asked jokingly.

"I have a steak with your name on it, right there." Billy pointed.

Dad made as if to run over to the grill to collect his food.

It was always good to see him in between his episodes when his true character, the one that wasn't burdened by all the demons inside his head, was evident.

The afternoon went by fast. We sat on the back porch and ate our barbecued meats and salads with gusto, pleasantly chitchatting. Sadly, part of me knew that this atmosphere wasn't going to last.

And I was right.

Once we ate every crumb of Emily's delicious cheesecake, Billy looked at Dad with concern. "Now that I've fed you, do want to tell me what really happened that started this mess?"

Dad hesitated. And I didn't like that, although it was understandable. He was ashamed of what happened. So it was hard to admit it, especially to people he considered family.

"I know it was no accident," Billy added.

Dad sighed, looking down. "I was thinking of Katarina," he said, and there was a rare kind of smile on his face, a smile reserved for my mother alone. "It was the anniversary of our first date. I remembered that day, feeling very excited and nervous when she finally agreed to go out with me."

He shook his head, the smile fading. "I started missing her like crazy, I started drinking, and the next thing I knew, I was spiraling out of control, drowning in all this ugliness inside my head, all the dark thoughts that I couldn't escape.

And that was when Sam found me." His face showed how much he was tormented by that event.

Although my heart was breaking for him, I was proud as well because he was here, talking about it, not hiding in some room, drinking. That was definitely progress.

"We've been all through that," Billy tried to reassure him. "I can't even remember how many times Emily had to bring me back from that same place, especially after losing my legs."

"I'm really sorry for putting you through it," Dad said, looking at his best friend before his eyes found the rest of us as well.

"We're all worried about you," Billy pointed out. "And this has showed us that something needs to change."

"I'm worried about me too," Dad tried to joke, but nobody laughed. That sobered him up. "I know something has to change; that's why I'm thinking about seeing a therapist." He put a business card on the table.

I glanced at it. *Dr. Amanda Sheldon.*

Will he go through with it?

"She's an ex-army doc who helps vets," he added.

Billy nodded as though that made a huge difference for him. "How did you hear of her?"

"An attendant from the hospital gave me her details," he explained.

So, although they couldn't keep him, they knew something was troubling him, I thought.

"I think that's a good idea," Billy said eventually.

"Would you ever consider going to a head doctor?" Dad asked him.

Billy stirred in his chair. It was obvious that the question caught him off guard, making him uncomfortable. "No, not really."

"But you think I should?" Dad challenged.

Billy gave him a look. "I've never put a gun against my head in front of my daughter."

Dad gritted his teeth, and I was really worried he would explode.

"I think going to therapy is a great idea," I said, trying to be supportive. "You should definitely do it. I'll go with you if you want me to."

"Thanks, Sam. I'm not sure yet. I need some time to think about it."

"What's there to think about?" I asked. In my mind, the situation was pretty simple. He needed help, and this was a great way to get it.

He shook his head. "It's just the notion of talking about what Billy and I went through to a stranger..." He trailed off.

I understood the gist of his fears. Being so vulnerable made his skin crawl. "You said she was a soldier too, so I'm sure she'll understand."

"We'll see," Dad said as though ready to finish this conversation.

"You need to figure this one out, brother, and fast, for your sake and Sam's," Billy pointed out, as though that wasn't painfully obvious already.

"I know, I know."

"In the meantime, I think that Sam should stay with us," Billy suggested.

My first instinct was to argue, and by the look of it, Dad wanted to as well. We needed to stay together. He needed me, and I needed him.

Something stopped me from speaking out.

"I would never hurt her, if that's what you're worried about," Dad said, clearly getting angry.

"We all know that, Jesse." Emily spoke up for the first time. "We simply believe that it would be for the best for the time being."

And why couldn't he stay here as well? I thought. Still, I already knew the answer to that; it was because Billy and Emily only had one spare bed – the couch I was using.

"Do you want to stay here or come to the motel with me?" Dad asked me.

I panicked for a moment, feeling like he'd put me on the spot. I didn't want to hurt his feelings, but I did want to stay. How to say that without sounding like a horrible daughter?

He took my hand, my good hand. "Are you afraid of me now?" he asked.

"Of course not," I reassured him instantly, squeezing his hand, allowing him to see the truth in my eyes. "I only want you to get better. I need you to get better."

"You must hate me for what I did," he said, closing his eyes.

"I could never hate you, Dad. And I'm not mad at you or scared of you or anything. I love you."

He opened his eyes, and I could see tears in them.

"I love you too, kiddo."

I sighed, gathering the courage to say the next part the right way. "I'm scared you might do something to yourself during one of your episodes, especially if I'm not there to stop you. You need to start taking care of yourself. So don't worry so much about me, and focus on yourself."

"I'll always worry about you, Sam. I'm your father, after all. I held you in my arms minutes after you were born. You're everything to me."

Hearing that almost broke me down, and it was hard holding back the tears that misted my eyes. "Then get better, for me," I pleaded.

He nodded. "Then it's settled. You'll stay here so I can show you how serious I am about getting better."

I was relieved he understood everything we were trying to tell him.

I reassured him one more time that I was all right as we hugged goodbye.

It felt strange to see him walk away from me like this, but we both understood it was something that needed to be done.

6

SAMANTHA

Billy and Emily provided stability in my life while I was living apart from Dad. The good thing was that he wasn't so far anymore, and I could go and visit him any time I wanted.

I worried he would start drinking again because he was frustrated that he couldn't return home and I was at Billy's. However, I hadn't seen him drunk, not once. So even if he drank a beer here or there, he was keeping it under control.

In the meantime, Billy and Emily made sure I kept up with my exercises and self-defense practices, did my home-work, ate properly, and got eight hours of sleep. They let me be without pestering me or asking unimportant questions. It was a relief they were so easy to get along with, because it made my existence there much more bearable.

This wasn't the first time I'd stayed with them. Dad had suffered similar bad experiences in the past, and while I was younger, I was always sent to their place so I wouldn't have to witness it. But it wasn't as often. Things were definitely different, if not easier while Mom was around to deal with him – and he wasn't having to cope with his grief and mine on top of everything else.

I banished all those thoughts from my head, realizing how useless they were. Tormenting myself about the past and wishing Mom were still here couldn't change anything.

This is my life now, and I had to adapt to it. It was time to move on so Dad could see I wasn't scared to live after what had happened. Besides, I had to have faith and trust Dad could deal with his own issues from now on. And I needed to focus on me. I would be out of high school in the blink of an eye, so I needed to figure out what I wanted to do for the rest of my life.

Going back to school was nerve-racking. Although I missed my friends, I dreaded seeing them because I knew they'd heard all kinds of stories about what had been happening to me.

Luckily the first person I stumbled on was my best friend, Helen. She hugged me tightly. "You're alive," she said theatrically.

"Was there ever a doubt, Hillie?" I asked, with a crooked smile, using my nickname for her.

"Well, you haven't been texting me back. Besides, there's a rumor going around you ended up in jail for shooting your dad."

I always liked that Hillie had no problems telling me absolutely anything without sugarcoating it. She was real when a lot of kids our age tended to be completely fake.

I rolled my eyes. "Are people actually buying that crap?"

"Some," Hillie said diplomatically.

"As you can see, I didn't end up in jail, and I definitely didn't shoot my dad."

"So what happened?" Hillie asked.

"It was just a stupid accident." I tried to brush it off.

Hillie didn't call me out, and I was grateful. I wasn't prepared to share what really happened with anyone, even her.

The other kids asked me all kinds of questions. I knew it was important to stick to the same story I told the police and the social workers: that it was all just an accident and nothing else. I also ditched the bandage to make my wound look less threatening. Since my hand wasn't completely healed yet, I opted for wearing Band-Aids, which spared me a lot of additional questions.

My friends had my back, so I didn't feel as though I was the biggest freak in school, thanks to them. But I still hoped something else would happen in our small town so everybody could move on from me and my father and talk about something else.

But my troubles weren't limited to my classmates. The school counselor wanted to speak to me, and the principal called me for a sit-down. All I wanted was to be left alone, to move on, yet all these people weren't letting me.

From my perspective, they were messing things up, making me feel horrible asking their uncomfortable questions about my family, my dad, and our life at home. I wasn't ashamed to speak about all those things, although at times it tended to get hard, especially talking about Mom. But their reactions to it all were making me feel anxious, confused, and small.

As though it was the police investigator's desire to make my life even harder, make me an even bigger pariah at school, they started pulling me out of class to chat with me. I was angry that the principal was allowing them to harass me during school hours. Unfortunately, there was nothing I could do about it. They had all the power. I was a minor, after all. A minor they thought was in trouble.

Then the principal, a social worker from CPS, and one of the deputies all came together to question me.

"Walk us through the day of the shooting one more time," the deputy said.

I groaned. "I've already told you everything."

"I want to hear it again."

He was hoping I would make a mistake, change a detail, and then that would be the proof he needed I was lying.

I sighed and repeated the same story I'd shared so many times before. I woke up, then did my homework and my chores. I was in the kitchen when the gun fired. It startled me, and I broke a glass, injuring my hand. I kept it pretty simple, without adding too many details.

"Now tell us about your father and the gun."

"For the last time," I said, stressing each word individually, trying not to show that I was losing patience, "it was an accident. Dad was cleaning his gun, and it just went off."

"Was he drinking at the time?" he asked.

"No, of course not," I lied like a pro. Then again, to be fair, he never drank while we trained with guns or while he cleaned them. He was very strict about that. It was drilled into my head to always be careful and to have respect toward firearms because stupidity and recklessness landed people in trouble.

"Samantha, we saw all the empty bottles. We know your father is an alcoholic. And alcohol and that much firepower is a very dangerous combination."

I just stared at him.

"Tell us the truth about what happened. Did your father drink and then recklessly handle his guns?"

I gritted my teeth. "I'm sick and tired of answering all the same questions over and over. What do you actually want from me?"

"How about being honest for a change? How about trusting us and the fact we're here to help you?"

"You want me to be honest? Here it is. Everything you've done so far is telling me not to trust you. Why do you keep pulling me out of class, asking me all these questions I've already answered? Why do you insist on harassing me? Why do you hate me and my dad? Why won't you just leave me alone? Honestly, it feels like you have some agenda."

The deputy looked at the social worker and then raised his hands as though in supplication. "It wasn't my intention to upset you."

Bullshit, I wanted to say.

"Samantha, we all simply have the best intentions for you."

I snorted. "Then stop pulling me from class. I actually have to be present to be able to pass them. Are we done? May I leave?"

They shared a look. A look I didn't like one bit.

"Yes, for now," the deputy answered.

I didn't have to be told twice. I stormed out of the principal's office, which they'd used for their interrogation.

I didn't like how it was implied I would be seeing them again. This was turning into a real problem, and I had no idea how to solve it.

7

JESSE

It was a wake-up call, a breaking point for me. I knew I'd said it before, but this time it felt different. I knew I had to change because deep down I was aware if I tried something like that ever again, I would be successful. Leaving Sam alone would be an even greater sin than taking my own life.

A piece of wisdom was stuck in my mind. And that was the importance of routines. Establishing a new routine or sticking to an old one helped retain balance in life, especially when a person felt out of it.

Since my old routines entailed drinking and feeling sorry for myself, I started to create healthier ones. It was easier said than done, but I was adamant about correcting my behavior, changing patterns, and abandoning thoughts and narratives that were harming me because I really wanted to be a better father to Sam. I wanted to create a safe place for her. I never wanted her to see me in that state again.

With some perseverance and threats that I would hire a lawyer and sue everyone involved, I managed to get the sheriff and his deputies out of my house. As expected, they ever so graciously decided my house wasn't a "crime scene" anymore and that I was free to return to it. Which was a relief because it meant I was closer to Sam.

The instant I returned home, I took a good look around and felt ashamed that I'd allowed us to live like that. I knew Sam did her best, but I was guilty for putting her in that position in the first place, as though it was her job to take care of the house as well as me. I was the parent, and it was time to show her I was capable of taking care of both of us.

In order to clean up my life, I had to take the first step and clean up my house. That was all part of creating a safe, happy environment for my daughter. At times I worried I'd trained her like a soldier too much. Perhaps it was time I taught her how to be a kid.

The sheriff had taken all my guns away, but now he had to return them, and I put them all in the gun cabinet I'd built. Then I locked it up. Next, I got rid of all the unnecessary junk I'd gathered over the years. I threw away the trash, dusted, vacuumed, and washed the dishes.

I decided to stay away from the guns from now on, but I returned to my regime of daily exercise. Doing my stretching, self-defense training, and light weights felt weird without Sam beside me.

Despite all these changes, unfortunately, I felt no difference in my head. I wasn't magically cured, as I'd hoped. My mind still felt mired in a shambles, I was still quick to anger when things didn't go according to plan. I was still plagued, contaminated by the darkness that had entered me during the war. And that darkness had definitely spread and deepened once Katarina died. I was still me, even in a clean house. That realization certainly made me lose some of my original elation.

Deciding it was time to bite the bullet, metaphorically speaking, I called the psychologist I'd been referred to. No matter how much I hated the fact that I was forced to beg some stranger for help because I was too weak to deal with all that shit on my own, I knew it needed to be done. Sam deserved a father who wasn't fractured, but sane and normal.

I will never be able to forgive myself that she saw me like that. Repeatedly.

Rewatching that scene inside my head, being confronted with such a look in her eyes, so scared and desperate, made me want to bang my head against the wall.

"I'm sorry, Dr. Sheldon is on vacation," a receptionist informed me. "She'll return next week."

I gritted my teeth, hanging up, although she'd started saying something else. "Fuck," I snapped in frustration. That was just my luck.

Then again, perhaps that was a sign I shouldn't be going to therapy in the first place. What good would talking to a stranger do anyway?

Feeling like a total failure, I decided that staying completely away from alcohol was one of the many stupid ideas I'd had as of late. All the same, I didn't allow myself to get drunk. Visiting Sam at Billy's was the highlight of my day, and even though I was completely worthless, she didn't have to see me drunk as well.

My daughter was truly the only good thing, the only pure thing in my life, and I'd be damned if I would screw that up.

When I went to see her, I tried really hard not to dwell on the fact she wasn't living with me anymore. *It's only temporary.*

I could see she was hesitant to share something with me.

"Did something happen in school, Sam?" I asked, worried that other kids were mean to her because of me. It wasn't easy being the daughter of a crazy man.

"A CPS social worker and some deputy came to speak with me."

That pissed me off. I couldn't believe they'd actually pulled her out of class to speak with her at school. Then again, it made perfect sense if they didn't want me around.

Those bastards.

"I'll have to speak with your principal because that's unacceptable," I practically growled. I tried not to get too riled up, but how could I not? They were harassing my daughter.

"Don't do anything, Dad," Sam pleaded. "It will only make matters worse."

"I agree with your daughter, Jesse. They'll stop once they find nothing," Billy added, trying to be the voice of reason, something I was lacking at the moment.

The urge to protect my child by any means necessary was so strong. I felt like tearing buildings apart—two in particular.

"Doing nothing feels wrong," I said eventually.

"I know, brother. It goes against our nature, but the situation calls for it."

I nodded. I still felt like raising hell for what they were doing. It was bad enough they continued to knock on my door, asking all kinds of stupid questions. It was unacceptable they were doing the same to Sam, especially when the kid was in school. She was innocent. All the same, I saw wisdom in what Billy said.

"I don't like it, but I won't do anything," I reassured them.

"Don't worry so much about me, Dad. I can take care of myself."

"I know you can. But I'll always worry about you."

She hugged me, which I knew was a rare treat coming from a teenager.

"What did they want anyways?" Billy asked.

I gave him a look, not knowing if he was asking me or Sam.

I answered because Sam hesitated. "The usual bullshit," I replied vaguely, not wanting Sam to hear the truth of how invasive they were with their questions.

Later, once Sam had gone to bed, I expressed my worries to Billy. This thing with CPS was really bothering me. They could take Sam away from me. "They have it in for me, and I don't know why."

"It is troubling," Billy agreed. "Just don't give them any more reasons to come after you."

"Right, right," I replied, although I still felt pretty restless.

Much later that night, after I'd returned to my freshly cleaned house from my visit, I started to doubt if I was causing Sam more harm than good. I knew she had a tough time in school because of me, because we were being labeled different and crazy, although she tried to hide that from me.

Was my lifestyle scarring her for life?

I took one of the whiskey bottles from my stash, opened it up, and poured myself a glass. Although overwhelmed with all kinds of feelings, I patted myself on the back for not drinking straight from the bottle. That showed restraint.

Let's see if it will last, I thought while having a drink, then another. Although I knew it was wrong, the sad reality was that I needed something to calm me down, quieten the thoughts inside my head, tame the raging storm in my heart, and the bottle of JD was it.

Luckily, I stopped myself in time. Somehow, I managed to drink enough without drinking too much.

This is a slippery slope.

I looked at the bottle in front of me. Every part of my being wanted more, yet I resisted.

That was when I decided to taper off. I would just finish what I had over a period of time and then be done with it. No more alcohol.

Or at least that was the hope.

8

SAMANTHA

I tried to move past what happened, return to my routines, go to school, hang out with Hillie, go home to Billy and Emily's, do homework, and see Dad for a little while before sleep. Rinse and repeat the next day all over again.

I was managing, especially since I had Hillie by my side to distract me from all my problems. She had been my best friend ever since I could remember. One day we started playing in the playground, and that was that, inseparable for life. Life was easier with her by my side. She was the only one I could actually speak with.

It wasn't a secret to Hillie that my father struggled, that he was an alcoholic. He'd even had a few episodes in front of her over the years, so it was no big deal to her when I told her how Dad had had an "accident" during one of those.

Hillie never judged me, no matter what I shared with her. Then again, her family was equally screwed up. Her oldest brother was in jail for trying to cook meth. He almost blew up himself and his girlfriend when it failed. And her mother was addicted to painkillers.

Even with all that in mind, I was ashamed to share Dad's failed suicide attempt. Failed only because I managed to stop him.

"That's so messed up, Sam, but I'm glad you were there in time," Hillie said.

"Me too."

My biggest fear was that there would be a next time, and then I wouldn't be so lucky. That he would choose some remote place, wanting to spare me witnessing it, then he would end his sufferings.

I will never forgive him if he kills himself.

Deep down, there was part of me I was deeply ashamed of that actually wanted him to end it all, end this suffering for the both of us. Luckily that part was easily silenced and buried inside.

"Did you tell the police what happened?"

"Of course not. I don't want them to lock him up."

Hillie nodded in agreement.

"I don't understand why they keep pestering me after we both told them it was an accident," I stressed.

Do they know I'm lying? I asked myself for the millionth time. But there was no way they could know, considering Dad and I were the only two people there, and our stories matched.

"Because that's what they do. You know they tried to take Susie's baby from her just because she fell asleep with her on the bus," Hillie said, getting visibly upset.

I'd heard about her cousin, Susie. She'd gotten pregnant at fifteen and had to quit school and start working. No wonder she fell asleep; she was probably exhausted from tending to her baby and working at the same time. Yet instead of helping the young mother, the authorities overreacted and tried to take her baby away. Insane.

"You know they all completely freaked out about my dad's gun collection, not to mention my training," I said.

Hillie gave me a look.

"What? Please don't tell me you think their reaction is okay."

"Of course not. You have every right to live how you want as long as you don't hurt anyone."

"Precisely, thank you, but they act as though we're criminals or something," I complained.

"The people in charge don't like it when regular people are too competent because that means they're not so easily controlled," Hillie said, sounding like a grown-up, like she was quoting someone.

"I wish they would just leave us alone," I said. "After all, we're nothing special."

Once again Hillie gave me a look.

I frowned. She was seriously starting to irritate me. "What's with your face now?"

"Sam, your family isn't normal."

I wanted to say something in our defense, but she went on.

"That's not a bad thing," she added. "Just different. I mean, not all dads are as cool as yours. Most don't teach their kids any kind of survivalist things, or any kind of martial arts that could be used outside of the sports arena. Not to mention you're the only girl I know who can shoot better than most hunters around here. Most kids our age play video games, not train to become some highly skilled superhero."

I tried to process what she was saying. If I wanted to shoot and do martial arts instead of play video games, I should be allowed to, right? This was a free country; we were supposed to be allowed to do what we wanted.

"Don't worry, Sam, it'll blow over soon," Hillie added, trying a little late to comfort me.

"You really think so?" I said, not bothering to hide my doubt.

"Yeah. Government people have to act like they're actually doing something so they can justify their jobs," Hillie replied. "Once they find nothing, they'll move on to pester someone else."

"You're right, I guess," I replied. "I just have to stick to my story, and they'll eventually give up."

"Exactly."

My dad'll be fine, and I'll be able to go home soon. He just has to prove that he won't try to harm himself ever again. And once that happens, we'll be together again. And those assholes from the CPS won't be able to tear us apart over licensed guns or Dad's disabilities no matter how hard they try.

But, as expected, CPS returned to ask me a series of uncomfortable questions I'd already given answers to.

And to make matters worse, the social worker pulled me out of school and took me to their office. The principal protested, but backed off after she mentioned disciplinary actions, performance reviews, and suspension.

I protested, too, since they tried to speak with me without a grown-up present, but they bombarded me with some legal terms I didn't understand. It seemed they had every right to do so if they deemed that I was in danger.

Danger from whom? My dad of course. To that, I commented they would all be in danger from me if they didn't stop ruining my life. I was dead serious about that. I had skills. And I was so tempted to use them.

"Hello, Samantha," the social worker said.

"This is harassment," I replied, leaning back in the chair.

"It's not harassment. We're all very concerned about your well-being and simply want to make sure you're growing up in the safest environment," she explained, sounding unbelievably condescending.

"If you're so concerned about my well-being," I mocked, "then stop pulling me out of school. You're disrupting my life and screwing up my grades."

"I understand your frustrations, but this is a process we have to go through."

"I'm not frustrated, I'm angry, there's a big difference."

"Why are you angry?"

I took a breath. "I just explained why. This is insane. Why won't you leave me alone?"

"I sense a lot of defensiveness in you. Tell me, are you afraid we'll discover something you don't want us to?"

I remained silent.

"We already know your father has been teaching you how to fight, how to shoot. Tell me, is that all he's been teaching you?"

"What are you talking about?" I asked, genuinely confused.

"Is making bombs part of your training?" she asked.

So now I was a terrorist, good to know. "That's crazy, of course not. And if you want me to be honest, you're right, I am afraid. Afraid I will fail all my classes wasting time here with you."

"What I'm hearing is that you're not satisfied with your current living accommodations. Do you feel like your current residence doesn't provide you with a place to study and focus on your schoolwork?"

"What? That's not what I said at all. Stop trying to twist around everything I say."

"Samantha, I understand you love your father; however, you have to stop covering for him. It's obvious how neglectful he has been toward you."

"What are you talking about?" I asked. "Did you forget to take some pills or something?"

"Your father is clearly a very dangerous man," she said, ignoring everything that I just said.

"You're wrong," I argued. "My dad is the best, he's the only family I have, and I won't let you use me to get to him."

"Get to him? Samantha, there is no conspiracy going on here; there's no personal agenda. We only want what's best for you."

"Yeah, right."

She looked at me long and hard before proceeding. "Did your father teach you to think that we're the enemy? Because he's wrong, Samantha; we're not. We're the good guys."

Being bombarded with so many questions, all about my dad, and with such negative connotations made me extremely worried I would be taken away from him. It was obvious they were looking for an excuse to do exactly that.

These people had already made up their minds; everything else was simply a formality. I feared that no matter what I said to this woman, I couldn't change their minds.

Please, Mom, don't let them separate us, I prayed with all my might.

A FEW DAYS after that meeting with the social worker, I returned to Billy and Emily's to find a different social worker with a terrible dye job, plus a deputy, sitting on Billy's couch.

This can't be good.

"Hello, Samantha, we've been waiting for you." The social worker greeted me in a falsely cheery voice.

"What's going on? Where's Dad?" I asked Billy, ignoring all the rest. I also stayed by the door, ready to flee if I had to.

"Why don't you sit down, Samantha; we need to speak with you." The social worker tried again.

I hated the way she said my name. It irked me that she was so calm as she tried to tell me what to do in Billy's house. I moved next to Billy but remained standing.

"Where's my dad?" I asked again.

"I don't know. I can't reach him on the phone," he replied.

The social worker turned to me, her face deadly serious as she delivered her killer blow. "Samantha," she said, "your father has lost custody of you."

9

SAMANTHA

"What?" I exclaimed. "How? When?" What a complete nightmare. This was what I'd feared from the start, that they would find a way to take me away from my dad.

"That's news to me too," Billy said glumly.

"Wait, if he was in court, why wasn't I asked to speak in front of the judge as well?" I asked. I was old enough to speak my mind. Wasn't it my right to be there and tell my side of the story?

"The judge believed you would be biased, so he made the decision without your statement," the social worker explained.

That pissed me off even more. Of course I would be biased; I wanted to be with my dad. "That can't be right. I want to see my dad."

"From now on, you will have limited contact with your father. The judge's rule is final."

"Your father will be appealing this ruling, don't worry," Billy tried to reassure me, sending dirty looks to the social worker.

"I want to see Dad right now." I moved as though to leave the room, to run back to our place to see Dad.

But the deputy blocked my exit and grabbed my arm.

I looked at him in outrage. "Let me go."

"Samantha, please calm down. Nothing bad is going to happen to you," the social worker tried to reassure me.

I looked at her incredulously. "You just told me my father lost custody of me. Something bad already happened."

"This is for the best, Samantha."

"I'm done listening to you. Now, let me go. You can't keep me here." I needed to see him, make sure he was all right. Why couldn't they understand that?

"You're not staying here."

That made me turn around to look at her, and I almost laughed out loud at her ridiculous hair. "Excuse me?"

"You're being placed in a foster home. I need you to pack your things and come with us."

"I'm not going anywhere with you," I rebelled.

"She stays here," Billy said. "We've known her, watched over her since she was a baby."

"We're her godparents," Emily said, coming into the room.

I rushed to her, and she hugged me tightly.

"I'm afraid that's not possible. You're not related to Samantha, godparents have no legal role in the matter, and you aren't registered foster parents," she explained, her mouth set in a tight, mean line.

"I don't want to go," I said in panic. I had a sinking feeling that if they made me leave this place, I would never be able to return. I'd never see Dad again. I'd never see Billy and Emily again.

"You have to," the social worker insisted. "It's the law."

"Billy and Emily are more family to me than any strangers you can place me with," I argued. I hated how powerless I felt. I felt like crying. I felt like raging, fighting my way out of that place.

Better to run away than to be forced to live with a bunch of strangers.

"We'll apply for guardianship or whatever it takes to keep Sam with us," Billy said to the social worker.

"Even if you do, that takes months to get approved, and Samantha can't stay here in the meantime. You need to come with us." That last part was for me.

"I refuse," I said stubbornly.

"There's no need to turn things into an ugly affair," the deputy warned, crossing his arms. It was obvious he was ready to drag me out of the house if necessary.

I was prepared to fight until the end, but I didn't want to cause problems for Billy and Emily. They were so kind to me and to Dad, I couldn't repay them with violence.

"We'll find a way to get you back to your father," Emily whispered to me.

I crossed my arms over my chest, mimicking the deputy's stance. "There's nothing to pack. The sheriff wouldn't allow me to go home and get my things."

And once Dad had managed to chase that mob away, I'd figured there was no point in doing something like that since I would be returning home soon. Apparently, I was wrong.

One phone call later, I was escorted back to my house so I could pack my things. I hoped I would be able to see Dad as well, but sadly he was nowhere to be seen.

The deputy informed me that he'd been taken away by another deputy so he wouldn't cause problems.

As soon as I walked in the front door, it broke my heart to

see how clean and tidy the house looked. He really was trying to make things better. And then this had happened. He must be devastated. It was hard to fight back the tears that filled my eyes.

While nobody was looking, I wrote a note for Dad. I told him how much I loved him and that we'd see each other soon. I needed him to have faith that things would turn out for the best.

Back next door, Emily was sniffling beside her husband. Billy promised me he would help Dad find a way to get me back as soon as possible.

I clung to that promise, but I wasn't an idiot. I was aware that parents who lost custody of their kids rarely got them back. Even so, I couldn't believe this was actually happening to me. That one stupid bullet had managed to destroy my entire life.

I thought about making a run for it. These idiots couldn't stop me. I knew the layout of the surrounding lands and all the farms better than anybody else. I could hide in some motel under a fake name and try to reach Dad. *And then what?*

If I became a runaway, I would have to leave everything and everyone I knew and loved. If I ran away, I couldn't return home or go back to school. Most importantly, I definitely couldn't live with Dad anymore.

What if we ran away together? Of course, I couldn't do that to him. I knew he needed to be surrounded by familiar things to feel safe and grounded. Running away would be the end of him.

So no matter how much it pained me, I did what I was told and packed my things.

I said goodbye to Billy and Emily. "Watch over Dad for me," I pleaded.

"Don't worry about anything," Emily reassured me.

"We'll see you soon, Sam," Billy promised.

I nodded, getting inside the car.

"This is for the best, Samantha, you'll see," the social worker said.

I could barely contain my fury as we drove to the foster house, to my new home.

To my prison, I corrected my thoughts. I refused to think of that place as home. My home was the farm, the place where I was born, where I grew up with my parents.

As we drove, I was extremely worried about Dad. How had he taken this news? How was he going to survive without me? They didn't even allow me to say goodbye to him. That hurt the most.

"I know this feels like the end of the world, but it's honestly for the best, Samantha," the social worker commented. "You'll love it at the Bradfords' house. And you'll make friends with the other girls in no time."

I was done listening to her condescending voice telling me how all of this was for the best, so I asked her what genuinely interested me. "Why did Dad lose custody of me? Why am I being taken away to live with these strangers?"

I felt like I had every right to know because this was my life, after all. And I didn't bother to hide how all of this made me extremely angry. If they labeled me a teenager with an attitude problem, all the better. Perhaps then the Bradfords wouldn't want me, and the social worker would have no choice but to take me back home.

"Your father lost custody because you were being

neglected, endangered, and abused." She sounded like she was quoting a report.

It took me a moment to process all those words. "None of those things are true. I have everything I need, and he's never raised a hand to me in my entire life."

"There are many kinds of abuse, Samantha, and you're too young to understand it all. It wasn't right, the way you were living."

I knew this was because we were survivalists, and she hadn't even denied it. "My father made me the way I am. He taught me everything I know, and I'm proud to be his daughter," I said, raising my chin.

The social worker turned to look at me. "Your father is a paranoid, dangerous nonconformist who is unfit to raise children."

I wanted to hit her so hard my knuckles tingled. I settled for kicking the back of her seat. "Don't you dare speak about my dad like that. You don't know him. You don't know anything about us. You're just a judgmental bitch who's trying to ruin our lives."

"Quit the attitude right now," she yelled.

I couldn't help flinching. I had no idea she could do that. *Isn't that abuse too?*

"I know plenty about you and your family, and this little show of yours tells me I did the right thing. You two need to be separated because he is clearly a bad influence. He needs help, and you need to be placed in a better, more conventional environment."

"If he's so unwell and dangerous, then why was he released from the hospital? Why didn't they lock him up and throw away the key?" I challenged.

She shook her head but didn't reply.

I felt victorious. She hadn't been able to reply because I was right.

I knew foster homes got paid to take care of all the children, so maybe, I thought, social workers were taking their cut too. They were disgusting, the whole lot of them, ripping families apart. And I wouldn't allow them to do the same to me. They couldn't make me stay. Dad needed me, and I needed him. I'd already lost Mom; I couldn't lose him too.

"Once you calm down and spend a few days with the Bradfords, you'll see how much better your life can be," the social worker insisted, her voice a normal volume again.

"Being kidnapped and uprooted can't be better; besides, this is temporary for me," I replied stubbornly. "He's going to get me back. He's stopped drinking, and he'll go to therapy, so the judge will have no choice but to undo this ridiculous decision."

"Even if what you say is true," she countered, "he may not end up being considered a fit father ever again."

I could only stare at her for a moment. "That's crazy," I said when I recovered. "Why not? He's the best person I know. He's fought in wars, he's helped a lot of people since he got back, and he even repairs cars for free if people don't have money to pay him. How can a person like that be unfit?"

"He's unfit because he has untreated medical issues and is an alcoholic," she pointed out.

"We all have problems," I admitted, "but he's handling it."

"Look, Samantha, I know this is stressful for you. You're not thinking rationally at the moment, but you'll be grateful for this opportunity."

"What opportunity?" I stressed the words.

"For a fresh start."

"I don't need a fresh start. My father is not the monster you're painting him to be, and I need him in my life," I insisted.

"What you need is help and healing, and that's exactly what you'll get staying with the Bradfords. They've helped a lot of girls like you in the past."

Girls like me! What's that supposed to mean?

"If they're so great, you live with them," I said, folding my arms over my chest and glaring through the window.

It was pointless speaking to that woman. She couldn't understand anything because she was programmed to think a certain way. In her mind, I was an anomaly that needed to be corrected. And they were sending me to these people to do just that. The more I heard about the Bradfords, the more I hated them because they were clearly part of the problem.

But the joke would soon be on them. I had no intention of changing.

I'll find a way to return to my dad, no matter what.

10

SAMANTHA

The social worker left me to calm down, and we drove in silence the rest of the way to the Bradfords' home.

I took advantage of her not paying attention to me to text Dad. I was relieved that I was allowed to bring my phone. I also texted Billy and then Hillie to let her know that I was being taken to some farm, to some people called the Bradfords. I wanted as many people as possible to know where I was. That made me feel safer for some reason.

Although I knew how foolish it was of me, I hoped they would all gather together and come to rescue me, even though I had no idea where I was being taken in the first place.

I was relieved when Dad texted me back.

> I'm sorry this happened, kiddo. I'll prove the judge wrong for taking you away, I swear.

Although it was good to hear from him, it irked me that he'd treated me like a kid who needed to be protected, as opposed to someone who could stand beside him and fight for our family. Perhaps if I'd known about the custody battle sooner, I might have been able to help. I could have changed things. I stopped myself there: going down that path was pointless. The damage had been done. It was time to create a plan that would get me out of this mess.

Although Dad's text was meant to be reassuring, and it was a relief that he wasn't simply giving up on me, I still felt uneasy and worried. And the texts I received from Billy, Emily, and Hillie didn't calm me down either.

Nobody knew what advice to give me because none of us had been in a position like this before. It was strange and terrifying for all of us. They were losing me just as much as I was losing them. All that made me feel really isolated and alone.

I really didn't want to be forced to live with these strangers. And it was very hard to not be angry at Dad, blaming him for getting us into this situation in the first place.

After an eternity we reached the farm. And it was huge. In the middle of the fields was a two-story farmhouse. It was a lot nicer than the one I grew up in.

An older man and a slightly younger woman came out of the house. They were traditionally dressed. He was very tall, dressed in black, with short hair that was graying at the sides. She was shorter, very thin, with natural blonde hair, and dressed in a hideous light gray dress. I felt like I was looking at a picture from the past.

Very reluctantly I got out of the car.

The woman smiled broadly as the man remained serious beside her.

"Samantha, meet the Bradfords. Reverend Gareth Bradford and his wife, Evangeline," the social worker introduced.

Reverend and his wife. I groaned inwardly. I couldn't
believe they put me in a pastor's house. My family wasn't
religious, so I hoped this wouldn't turn into a problem. If
they expected me to know the scriptures, I would have to
disappoint them. I had no intention of reading the Bible
either.

"Nice to meet you, Samantha," Mrs. Bradford said, still
smiling. Despite this, her mannerisms were pretty brusque.

"Let's get you settled," the social worker said, seemingly
keen to rush me inside.

As I walked into the Bradfords' house, I was still baffled
as to how some social worker could just come and get me,
pack me up, then ship me to a stranger's house without bothering to ask me how I felt about it. Although I was sure they
already knew how I felt; after all, I had been pretty vocal in
the car – it was only that nobody cared.

I wanted to go home. I wanted to wake up from this
nightmare.

"Welcome to our home." Mrs. Bradford's words snapped
me from my thoughts.

The social worker had said there were other girls living
here, so I expected to see them, but there was nobody there.
And the house was very quiet like nobody apart from us was
there.

Settling into the living room, which had no TV, it was
more than obvious these people were very pious. Religious
things were everywhere, crosses on the walls, embroidered
quotes from the Bible on the cushions, and a Bible was
placed squarely on the coffee table.

"I'm really happy to meet you, and I hope your stay with us will be a healthy change of lifestyle," the reverend said.

That sounded as though they wanted to convert me or something. I wasn't sure how to reply, especially since I didn't want to lie. I wasn't happy I was here. *Is it a sin to lie to religious people?*

"What's wrong, Samantha? You were more talkative in the car," the social worker jibed.

"It's very nice meeting you, Mr. Bradford, Mrs. Bradford," I said eventually.

"Call me Reverend," he corrected. "I am known as Reverend Bradford."

The two of them asked a few questions about my life, and I replied as best I could. I felt awkward, and aware that they were super religious, with their congregation and everything, I constantly worried I might say the wrong thing, while not knowing what the right thing would be either, which was why I opted to keep quiet whenever I could.

Hillie would tease me about it no end, since that wasn't in my character at all, but what could I say? I felt misplaced, trapped even, and I already hated every second of it.

11

SAMANTHA

After filling out some paperwork, the social worker promised to return to see how I was settling in, gave me her number, and then just left me there.

I couldn't believe that was it. Was this really how the system worked? I was being dumped to live with complete strangers, as though that was normal and safe. And after making such a fuss to insist that my dad was unfit to be a father, this felt very strange.

It was unnerving how the reverend and his wife kept looking at me, as though anticipating something, but sadly I was in the dark about what was expected of me.

The silence dragged on, and I stirred on the couch. Everything looked so pristine, so clean. I sat on the edge, feeling like I might dirty it otherwise.

I kept expecting the reverend to ask if I had been baptized or if I went to church regularly. *How will he react when I tell him I'm not baptized?* I didn't go to church either.

Would they return me to the social workers? Perhaps they wouldn't want someone like me living among them.

That thought almost cheered me up, but then I remembered something. *Don't religious people love to save people who've strayed from the path?*

I'm no stray, a rebellious voice inside my head insisted.

Mrs. Bradford looked at her husband, who gave a barely noticeable nod before she smiled at me. "There will be time to properly get to know one another in the days to come." She rose from her seat. "You must be tired from the drive," she said as she gestured for me to get up as well, and I did. "Let me show you your room."

I grabbed my small bag and followed her, wondering if I should say something to the reverend, who remained sitting in a chair. I opted to say nothing. That sounded like the smartest choice. He unnerved me for some reason.

I banished all that and focused on what Mrs. Bradford was telling me. My room was located on the second floor, where the other girls lived.

The corridor to the left was where the girls' rooms were located, and the corridor on the right was where the Bradfords' master bedroom was, alongside some private rooms that I was cautioned not to roam in.

The room I was to sleep in was on the small side and contained only the most basic pieces of furniture, which was something I was accustomed to anyway. What confused me were the two beds inside. I looked at Mrs. Bradford questioningly.

"You'll be sharing this room with Grace," she informed me. "She's one of our other foster daughters. You'll meet all of them later after you rest."

I was relieved to hear there were in fact other girls living here. I just knew it would be super weird and uncomfortable if I was the only one living with these strangers. There was safety in numbers. Even though the rest of the girls were strangers as well, they were foster kids like me, and that was comforting in a way.

"The left side of the closet is prepared for your things. I'll leave you to settle in." And with that, she left.

I had to admit, I found Mrs. Bradford a bit odd.

I sat on the bed for a moment and noted it was very firm. Standing up again, I went to the closet. True enough, the left side was completely empty. On the right were neatly folded clothes. Very ugly clothes, not that I was judging.

It didn't take me long to put my things in the closet. I didn't bring much because I still firmly believed this situation was only temporary. I would be out of this place in a matter of days, as soon as the judge realized he'd made a huge mistake about my dad.

Part of me wanted to leave all my things in the bag; however, I got the feeling something like this was expected from me. Mrs. Bradford had made a point of it, so I complied.

I had promised the people who really knew and loved me that I would behave, so I did. Dad had specifically told me to be on my best behavior, and I would do that for him. I knew if I caused problems, he would have problems as well. And I had to avoid that if I wanted to leave this house.

After getting my things sorted, it took me another minute to get familiar with everything in the small room. There was no bathroom, which meant I would have to share it with other girls. I had no problem with that. I looked through the window at the fields below. I was in the middle of nowhere. I didn't like the idea of that.

Once I got bored, I sat on the bed and just waited.

I took a few photos of my new room and sent them to

Hillie. We texted for a bit as she tried to cheer me up. I already missed her, missed everybody. I couldn't believe I had been in school with her this very morning and now I was in the middle of nowhere, unsure when I would see her again. See any of my friends.

A few hours passed, and I simply stayed in the room, unsure of the protocols and rules of this place.

All of a sudden, while I was lost in my thoughts, a girl burst into the room.

I got to my feet immediately. Normally, I would also grab for a weapon, but sadly there was nothing to grab in such a bare room. Perhaps that was a blessing in disguise, since I didn't want to look like a complete freak.

"So you're the new girl," she commented, checking me out from head to toe. "My condolences for ending up in this place."

Her phrasing suggested this was a prison or worse. I wasn't allowed to leave and go to my dad's, so perhaps this place was like a prison.

Since she was scrutinizing me, I did the same with her. She was taller and slightly older than me, and she wore a really formal dress, the same type Mrs. Bradford was wearing. She was dark-skinned, her tightly curled black hair was in braids, and her eyes were brown. "Are you Grace?" I asked.

"Yes," she replied.

"So it looks like we'll be roommates, at least for the time being," I said, simply to say something.

"I'm here to teach you some rules while staying with the Bradfords," she said, ignoring my previous sentence.

"Okay," I said a bit warily.

I feared something like that might happen after seeing

how the pair lived and all the crosses on the walls. I hoped they weren't into some weird stuff, like singing after dinner or knitting. Obviously, I had no idea what I was talking about. I had no idea how religious people lived.

"First of all," Grace said, breaking my chain of thoughts. "No swearing – and by the way, oh my God definitely counts as swearing – and no taking God's name in vain, either. Second, no fighting."

That took me by surprise: with whom was I going to fight anyway? And then I realized she meant verbally, not physically.

Her next words confirmed as much. "Even raised voices among us girls aren't allowed."

"That's a bit extreme, but okay," I commented.

Grace rolled her eyes. "You have no idea. I'm just getting started."

"There's more?"

She simply gave me a look before continuing, "All our means of communication are closely monitored."

"Meaning?"

"If you have a phone, they'll check it at random times."

I was shocked. *That can't be legal. Was it legal?*

"And when you're on the internet at the shared computer, your browsing history will be inspected," she said.

I frowned. There was no way I was giving them my phone for inspection. I didn't care so much about the internet. Their computer, their rules; however, my phone was my property, my thing, end of story. And I would fight them on it if I had to.

"We all go to church on Sunday morning, after which we do some volunteer stuff, so you'll need to look your best for it."

I definitely didn't have anything similar to what she was wearing. I didn't own a dress or a skirt for that matter, so they would have to deal with me going to church in jeans and a long-sleeved T-shirt. That was appropriate, right?

"And I'll show you how to braid your hair," she offered.

I groaned inwardly. I hated it when people touched my hair. Being the only redhead in my small town, kids often wanted to play with it and pull at it, so I'd developed an aversion.

I guess I'll have to get over it.

"Is going to church mandatory? What if I'm not Christian?" I challenged.

Grace's eyes went wide. "Don't ever say something like that again," she snapped, and I was shocked to hear that there was real panic in her voice. "You have to go, like the rest of us."

"Okay," I said, just so she would calm down. I truly didn't expect a freak-out. Perhaps it was foolish of me to think I could skip it. The man was a reverend, for crying out loud.

"Anything else?"

Grace nodded. "There's a chore list we all have to go through each day."

Now the fact of the Bradfords living in such a pristine-looking house made perfect sense. We had to clean it. *Child labor at its best*, I mocked.

"And make sure not to slack off because then all of us will end up in trouble," she warned.

"You mean punished?"

She nodded.

So the Bradfords were pretty old-fashioned in every

sense of the word. All the more reason not to stay with them longer than I had to.

"What about school?" I asked.

Suddenly, Mrs. Bradford appeared at the door, like some kind of apparition. She walked so lightly that I didn't hear her approach until she was already there. Her presence startled me.

"You won't be returning to school for the time being," Mrs. Bradford told me.

I didn't like her answer one bit. "Why not?"

"The county is still sorting out the logistics, whether to bus you to your old school or enroll you at the local school."

"I would prefer to go to my school," I said.

Mrs. Bradford made a face. "That's up to the county, not you."

I simply nodded because it was very obvious this wasn't actually a conversation. She was just informing me how things stood. Apparently, all the politeness, all the warm welcomes were for show in front of the social worker, but now I was seeing the real Mrs. Bradford.

For some reason, I preferred that way to that smiling robotic wife version she was trying to pull.

"Grace, let's go," Mrs. Bradford said.

They left me again, alone in the room, with nothing to do. This whole situation – all the rules and all the strangeness – made me feel uncomfortable.

The emotion intensified knowing I was stuck here.

What am I going to do now?

12

JESSE

I couldn't believe those assholes came and took Sam away.

I knew she was getting out of school, so I was about to go to Billy's to see her when the police came with a social service cleric and handed me some court documents, notifying me that I had lost custody of Sam.

Just like that. It had all been decided without me. And the police were there to make sure I didn't cause any problems once I got upset. And damn right I got upset. It was such a sneaky move, deliberately excluding me from everything.

All I knew was that the sheriff and some social worker Sam had spoken with asked a judge to take custody from me. And the bastard did, without even speaking with me. He read some files, listened to people who didn't actually know me make judgments about me, and decided I wasn't fit to be a father.

I was furious. Especially after finding Sam's note. I wanted to tear the whole house down, then set it on fire, but managed to stop myself. I knew that was exactly what they wanted. That would simply hand them proof they did the right thing.

I was extremely worried for Sam. I worried the longer she stayed away from me, the harder it would be to get her back, which meant I had to work fast. I also felt like she was in extreme danger; however, I told myself that was only my broken mind playing tricks on me, making me paranoid.

It was pure hell not knowing where Sam was at the moment. Was she all right? How did she take the news? Was she angry with me? Did she feel betrayed? All kinds of thoughts plagued me, making me feel so much rage. The urge to drink myself stupid was so strong I sank a few glasses of JD, but I made sure that I resisted getting drunk.

Sam needed me now more than ever, so I couldn't allow myself to relapse. I couldn't let myself return to that dark place, no matter how much my demons tried to drag me there, no matter how much I wanted to take their hands and let them.

All of this was my fault. If I wasn't such a basket case, then they wouldn't have been able to swoop in and take my daughter away. It was devastating knowing that I had managed to lose her. I'd promised Katarina I would take good care of our girl, and then this happened.

I will get her back.

The problem with that plan was that I had no idea where to start searching for her. The assholes from the CPS refused to tell me where she was. They just told me that I could appeal to a judge if I felt wronged.

The same guy who took Sam away from me. *Yeah, right.* That seemed fair.

Even though it wasn't in my nature, I had to calm down

and think rationally. Create a plan, not simply act, not simply storm in all guns blazing.

If I wanted Sam back, I had to clean up my act. Also, I had to hire a lawyer to fight my battles. The only way to fight them was from within. I needed to play the system at their own game. That was my path back to Sam.

And then, in the midst of my despair, Sam texted me and said she was with a family called the Bradfords and stuck on a farm in the middle of nowhere. There was so much I wanted to say to her, but I didn't want to dump my own issues on my daughter, so I opted for some generic shit and felt awful about it as soon as I'd sent the message.

I went to Billy's to share my thoughts with him and Emily. After expressing my outrage and telling them about my recent experiences with the people from CPS, I told them my plan to hire a lawyer. "I think that's my only option," I concluded.

Billy nodded. "I agree."

"I'm so worried about her."

Billy placed a hand on my shoulder. "I'm here for you, and I'll do everything in my power to help you get her back."

"Both of us will," Emily said, returning from the kitchen and setting a plate of hot food in front of me.

"Thanks," I said, although I didn't know if I was thanking them for the food or their support. Probably both.

"Do you have a lawyer in mind?" Billy asked.

I nodded. "Johnny's younger brother."

Billy's expression immediately turned sober: Johnny was one of our military brothers who'd never returned home. We'd lost so many in the various wars and overseas campaigns.

"Is he any good?" he asked.

I had no idea. But, nevertheless, he was someone I trusted given that he was from a military family. "Johnny always spoke highly of his lawyer brother." The brother who broke tradition, who replaced a rifle with a law book. "I just hope legal actions will actually change something and I'll be able to get Sam back."

It was obvious something was on Billy's mind, but he was reluctant to share it. Clearly not wanting to bring me down. I could guess all the same.

We had trusted the government less and less ever since returning from our last tour, so sitting around and doing nothing while some lawyer did everything for me felt like going against my very nature.

Nonetheless, I would walk through hell itself to get Sam back. I had been surrounded by death and despair before, so that was nothing new. Compared to that, going to court, having my life shredded, and fighting with social workers felt like nothing at all.

War is war, I realized; this one was just a different kind.

THE NEXT MORNING, I went to see my new lawyer, Peter Molon.

I explained how they took Sam away without me being arrested or taken in front of a judge. It was obvious from the look on his face that that wasn't standard procedure.

"We'll definitely appeal that and the decisions made as a result," he said.

I nodded.

I also asked if there was a chance Billy and Emily could act as foster parents for Sam while I battled for custody. "I just want her close and safe; even if she's not with me, she should be with her godparents."

"Are they legally her godparents?" he questioned. "Do you have it in a will or other legal form that gives them guardianship over her in your absence?"

My shoulders dropped. "No."

Peter nodded. "I'm not sure about the procedure to make them her guardians, but I'll look into it and then report back to you."

After our meeting ended, I still felt like I hadn't done enough. So I did something I never believed I would. I bought a laptop. It was a used one, cheap, but it worked.

Once I got home and hooked it up, I looked up everything I could find about family law to determine exactly how this situation had come about and what Peter and I could do about it.

He'd tried explaining it to me, but we had limited time together before he had to go to court, so we'd focused on more important issues. All the same, nothing was stopping me from doing some research on my own.

A couple of hours later I was none the wiser, which was why it was a relief when Peter called me back.

"Becoming a foster parent isn't an easy task," he informed me. "It can take months to jump through all the hoops. And you signing over guardianship now won't do any good because they've already terminated your parental rights. We would have to get those back before you could legally make Billy and Emily your daughter's legal guardians, if you were wanting to do that, which I wouldn't recommend because in that case you'd be giving up your rights all over again."

I made a face even though he couldn't see me. "Well, fuck." Sam didn't have months or years.

"For now, I would like us to focus on you," Peter continued. "Prove you're fit to be a parent and that your rights shouldn't have been terminated in the first place. I'm not going to lie. It's not going to be easy."

Between my research and what Peter told me about the situation, proving I was fit to get Sam back would be more complicated than I could have imagined. It would involve thorough background checks, psychological evaluations, mental tests, and substance control tests, which meant I would definitely have to enroll in AA and stop drinking altogether. I would also have to start seeing a shrink.

"I'll do whatever it takes to get Sam back with me," I said.

"That's good to hear," Peter said. "And considering how all of this started, I'm advising you to make an appointment with that therapist you told me about."

"I planned on doing that," I said.

"Good. I'll set things in motion here, and I'll inform you about our next course of action as soon as I can."

I hated all of this. All the things I would have to do, all the changes I would have to make just to prove to the government that my daughter belonged by my side.

But all I had to do was think of Sam and the look on her face when she saw that gun pressed against my head to know that I would endure much worse than this to get her back home.

13

SAMANTHA

I tried to settle in my temporary home and not ruffle any feathers. However, I soon discovered that wasn't easy because no matter what I did around the house, Mrs. Bradford looked displeased.

And then I discovered why. There were a lot of unspoken rules in addition to those Grace had recited for me on my first day.

Do not eat too loud, do not make noise while washing dishes, be light on your feet, and do not speak unless spoken to, to name a few. Grace was right when sharing her condolences with me. I felt worn out even though only a few days had passed since I'd first arrived.

And I couldn't even start sharing my thoughts about the reverend. He constantly looked like he was in a bad mood, and his voice, when he chose to say anything, was so strong and commanding that it gave me chills.

When I'd finally met the other girls, I'd learned they had been ordered to stay in their rooms on the day of my arrival so they wouldn't bother me, which I found odd. Besides

Grace, there were two other girls, Chloe, who was thirteen, and Patricia, who was twelve.

Chloe had blonde hair, brown eyes, and olive skin. She didn't speak much with me, and I figured she was just shy.

Patricia was small, skinny, pale, and looked younger than she was, with light blonde hair and green eyes. I thought she looked way too serious for her age, and then I was told she had autism. That was why her parents had abandoned her when she was a baby – because they didn't want to deal with a child who was different, and I found that very sad.

It was obvious that Chloe was protective of Patricia and constantly helped her with her chores.

No matter how different they were, all the girls had something in common. I couldn't put my finger on what it was, but I knew it would come to me, eventually.

And that wasn't all. The vibe around the house was all wrong. It wasn't a happy house filled with laughter. On the surface, the girls were polite and doing what they were told, but rippling beneath that there was this undercurrent, this tension, which was making everyone, including me, nervous, and I couldn't understand why.

My gut told me that something was wrong. But I was definitely missing some piece of information to understand it all. And I refrained from asking, even Grace with whom I was the closest. And I meant that strictly geographically since we were sharing a room.

For the time being, I kept silent about everything that I observed and kept watching. My father told me I should always listen to my gut feeling, that I needed to respect it, because his gut feeling had saved his life more times than he could count, and mine would do the same for me.

That night, after finishing all my chores and going to

bed, I texted my dad. We hadn't spoken since the day I was brought to this farm, and I wanted to check in.

> This place is super weird and full of crazy rules and chores. It's like I'm in the army, but the religious kind, without all the fun parts. The fields around the house would be awesome for shooting practice.

His message came straight back:

> Sorry to hear that, but hang in there. You'll be coming home soon.

With that thought in mind, I started to doze off.

"What is the meaning of this?" a voice yelled, snapping me from my sleep.

"What time is it?" I was startled to see Mrs. Bradford looming over my bed. To my shock, she was holding my phone. She'd definitely read the text I'd sent to my dad.

"What are you doing with my phone?" I asked angrily.

Her head looked ready to explode. Apparently, I wasn't supposed to talk back to her.

"It is rude to gossip and lie behind our backs. We took you in, we've been nothing but kind to you, and this is how you repay us?" she berated. "I won't tolerate something like this. You need to make sure it doesn't happen again."

I glared at her. Who even was she? She couldn't boss me around. She wasn't my mother. She was just some lady I was stuck with for the time being, who got paid to take care of me.

"I can speak with my father and share my thoughts and opinions with him whenever I want," I pointed out.

"Starting tomorrow..." Mrs. Bradford pursed her lips.

"You will be in charge of the barn, on top of the rest of your chores. Perhaps that will teach you not to speak back when you're wrong," she snapped at me, and with that she left, taking my phone with her.

That was how I learned that despite the fact I always kept my phone close to me at night, it was checked at random times, just as Grace had warned me.

As it turned out, Grace wasn't exaggerating about the internet being monitored either. There was a family computer in the kitchen, and the Bradfords checked our browsing history. Most of the fun sites, including YouTube, were blocked altogether, so I simply used the computer for school research.

I wasn't allowed to go to actual school, as the county was sorting things out, but I still tried to stay up to date. I'd spoken to Hillie, and now she sent me everything they did in class. I tried to learn on my own, but I was terribly behind, at least partly because I was allowed only fifteen minutes on the computer each day, and I had none of my books with me.

More rules were revealed to me along the way. I wasn't allowed to lock any door, including the bathroom door, which horrified me since I shared it with other girls, and some of them, especially Grace, had no boundaries. She'd burst in a couple of times while I showered, and she almost looked offended when I told her to leave.

It also bothered me when Mrs. Bradford locked Patricia up in her room during one of her tantrums. That was what she called her episodes.

As it turned out, the Bradfords were complete religious nutcases who ruled the house with an iron fist. That was the undercurrent I'd sensed. I realized that was what all the girls had in common – fear. They were all afraid of what the

Bradfords would do next. What new rule would they impose on the girls?

It went without saying I hated that place, and I was definitely starting to hate them.

"How do you like living with the Bradfords so far?" Grace asked me one night.

I was surprised because Grace and the other girls didn't interact with me during the day much, other than to tell me what needed to be done. And she was breaking one of the rules, which said we weren't allowed to speak with one another after Mrs. Bradford came to turn our lights off. The nighttime was reserved for reflection, prayer, and sleep.

Nonetheless, I replied because I liked the fact that we were breaking at least one of the rules. "It's definitely different from what I'm used to," I said, deciding to be diplomatic, not really sure why.

Perhaps I was afraid Mrs. Bradford was eavesdropping. It wouldn't be the first time. Each day I was confronted by some other controlling madness, and I really tried not to get bothered by it all because I was sure this was temporary for me, yet it was getting harder and harder to keep my cool.

I felt sorry for the other girls who were stuck with the Bradfords, especially Grace, who was with them the longest.

"I would like to say things will get better, but they won't," she answered.

Of course, I had a million follow-up questions, but we could both hear Mrs. Bradford scolding Patricia for still being up, so I remained silent, not wanting her to check up on us as well. That woman gave me the creeps; it was so obvious she was pretending to be something she clearly wasn't.

The next morning, while I was choosing a clean shirt to

wear, I noticed that a few of my things were missing, all my jeans, plus a pair of underwear.

"Did you take some of my clothes?" I asked Grace, who was in the process of dressing. She had a variety of very ugly dresses, I noted. More to the point, all the girls did.

Was that one of the rules I wasn't familiar with? I suddenly had a fleeting thought.

"Mrs. Bradford threw them away," she informed me as though it wasn't a big deal.

I looked at her incredulously. "What? When? Why?"

My family wasn't downright poor, but we definitely had to manage our income, so to have someone throw my things away was unacceptable.

"Yesterday," she said, ignoring my other two questions.

How did I not see it before? Then again, between all the chores I had to do, I was pretty busy throughout the day.

I grabbed the first clean shirt I saw so I could dress and go look for Mrs. Bradford. I had to confront her about this.

"I wouldn't do that if I were you," Grace warned.

"What do you mean?" I asked, lingering at the door.

"You want to go and yell at Mrs. Bradford for this. Don't."

"I'm not you, Grace. I have to stand up for myself," I snapped, leaving the room in a whirl of indignation.

As I looked for Mrs. Bradford, I wondered if I had been too hard on Grace. She simply gave me friendly advice. Of course, I couldn't take it because I didn't want to live in fear: I didn't want to be like her. The Bradfords had to know they weren't my parents, and I didn't have to listen to their crazy rules.

I found her leaving her sewing room.

"Why did you throw my things away?" I demanded, not

bothering with all the morning pleasantries I was constantly reminded I had to say.

"They were too revealing, and the colors were downright vulgar," she replied, making a face in disgust.

To someone wearing nothing but beige, gray, and brown, colors like red, yellow, and orange were bound to be too much, I thought sarcastically.

"Those were my clothes; you had no right."

"You live here now, and you need to dress accordingly. It reflects poorly on the reverend if his girls are dressed like common trollops."

Trollops? Common? What century is this woman living in?

"I want my clothes back," I insisted.

She went to her sewing room and returned seconds later, dumping a pile of something into my hands. "Here you are, these are suitable replacements."

I needed only one glance to realize I'd received a few ugly dresses like the ones Grace wore. They were from the same material too. "I won't wear these," I rebelled.

Mrs. Bradford narrowed her eyes. "You will if you know what's good for you; now go to your room and change. You have a lot of chores to do today, and you're already behind schedule," she hissed in a dismissive tone, moving past me and going downstairs.

The reverend appeared by the door of his bedroom.

I scurried back to my room, feeling like my head was spinning. I couldn't believe that interaction actually happened. At times I felt like I was living in a parallel universe or something.

What the hell? I thought, throwing the dresses on the bed.

"Told you," Grace said while making sure her hair was neat and properly, tightly braided.

Reminding myself I had to play nice while Dad worked on getting me out of there, I sighed and got changed. The clothes were uncomfortable. Not to mention it was hard to move around in them. I wasn't used to walking around in a skirt, and now I was supposed to be in one that was so long it touched my ankles.

I hated it.

To make matters worse, Mrs. Bradford looked at me approvingly as I got downstairs. "Now you look like the proper modest young lady you're supposed to."

At some point, feeling like I'd had enough, I grabbed a pair of scissors and sat on the kitchen chair. I wanted to cut the fabric of the dress. I couldn't walk around in this thing. Not to mention the sleeves were so restricting I felt like I was suffocating.

"What are you doing?" Mrs. Bradford yelled, appalled, snatching the scissors from my hand.

"I can't move in this," I argued. "I want my old clothes back. This is insane. You have no right to steal my things and throw them away."

Mrs. Bradford slammed her hand against the kitchen table. "How dare you speak to me in such a manner, disrespecting my generosity."

"I didn't ask for any of it."

"Silence! I won't have some disobedient brat tell me what I can or can't do in my own house. You are here by our grace, and to hear you sully all that was done for you is unacceptable."

Realizing this showdown could turn into a real problem for me, I said, "I wasn't doing that. I just..."

"I said keep quiet," she snapped, raising her voice again. "Return to your room immediately. You clearly need to pray on some of your actions. And don't bother coming down for dinner."

In a fury, I left the kitchen and stomped back to the room, making as much noise as possible, no matter how petty that was of me.

I couldn't believe she'd grounded me as though I were some small child. I was gritting my teeth hard until at last I managed to fall asleep, hungry.

14

SAMANTHA

The Bradfords were trying to make me like the other girls, perfectly modest, obedient, religious. I had to braid my hair and wear dresses. Not to mention my sneakers had disappeared in the middle of the night and were replaced with a pair of ugly black shoes like the rest of the girls wore. They were tight and uncomfortable and blistered my feet all around.

This place wasn't a prison, it was even worse. It was hell.

They monitored us twenty-four seven, and to my horror, I noted there were cameras installed around the house. They demanded we dress a certain way, speak a certain way, and act a certain way.

It was masked as concern for our well-being. To make sure we stayed on the right path, the path of God. I now knew it was all a lie. And when I confronted them about it, about the hypocrisy of it all, they grounded me.

The reverend and his wife pretended to be nice, but they weren't. They had masks for the world, for their congregation, and those masks were definitely off in the privacy of their home. It frustrated me that nobody except us, who lived with them, was aware of that. Not to mention how furious I was at Social Services. They had definitely failed us, placing us with these religious nutcases.

They were a couple of hypocrites. We were slaves to them, free labor. The house always looked pristine thanks to us, but still, Mrs. Bradford always complained and yelled at us for being lazy.

After doing all my chores one afternoon – there were a lot of them; I felt like Cinderella, although all the stepsisters were slaving away beside me – I figured I needed to know this place, just in case something happened and I needed to evacuate quickly. That was one of the things Dad taught me. *Always get familiar with the grounds.* I decided to start with the house and then spread to the lands beyond.

Snooping around the house proved to be mission impossible. First Grace warned me to stop sneaking around. Then the reverend caught me near Mrs. Bradford's sewing room. He grabbed me by the ear and dragged me back downstairs, giving me more chores to do as penance for my behavior. I tried one more time, but was caught by Mrs. Bradford, which resulted in me missing dinner again.

So I proceeded with the other part of my plan. I investigated the farm while doing my chores outside. Some of the fields were left unattended, with tall grass and wildflowers freely growing. The other fields were planted with corn and wheat. And Mrs. Bradford had a large vegetable garden she expected us to tend to. That was one of the things I didn't mind doing, actually. My mom had loved growing vegetables and had taught me how to tend her neat rows of carrots, lettuce, and spinach; I could think of her as I worked, my hands dark with soil.

Unfortunately, all that land meant the farm was way farther from the highway than I originally thought. I regretted not paying more attention when I was brought here.

All in all, the farm was a bleak and lonely place. I honestly couldn't bear this torture any longer. I felt like a prisoner sentenced to hard labor, and there was nothing I could do about it because there was nobody I could rely on.

I can rely on Dad, I reminded myself. He'd told me that he'd hired a lawyer, and he'd promised to get me back. But how long would that take? I really wanted to run away, but I feared Dad would get in trouble if I misbehaved in any way, so reluctantly I stayed in line.

I gazed out across the cornfields, trying to see beyond them. It looked like only more cornfields followed. Even if I started running right now, I wouldn't know which direction to go in. I had no idea where the nearest town was. And I had no money for a bus ticket.

I'm stuck. At least for the time being.

"What are you doing here?" Grace asked, behind me, startling me.

She acted like their watchdog or something. Then again, I understood she was acting out of fear because the Bradfords had one simple and most important rule. If one girl was making trouble, all girls were in trouble. All of us could get punished.

Grace didn't know me, so I understood her suspicions of me. She didn't want me causing trouble for her, making her already hard life even harder. Although I sympathized, I had no intention not to snoop around. There were things I had to know about this place.

"I was wondering why all the fields aren't cultivated," I said, which was the first thing that came to mind.

In truth, I could already guess the answer to that question. The reverend couldn't do it all by himself. And he was either too stingy or too secretive to hire help. I bet it was the latter. He looked like the type who didn't want strangers milling about.

"It's really stupid to be curious about something like that," Grace said, with a hint of attitude.

I wondered if I'd done something to her to make her act like that toward me. And then I reminded myself I was the new kid.

"It's never stupid to be curious," I replied with a shrug.

She rolled her eyes. "Come on, I need your help with the pantry. Mrs. Bradford wants it reorganized."

I followed her, although I wasn't done exploring. I planned on resuming my investigations as soon as possible.

I also decided to look for local maps so I could get my bearings and see exactly where I was. See where the nearest town was located, or even a gas station. That kind of information was important. It could be a lifesaver in certain situations. Dad made sure I always remembered that. So if there was a reason I needed to run away, and fast, I wanted to know which direction to run in.

Once Grace and I had cleaned and reorganized the entire pantry, she left me alone in the kitchen and went to Bible study.

I was very tempted to use the computer, but I didn't dare. And not simply because it was monitored. It wasn't my time to use it, and I knew without a shadow of a doubt I would be punished if I used it without permission. Besides, if

I googled maps, then the Bradfords would know what I was up to. And that would be a bad thing.

That was why I would look up what I needed to on my phone, which had finally been returned to me, after we went to sleep and then simply delete the search history. I would even return it to its default settings if I had to. It was imperative they didn't know I planned on escaping.

As I pondered my dilemmas, I noted how the house was super quiet all of a sudden, and that didn't happen often. The girls were always quiet, of course, but usually Mrs. Bradford was yelling at one of us, or the reverend was practicing his sermons for Sundays.

As I walked about, I realized the reverend and his wife were nowhere to be seen. That was surprising – and rare – given how much they liked lurking in the shadows, watching our every move. At least, it looked like that to me. Creepy.

As though compelled, I picked up one of the dusters and went upstairs. I knew the rest of the girls were having their Bible study, so I was the only one left free to do what I wanted.

I went to the part of the house that was off-limits. I tried the first room only to find it locked. The same thing happened with the next one.

Strange, I thought.

I wanted to try the third, but I heard a rumble from inside, like people walking about, and I ran out of there immediately. I barely managed to get to the foot of the stairs when the door opened. Both the reverend and his wife left the room, and I couldn't help but notice that they looked kind of odd. Were they fighting?

I took a few steps down so they wouldn't see me, pretending to dust the paintings. As I might have expected, all of them had religious motifs. Translation, they were all dark, gloomy, depressing.

I could hear Mrs. Bradford sniffing. Was she crying?

"Do not walk away from me," he commanded.

"Stop following me," she countered.

Yup, she was definitely crying, which meant they were arguing about something. That piqued my interest.

"Obey me, Evangeline. You must obey me."

It was obvious he was following her around, looming over her as she tried to get away. This was the first time I'd heard them at odds.

Despite the pretty weird, not to mention uncomfortable scene, the reverend remembered to lock the room they'd been in. Were they worried that the girls would steal some of their valuables?

And then they spotted me.

She quickly wiped the tears from her face, scowling at me. "What are you doing here?"

The reverend still loomed over her. It was obvious he wasn't done arguing with her. Or whatever it was they'd been doing behind locked doors.

"Dusting the picture frames, Mrs. Bradford." I looked down, trying to keep my face neutral as though I hadn't heard their exchange just now.

Her eyes narrowed, as she clearly realized nobody told me to do that. But apparently, she decided to brush it off. "Go back to your room immediately," she ordered.

"Yes, ma'am," I replied with a nod, not daring to look at either one of them. I left, relieved not to be in their presence anymore.

What was that all about? I couldn't help wondering. *This place is getting weirder and weirder by the second.*

Next, I could hear Mrs. Bradford yelling at the other girls downstairs, sending them back to their rooms as well. Her fight with the reverend must have been fierce to leave her in such a bad mood.

Thirty seconds later Grace entered the room.

"What's that all about?" I asked her.

She shrugged, then went to her desk and continued reading the Bible.

"You know, I just saw her crying," I tried again. "She and the reverend clearly had a fight."

Grace's expression was weird.

"What is it, Grace?" I prompted.

She shook her head. "Just stay away from the reverend when he's angry," she advised.

I looked hard at her, hoping she might say more, but she ignored me and simply continued reading the Bible.

15

SAMANTHA

Something strange was definitely going on between the Bradfords, especially when they thought nobody was watching them.

That was why I'd been keeping a close eye on them ever since I saw Mrs. Bradford crying. Although she appeared to be the perfect obedient wife, she showed the sharpness of her teeth when they were alone. On the other hand, it was more than obvious how much the reverend hated it when she tried to defy him.

The couple from hell had a pattern of behavior. They always treated us way worse after they'd been arguing behind locked doors. He would make us girls recite parts from the Bible by heart. He would drill us relentlessly, and whoever dared to make a single mistake was severely punished. And she would criticize everything we did and call us a useless bunch of orphans who came to this world only to torture her.

Since I'd arrived, I'd noticed the other girls were always

on their best behavior while the Bradfords were fighting, while their joint bad moods were palpable in the air. No matter how good all the girls were, they still found ways to punish us.

To be perfectly honest, I couldn't care less if the Bradfords had marital problems. However, since they were affecting me and the other girls, I had to care.

The problem was I needed answers that couldn't be given simply by observing someone's behavior, so I tried speaking to the other girls about the Bradfords. Unfortunately, they wouldn't tell me a thing.

I could understand it. The girls were afraid. The Bradfords hadn't hurt me, and I hadn't seen them hurting the other girls, but I'd seen the aftermath. The girls had bruises and marks on their bodies, and Patricia couldn't have fallen down the stairs as many times as she claimed.

But I still felt like I could be an ally to them no matter what was happening around the house, and it bothered me that they mistrusted me.

What were they afraid I would do anyway?

Tell on them to the Bradfords?

I would never do something like that. Then again, they didn't know me that well.

I'll prove my loyalty somehow, and then perhaps they'll trust me with the secrets of this place. That thought made me frown. It sounded like a long-term endeavor, and I really hoped like hell I wouldn't be staying that long.

I wondered if the Bradfords acted the way they did because of the strictness of their religious beliefs, or if they chose religion as a way of hiding their true nature. That thought made my head hurt. Perhaps learning such details didn't really matter. What did matter was learning the truth. It wasn't like there was really anything else to do around the house, all day long.

The chores were hard, and we weren't allowed to watch television or movies, plus not going to school was driving me insane.

I realized it was imperative to return to my daily routines. No matter where I was, I couldn't neglect my training. Now more than ever I had to stay sharp and in shape. I knew it would be impossible to practice shooting, but I was definitely going to do all the rest.

I found a perfect place to practice by the barn. And the best part was that I couldn't be seen from the house. If I did all my chores a little bit faster, I knew I could steal an hour to go through my exercises and self-defense moves early in the morning.

It was pretty easy for me to thoroughly hate this place. I would hate it even if the Bradfords were the best people in the world. The fact that they weren't, that they had all these rules that they imposed on me, that I lacked privacy and couldn't speak with Hillie or Dad whenever I wanted made me hate them even more. It was exhausting walking around them on tiptoes, having to pick and choose each word spoken.

I was berated for crying to my father over the phone.

Once again Mrs. Bradford came furiously to my room. "You selfish girl. Your father lost you. He can't help you anymore, yet you hurt him with your words. Hurt us as well," she lectured me.

I kept my mouth shut and just stared at her.

"It was very disrespectful talking about me and my

husband in such a manner. If you don't change your ways, I'll be forced to take drastic matters," she threatened before leaving.

I could have sworn I heard the key turn in its lock as she left.

True enough, she had locked me in the room. Luckily, I was used to going to bed without dinner, I joked to myself, so I wouldn't completely freak out. After all, I was actually locked up, imprisoned.

And the worst part? Grace acted as though that was the most normal thing in the world.

You misbehave, you get punished, it was as simple as that. Perhaps to her, not to me. Because of the Bradfords, I was constantly on guard. And found it really hard to sleep properly too. All the same, each morning I made a conscious decision to play along and do everything I was supposed to. At least for now.

The discipline and all the skills Dad had taught me were what kept me focused. They gave me the confidence to feel at least a little bit safer in a house that was full of uncertainty.

No matter what the Bradfords threw my way, I knew I could take it, survive it, and thrive despite it because I was much stronger than they thought.

"I know you think you have been a clever girl, but you haven't," Mrs. Bradford said as she cornered me that afternoon. "I know you've been sneaking out each morning before breakfast."

I cursed to myself, not liking the fact I had been discovered.

"I was doing my exercises," I explained, keeping my face

and voice neutral, as though I didn't see anything wrong with that.

Truth be told, *I* didn't see anything wrong with that, but this freak might. Everything was forbidden around here, so why not exercises too?

Mrs. Bradford made a face as though she smelled something nasty. "It looked like fighting, and you know we don't tolerate violence in this house."

I was tempted to ask her if she was joking, but the woman actually crossed herself after saying that.

"It wasn't fighting. Just some exercises Dad taught me to stay in shape."

"I would like you to focus on your tasks more and try to be more ladylike from now on, not waste time on such foolish things," she urged.

Although it was phrased like a plea, I knew it was a command.

I said nothing because I knew that if I flat-out refused to listen to her, she would just ground me again. And I needed to be free to roam about, to spy on her and her husband. So I simply planned on continuing to practice behind her back. However, that would definitely require me to find a more private place because this house and the barn weren't safe. Sometimes it felt like the ground itself had eyes to spy on me as well.

Mrs. Bradford could warn me all she liked, but she wouldn't stop me exercising, and she wouldn't stop me sending my regular messages to Dad either, encouraging him to get me out of here as soon as possible. Though I phrased it a little better than that. In return, he told me of his progress with his new lawyer.

They were trying to make the judge reconsider his ruling

and hear Dad out, because the first time around it had all been done behind closed doors.

Hearing that he was fighting as hard as he could to get me back was comforting. I also spoke with Billy, making him promise he would take care of Dad while I was away, and I texted with Hillie almost every night. She spoke about school, and I spoke about my current life in the country. All of that kept me sane, in a way.

I refrained from messaging anything too controversial so I wouldn't have to deal with Mrs. Bradford screaming at me each night after her phone inspection. I kept my messages short and positive, leaving out how I really felt about this place unless I was speaking in codes. I slipped a few things in that I knew they'd not find suspect.

Although I censored my messages to keep them PG friendly, Mrs. Bradford still chastised me for spending too much time on my phone.

I promised I would try to speak less with my dad and my friends in the future, which earned me a strange, unsettled look because she couldn't decide if I was serious or sarcastic. That pleased me.

It was exhausting playing nice, minding my words and texts, but it had to be done because I didn't want to be grounded or get my phone confiscated. And the last thing I needed was to be labeled a troublemaker because then they would keep an even closer watch on me. I had to avoid that at any cost so that I could continue doing all the sneaky things I wanted to.

Besides, if I lost my time outside, I would go absolutely crazy. Being outside and doing my exercises were the only times I truly felt like myself, free.

I really wished Dad would get me out of this prison soon

because everything about this place was wearing me down. Perhaps that was the point. Perhaps that was what the Bradfords wanted, to break me, so they could shape me into one of the other girls.

I refused to be like the rest. And I would fight them no matter what.

16

SAMANTHA

I tried to remain self-sufficient, just as my parents had taught me, while I lived in that prison. At the same time, I wanted to make friends with the other girls, and not simply because I wanted to extract secrets about the Bradfords from them. The truth was there wasn't much to do while living on that farm. We worked, prayed, or slept and that was all, so of course it would be nice to exchange friendly words with others. Or simply gossip about something. I missed gossiping.

But it seemed like they didn't like me, and I had no idea why. At first, I thought they acted like that because they didn't know me, were suspicious of me, and feared I could cause problems for them, but as the days went by, I started to wonder if they were under orders not to interact with me.

Luckily, learning how to fight wasn't the only thing that my parents had taught me. They taught me how to observe my adversaries, or in this case, the girls I wanted to be friends with, note their behavior and character traits, and use that knowledge to my advantage. Thanks to those skills, I knew I would get to the bottom of things no matter what.

Pretty easily, I noted how all the girls shared a few similar traits. They rarely spoke, even among themselves, and Patricia flat out refused to speak with me. Not even a single word. They did everything that was asked of them without complaint. The only exception to that was Patricia. I believed her autism made her act out because she liked her routines, and anything that disrupted them caused her stress.

Finally, all three girls were very pretty. And it was obvious how much pride that gave the reverend when "his girls" were praised each Sunday while we had to do our charity work for the community.

Despite my observations, I still had no idea how to get closer to them. Hillie was much better at social interactions than I was. Unfortunately, I couldn't ask her for advice because I didn't want Mrs. Bradford to know what I was up to.

"That is a really pretty braid," I complimented Chloe while we got ready for church. "I wish I knew how to style my hair like that."

She gestured as though she wanted me to sit down, and once I did, she started untangling the mess that was my hair.

Is this progress? I wondered. I felt like it was. "Did your mother teach you to do this?"

"No." Her reply was curt.

It's still a reply.

I'd decided to start with Chloe because there were moments when I saw a sliver of defiance in her eyes when she thought nobody was looking. It was just a little bit of attitude or an eye roll, but all the same it gave me hope she would be more open to breaking a few rules with me.

Perhaps I was wrong because she refused to say anything

else. And when I tried asking another question, she shushed me. After finishing my braid, she left.

That made me frown. I was finding it frustrating that none of my tactics were working.

Or so I thought.

"I've noticed how you're trying to be friendly with the other girls," Grace said once we were in our room again.

"We all live together. I figured it's time to get to know you guys," I replied honestly.

Grace shook her head. "The Bradfords don't like it when people ask too many questions."

"I'm not people," I corrected. "I'm one of the girls."

She gave me a strange look. "Not yet, but you will be."

It was my turn to shake my head. I was tired of her cryptic words. "So what you're telling me is that talking and being friendly are forbidden too? What kind of a place is this?" I added since she didn't say anything else. "I hate it here," I confessed, suddenly unable to hold it in any longer.

"You've been pretty vocal about that since day one," Grace countered dryly.

"I'm serious. I don't feel safe with those two always lurking about."

Although nothing truly bad had happened to me since I came here, some of my things had been stolen, and I went to sleep without dinner a lot. I still felt like I was in danger. It sounded crazy and paranoid, yet I felt like I was the prey being hunted by a predator.

"I'm going to ask the social worker to take me someplace else."

I'll swallow my pride, and I'll ask for help. I would do anything to get the hell out of this place. If this was the best they had to offer, then I didn't want to see the worst. At the same time, I was sure that any place at all would be better than here.

I still had that social worker's number, and if she didn't show up soon, I would call and threaten I would do something drastic if she refused to transfer me. I wasn't joking around. As a last resort, I would make a living hell out of the Bradfords' life and force them to kick me out if I had to.

Come to think of it, that sounded like an amazing plan. I wished I'd thought of it sooner; it could have saved me a lot of trouble. Then again, I had promised to play nice. And I still couldn't help worrying that my behavior would reflect poorly on Dad.

"I don't think that'll change anything," Grace said. "You'll just end up someplace even worse."

"I'll take my chances, anywhere is better than here," I insisted. "And I think you should do the same," I added as an afterthought. *All us girls should leave this place*, I thought. The Bradfords weren't good people, and they certainly shouldn't be raising children.

Grace looked at me as though I'd just said the most ridiculous thing in the world. "This is my home."

The certainty and conviction in her voice really surprised me. *How can she say something like that about this place?*

Then I reminded myself that she had been here the longest. I felt sorry for her.

"Besides, I'm going to age out in a few months anyways," she added glumly.

"What's going to happen to you then?" I asked. I knew one couldn't be a foster child above the age of eighteen, but I'd never stopped to think what that actually meant.

"I'll have to leave the farm for good unless the Bradfords decide to keep me for real, as their daughter," she explained.

"As in adopt you?" I asked incredulously.

She nodded.

It was on the tip of my tongue to ask if she was joking because I couldn't fathom that she could actually want to be adopted by those people and live with them forever. That idea sent chills down my spine. I would rather live on the street than accept a deal like that.

But I said nothing, and then, since the conversation was apparently over, I grabbed my phone and called the social worker. It rang and rang, but no one answered.

I gritted my teeth, checking the time. *Am I calling after hours?* I had to wonder.

I tried again, early in the morning. Still, nobody answered the phone. *I need a new plan*, I thought after trying unsuccessfully to reach the social worker throughout the day.

That was when I decided to slip a note to the social worker during her check-in. I had no idea when she would arrive, as I wasn't privy to such things, and if I asked Mrs. Bradford, she would just yell at me. But in the meantime, I started compiling a list of all the weird, intrusive, borderline abusive – and downright abusive – things the Bradfords were doing to us.

I was convinced that once the CPS was aware of what kind of people they were, they would be stopped from being foster parents ever again.

But as I read my list, I had a moment of doubt. What if they simply refuse to believe me and a bunch of vulnerable, lost girls? The reverend and his wife were respected members of society: he was a pastor, for crying out loud, and everybody loved them. And who was I? *Just a nobody, pointing a finger.*

Even if the social worker doubted my words, she would still have to look into it. She was a government official, and all complaints had to be investigated, or so I hoped. And once she started investigating, she would soon uncover all the dirt the Bradfords were trying to hide.

Overcoming that dreadful moment of doubt, I started writing my letter whenever I could, always in fear of being discovered. I talked about how unsafe I felt, and how worried I was about my foster sisters. It was strange to refer to them in such a manner, but I believed my letter would be better received that way if I acknowledged a relationship between us.

That conversation with Grace really bothered me, scared me even. She had been with the Bradfords the longest. Was it possible they had her brainwashed?

Will she be on my side when this letter becomes public, or will she call me a liar? I worried. *I guess I'll discover that when the time comes.* And in the meantime, I would continue to be her friend, no matter what.

Once I finished the letter, I kept it carefully hidden. My first thought was to keep it on me so I would be ready to deliver it when the social worker arrived, but I ruled against that as a plan. Keeping it on me would wrinkle it, dirty it, and I had to make sure my words could be clearly read because, otherwise, all my efforts would be for nothing.

While I waited for my check-in with the social worker, I hoped I would start going to school soon. Whatever happened, I really needed to escape this grim place at least for a few hours a day.

I tried not to think about how small my dreams had

become as of late. The Bradfords were making me small, and sometimes it felt like they were winning, but I kept fighting because I knew how much my parents would be disappointed in me otherwise.

I have to become one of the girls. I need to make them trust me.

17

JESSE

Things were not moving nearly as fast as I wanted them to. And that was infuriating.

I tried to focus on my routine simply in order not to go completely mad. I also started working again at a car shop that was run by one of Billy's cousins, and I did some handyman work on the side, knowing I would need a lot of money to pay for my lawyer and therapist.

Working full-time kept my mind busy, although it wasn't easy for me to deal with other people. My fuse was too short when confronted with stupid or rude people. I would have to work on that, among other things.

I'd promised Sam and Peter that I would go to therapy, and I kept that promise. One mandatory session with Dr. Sheldon turned into a regular thing.

Dr. Amanda Sheldon wasn't what I expected. She was close to my age. I liked that because it meant she had life experience, not simply book experience, and that was very important to me. I had to admit that I liked speaking with her. She made me feel as though I wasn't a completely lost cause. That I wasn't alone in my struggles. She really opened my eyes a great deal. Dr. Sheldon had a way of explaining things to me without making me feel stupid or broken.

There were still times, especially if I was having a bad day, when I felt like therapy was a waste of time, but considering my lawyer advised me it would be a good thing for the judge to hear I was in therapy, I sucked it up.

At first, I tried not to open up too much to her – I tried not to share all my secrets, troubles, and all the ugliness that was pressing in on me, because I was trying to focus on my need to qualify as a fit parent. I basically wanted her to teach me how to act and what to say to the judge so he would think I was a fully functioning human being who was a good parent.

Of course, Dr. Sheldon saw right through all that bullshit and made me talk about real issues because it was only then, by honestly working on my problems, that I would actually be able to be a good parent to Sam.

Unfortunately, knowing that and acting accordingly were two very different things. Part of me still wanted to fight against it at every turn. It wasn't in my nature to show weakness.

In a war, if you're weak, you die. That was a mantra I had lived my life by. And it was hard for me to open up, especially if she asked me a particularly hard question.

"Has your sleep improved?"

I shrugged. "I sleep."

She narrowed her eyes. "You need to stop evading, Jesse, and be honest with me. Tell me about your latest nightmares."

I groaned to myself. I should have known this was

coming. Every time I refused to answer a question to a level that satisfied her, she would ask an even harder one.

"My latest nightmare?" I repeated, not sure why.

"I know you have them," she insisted. "The dark circles around your eyes are a dead giveaway."

"I don't remember what I dream about," I lied.

"Do you dream about your time away?"

That was her fancy way of asking if I dreamed about the war.

I shrugged again. "Sometimes."

"Do you have nightmares every night?"

"Maybe," I replied reluctantly.

"Tell me about the reason you ended up in the hospital." She abruptly changed the subject. She did that at times.

"It was just an accident," I insisted. By this point, my self-defensiveness came out completely on default.

She looked at me through her big round glasses. "Nobody ends up on a psychiatric evaluation by accident."

"I got released," I pointed out stubbornly.

"Only because you managed to trick the system. My colleague told me about your stay in detail."

Colleague? I wondered if she was talking about the shrink who pestered me every day or the guy who gave me her business card.

"That was a fun little holiday," I tried to joke.

She wasn't amused. "Did you try to kill yourself?" she asked directly.

I remained silent. I didn't want to answer that question.

"Was your daughter present?"

I said nothing.

"Did you tell her to lie for you? Is covering for you something she is forced to do on a regular basis?"

I looked through the window. I knew she was trying to rile me up so I would open my mouth, and I wasn't falling for that trick. At the same time, I had to wonder how she knew all those things, personal things. I hadn't said shit to her, but someone must have blabbed.

Was it Billy who told her I'd tried to off myself? Was it Sam? No, Sam wouldn't speak to some stranger behind my back.

"Do you think that teaching her to be dishonest is the way to go?"

"I teach Sam to be loyal, honest, and righteous," I snapped.

"Not that day, right?" she challenged. "That day she chose to be loyal to you, and that meant she had to lie about what happened."

"Yeah. She caught me trying to blow my brains out because I couldn't get rid of all the images in my head. She managed to take the gun from me in time. Is that what you wanted to hear?" I asked, raising my voice.

"What images, Jesse?" she asked softly.

I shook my head. I didn't want to speak about that.

"You have to get it out sometime. Why not here, with me?" she added as though she could read my mind.

I closed my eyes for a moment. "We got ambushed one night," I said slowly. "We were cut away from the rest of our unit. It was complete chaos, and we couldn't see anything." I took a deep breath, exhaled as I looked down at my hands. "They threw smoke grenades at us."

I paused, remembering that night as though it happened yesterday. "I lost three squad-mates then; two died from friendly fire. The newbie panicked and started shooting in the wrong direction. One of the others managed to grab the gun from his hand before he caused an even bigger tragedy."

The damage was done all the same...

"Later that night, he killed himself," I said bluntly, "overwhelmed by the guilt of what he had done."

And the worst part? I couldn't even remember why I started thinking about that night in the first place. Katarina was on my mind and our first date. But one thing led to another, and the next thing I knew, I was crying and had a gun pressed against my head, wanting to end it all, with Sam begging me to put the gun down.

"How did that make you feel?"

At the time I thought the kid did the right thing. He absolutely should have offed himself for making such a huge mistake. But my attitude had changed since then.

"That pissed me off. Boys like that have no place in the army. War is a nasty business and no place for the faint of heart. War is a man's job." I crossed my arms over my chest, adamant.

"Are you a man, Jesse?"

What kind of a question was that? "Of course I'm a man."

"What is the definition of a man?"

"Men take care of business," I replied simply.

"Men are strong and powerful?"

"Yes."

"Men never ask for help?"

I just looked at her. Where was this going? Was she mocking me? My beliefs?

"Does coming here make you angry?" she asked.

I decided to be perfectly honest. "Yes."

"Why?"

I should have known she wouldn't let it go. "Because I'm not supposed to be weak. I should be able to handle all the memories and nightmares on my own. Men don't need to cry on some therapist's couch," I spat.

"Yet, here you are," she said in that same soft yet professional manner.

It should have pissed me off, yet it didn't.

"I managed my life and all the moods just fine while I had Katarina..."

"Did you really, or was that simply a bandage on a gunshot wound?" she challenged.

"She was my center," I insisted. "But since I've lost her, I've completely shattered, and I just don't know how to pick up all the pieces and glue them back together. And now I'm being punished for letting Sam down."

I sat quietly for a moment. I couldn't believe I had said all those things, yet I'd received no judgment from her. It was true. Dr. Sheldon accepted me no matter how broken I was, all the while trying to make me see things from a different angle, help me cope with things I couldn't change, and heal me. She didn't start berating me about my weaknesses. That was a strange experience for me.

"This isn't a punishment, Jesse. As a soldier you're simply wired to act in a certain manner, that's all."

I wasn't following. "What do you mean?"

"If someone attacks, you defend. If someone's in trouble, you go to save him, correct?"

"Yeah."

"And if you get shot in the process, you go to treat that wound because you can't be of service wounded."

"Exactly," I replied, impressed that she understood so clearly.

"Your PTSD is simply another wound that you need to take care of, and the right way this time, so it can heal," she explained gently.

"I don't know how to do that," I confessed.

She offered a small, reassuring smile. "That's where I come into the picture. This isn't a question about how weak you are. I know you're not weak. And there is nothing wrong with asking for help; we all have to do that sometimes. This is about taking care of yourself, and that definitely requires strength."

At the end of our session, she prescribed me some pills I had to take from now on, and I didn't mind. She'd really given me something to think about. It was all about perspective, and perhaps mine was wrong.

I realized I was man enough to admit that.

Once I got home, I called Sam. I worried about her a lot. I needed to make sure she was all right.

"How are you feeling?" I asked. I wondered if talking with Dr. Sheldon was rubbing off on me. It wasn't like me to ask that question, in that manner.

"I feel great, Dad. I spent the entire day outside, minding Mrs. Bradford's garden."

That startled me. She sounded completely different. "How are the reverend and his wife?"

"The Bradfords take such great care of me. Each day is a blessing. And reading the Bible really has a great effect on me."

She's being forced to read the Bible? And she's used great three times already. I was starting to worry.

This really didn't sound like my daughter. She was clearly faking her positivity. *Is she trying to tell me she's in danger or something?* Or was I reading too much into things, needing her to hate it there so I would feel better about myself? So I could act like a hero.

"I'm glad to hear that, Sam."

"I miss you, Dad. And don't worry about me, I am well taken care of."

"I miss you too."

"Oh, I meant to ask, Dad. Can you say hi to Ralph for me?"

Ralph?

And then I remembered. We had a code in case we couldn't talk freely. To alert me to any kind of danger, she only had to say one word. And there it was.

Well, fuck.

My daughter was in danger. And I hated being right.

18

SAMANTHA

My fourth week staying with the Bradfords had just started, but I felt like I had been staying with them for years. Time moved slowly inside that house, and if it weren't so filled with uncertainty and trepidation, it would be super boring.

Even with all the chores I had to do, the days felt too long. All the restrictions, rules, secretiveness, and religious way of living were taking their toll on me.

And then something even more bizarre happened. Mrs. Bradford smiled at me as we were cleaning up the table after breakfast. "I have something to show you; come with me."

I knew I wouldn't like it, but I followed her without saying anything. I had learned by now that she didn't like it when we talked back to her or talked to her at all. Unfortunately, I couldn't always rein in my temper. I was my father's daughter, after all. And I wasn't raised to endure injustice.

On the desk in the living room was a stack of books. It took me just one glance to know they were heavily religious homeschooling textbooks. I knew what they were because I saw the other girls using them. All the school supplies were provided as well.

No, no, no. I had a sinking feeling I knew what this was about. *Please let me be wrong,* I prayed, although I wasn't really sure to whom.

Mrs. Bradford handed me a list of assignments to do alongside my chores. "I expect you to take your studies seriously," she warned. "I will test you on these."

"I don't understand," I managed to choke out.

She gave me a look. "It's time to resume your studies," she said somewhat impatiently.

"I thought I would be returning to school; you said I would be," I challenged.

She smiled. It was creeping me out. It was far better, more natural when she frowned. "You won't be returning to your high school. You will be homeschooled like the rest of the girls."

Every part of me was screaming on the inside. I didn't want to be homeschooled. I wanted to return to my high school and be with my friends, and I definitely didn't want to learn from those books. I'd skimmed through one of Grace's books, and it was as bad as I expected. No matter what, the answer to each question was always the same: God.

Being homeschooled meant I would have Bible studies every day as well, and I didn't want to be forced to learn about God, about a religion I wasn't part of. It wasn't that I didn't believe in God. Truth be told, I never thought much about it all. I accepted the existence of God but never felt the need to participate in learning about him. And to be forced to do so, on top of everything else, made me feel as though I was close to breaking.

I shook my head. "My parents wanted me to go to a proper school," I insisted.

The smile disappeared from her face. "We're your foster parents now, and we've decided this is for the best," she said with finality.

"That's not what the social worker promised me. She said I would return to real school." I hoped I could scare her by mentioning the CPS worker, that it would make her reconsider.

"I have little patience for your complaints. I am telling you how things are going to be from now on."

"I want to hear that from the social worker." I held my ground, though she was making me uneasy.

"Is there a problem?" the reverend asked, appearing seemingly out of nowhere.

"Samantha doesn't want to be homeschooled," Mrs. Bradford explained.

His already grim face became even grimmer. "That is my decision. You will obey, or you will be punished."

I took a step back. It was more than obvious he was speaking about physical punishment.

I want to see you try to punish me. Those words were on the tip of my tongue. I wanted to create the biggest scene imaginable, throw a tantrum, perhaps even break a few things, get one of the crosses from the wall, or call the police. Unfortunately, I was simply a girl with a survivalist father going against a reverend, so I would accomplish nothing.

My biggest fear was that nobody would believe me.

"What are you still doing here? You are dismissed," he snapped.

I turned on my heel, ready to march to the bedroom. The room I was sleeping in. I refused to think of it as my own. I wasn't staying here. I couldn't care less that I didn't finish all my chores. I was beyond furious. I couldn't believe this was happening. It was so unfair.

"Don't forget your books," Mrs. Bradford called out.

I collected them, making as much noise as possible. If a small defiance was all I could get away with, I was going to do it whenever I could.

Grumbling to myself, I went upstairs. *I hate this.* I didn't want to learn anything from their stupid books.

Grace was sitting at her desk, studying, as I marched inside.

Unceremoniously, and with a lot of attitude, I dumped all the books beside her. "I can't believe this. I have to homeschool."

"It's really not that different from other textbooks," Grace said. "And the Bible study isn't that difficult, at least not in the beginning."

"I don't care if it's easy or not," I stressed. "I want to go back to my school and not be forced to do this."

She turned in her chair so she could look at me. "We're all homeschooled, so why would you be any different?"

Her outburst surprised me, so I didn't say anything else. I lay down on the bed, crossed my arms over my chest, staring at the ceiling, stewing.

The more I thought about it, the angrier I got. At myself. I should have seen this coming. It was naive of me to expect I would be an exception, returning to my school when all the rest were homeschooled and went to Bible studies.

I am so stupid, I fumed. It bothered me that I had allowed myself to get my hopes up. I should have known better.

And it was more than obvious that no matter how much

I tried, these girls would never be my friends, my allies. The Bradfords clearly had them brainwashed, especially Grace.

Deep down, I was terrified I would end up like them if I stayed here too long. But I also knew I had to force myself to stop thinking like that. *Dad will come to get me.* I knew he would. And I would never end up like those other girls because I would fight no matter what.

Instead of looking for help within, I had to find a way to reach out for help beyond the farm. I still believed the social worker coming to check up on me was my safest bet, but if that failed, I needed a contingency plan. My dad had taught me that it was always prudent to have a few spare plans up my sleeve, just in case.

I also hoped Dad got my message loud and clear the last time we spoke. *Ralph.* I feared he might have forgotten about our code, but the way he ended the conversation with, "I will, and I'll see you soon," gave me confidence that he remembered.

It was difficult to say anything negative about the Bradfords while they were listening to all my conversations. Mrs. Bradford liked to stand right beside me each time I received a phone call now, which was beyond maddening. I also suspected Grace was spying on me and reporting back to that woman everything I did, everything I said. I didn't have proof, so perhaps I was wrong, but it was a feeling I couldn't shake.

Although I knew it was completely stupid of me, I texted Dad to complain about my current situation. I couldn't stop myself even if I wanted to. And I didn't want to. I wanted him to know they were making me homeschool. And I wanted the Bradfords to know as well that I wasn't so easily breakable. That I would continue to be rebellious no matter how many times they punished me.

I am not like those other girls.

I knew I should have had a little bit more tact. I knew I could have written the message in code. But there was part, a strong part, of me that wanted to be petty, and that was why I wrote it as plainly as possible.

> I really don't like my foster parents. They're making me homeschool. All the books are religious and heavily censored.

I pressed send with pure delight.

Although Grace had tried to warn me not to act so stubbornly, defiantly because the Bradfords didn't like that, I refused to leave my room that day. I refused to study; I refused to finish my chores. I wanted to see what they would do to me if I stopped cooperating.

What could they do, anyway? They were trying to rule by fear and intimidation; however, they held no real power. They weren't my real parents, which meant they couldn't tell me what to do. Now that I'd realized that particular truth, I planned on throwing it in their faces the first chance I got.

I told Hillie that I wouldn't be returning to school, and she shared my outrage. She promised she would stage a prison break to get me out of this place. I told her I liked that idea very much.

But then I was surprised when Mrs. Bradford didn't come during dinnertime to drag me downstairs and make me pray in the corner for being such a disobedient spiteful girl.

Feeling like I'd actually managed to accomplish something, I fell asleep.

I was woken up from my sleep when Mrs. Bradford stormed into the room and loomed over my bed as though she were some storybook monster. "You still dare to defy me, after everything?" she screeched.

"I didn't do anything wrong," I argued. I knew what this was about, but all the same, I wasn't going to hold my tongue anymore. "You can't forbid me from speaking to my dad."

"I can, and I will," she snapped. "For this insolence, for not learning from your mistakes, your phone will be taken away from you for three days." She even waved it in front of me as she spoke, as though taunting me.

I had a sudden urge to snatch it from her hands, but I didn't. I knew nothing good would come of it if this turned physical. I knew I could take her. She was practically my height and very thin, and I worked out a lot. Sadly, the same couldn't be said for the reverend. And no matter what, I didn't want him involved.

"You can't do that."

"Watch me. And you can expect many more restrictions in the future if you don't change your ways." She left, locking the door.

I growled in pure frustration. I grabbed the first thing that was near me. It was a revised version of a biology book, and I flung it at the closed door. It smacked against it loudly.

It brought me no comfort.

I couldn't believe that bitch actually took my phone away. What was I supposed to do now?

What will Dad think if I stop answering him? I worried.

I could only hope he wouldn't do something reckless because of it.

On second thought, perhaps that was exactly what he had to do. These people deserved it.

Raise hell, Dad.

19

SAMANTHA

I really hated the Bradfords and their religious house of weirdness. At the same time, I only had myself to blame for losing my phone. I'd been overconfident. I'd convinced myself there was nothing she could do about my disobedience.

I was wrong.

Each time I rebelled, I got punished. And the reverend and his wife were ruthless about it.

I felt on edge without my phone. It was my only window into the real world. The Bradfords lived in some other time. Ancient time. I felt all alone with nobody I could turn to. The other girls avoided me like the plague, and now I couldn't speak with Hillie or Dad. The worst part was that there was nothing I could do about it. Without my phone, I couldn't even call social services or the police to complain about the Bradfords' mistreatment of me.

The reverend and his wife hid behind their Bible and found quotes within it to justify their behavior, yet they were nothing but bullies. He was a totalitarian Bible beater. Literally, as it turned out. I once overheard Patricia complaining to Chloe how the reverend beat her with his Bible because she couldn't remember a specific verse about chastity. That was horrifying to me.

At times I found Mrs. Bradford even worse than her husband. She hid behind the facade of being a perfect motherly figure, but she had the shortest fuse imaginable. She could explode over anything and was verbally abusive. She constantly called Patricia stupid and acted as though she couldn't stand her, although I reckoned I was the biggest thorn in her side.

"You will burn in hell for being such a wicked, rebellious child," she screamed at me once just because I helped Chloe fix lunch instead of letting her do it all by herself because that was her penance for burning the bacon and eggs that morning.

I was lucky up until that point that neither the reverend nor his wife tried to physically harm me, but I feared that day was coming fast. Although I could see in Mrs. Bradford's eyes that she would like nothing more than to slap me, I suspected they were reluctant to do so because the social worker was due to check up on me. And it wouldn't be easy explaining my bruises, especially since there was no way I would lie for them.

I added a few more things to the note I planned on giving to the social worker during our next meeting. I knew it wouldn't be easy to slip her the note. Of course, it would be best if one of the girls could create a diversion. However, I knew I couldn't rely on the others to help me with my plans.

I hadn't told anyone about my note, and I didn't intend to. No matter how much I pitied all the girls who were forced to live in that house with me, I didn't trust them either. So it was on me to create a plan and execute it.

The days went by, and nobody came to pay me a visit. I was endlessly worried the Bradfords had told the social worker not to come anymore because all was well.

What if they lied, what if they said I had fully adjusted and wanted to stay here?

They couldn't do that, could they?

The social worker had an obligation to check up on me no matter what, right – right? I realized I had no idea. And I didn't like the fact that I didn't know. I felt like I was constantly walking through the dark.

All the same, the note was ready, and I would give it to the social worker as soon as she came to see me. Still, it was maddening, waiting.

The best time of my day was nighttime because it meant I could go to sleep, surrender to my dreams, and forget about this horrible place for a few hours.

But that particular night, a scream woke me up from sleep. It pierced the silence so suddenly, so intensely that I jumped out of bed prepared to fight. And then it happened again, and I realized it was Patricia or Chloe.

It was apparent that Mrs. Bradford was beating the screaming girl savagely. She was screaming, crying, begging for mercy, promising she would be good from now on, but however desperate or anguished her words became, nothing worked on Mrs. Bradford or made her stop.

My heart was beating like crazy. I had never been this disturbed in my entire life. And there were certainly moments from the past that could qualify as genuinely disturbing. I'd stopped my father from committing suicide, yet this bothered me more.

That was probably because that terrible Bradford woman was beating an innocent girl.

I looked around the room and noticed that Grace was now awake as well.

"It's very painful when she uses the wooden spoon," she said with a strange expression on her face.

Mrs. Bradford was beating a child with a wooden spoon. What the hell? *I have to stop this*, I thought, going toward the door.

"What are you doing?" Grace asked, looking genuinely confused.

I could only stare at her for a moment, yet the girl's crying prevented me from wasting time. "Someone needs to stop this savagery," I snapped.

"You won't stop anything," Grace replied calmly. "The only thing that will happen is you'll get beaten too. Let it go."

Her neutral tone shook me to the core. It was horrifying to me that she could accept this torture as normal.

Is that true? Will I get beaten as well? I had no reason to doubt her, yet my mind still refused to accept that.

The girl kept crying. Somehow, from the half-formed words amid her tears, I started to suspect it was Patricia.

"I can't just do nothing," I rebelled. It wasn't in my nature to allow something like this to happen. My parents had taught me to help out when others were in trouble, and to have my family's back, no matter what.

"Suit yourself," she said, shrugging. "Oh, just so you know, she probably deserves it."

"Who?"

"Patricia."

"How can you say that?" I demanded.

"It's true," Grace said, her voice completely flat. "She always provokes Mrs. Bradford."

I felt like my head was spinning. I didn't know what to do.

"Whatever you choose to do, keep it quiet. I need to sleep." And with that, she returned to bed, turning away from me and placing a comforter over her head.

Gritting my teeth, I reached the door. It was locked.

I cursed like never before. Of course, I knew how to pick locks, especially old-fashioned ones like this one. Only trouble was, however, I didn't have any tools with me.

While I fumed, the house went completely silent. It felt unnatural after all that noise.

Did she kill her? I wondered.

I waited a little bit longer and couldn't hear anything else. Although it felt completely surreal to me, I returned to bed, still shaking.

I need to get the hell out of this place.

In the days that followed, I did my best to stay under the radar. I did all my homework, knowing I would have a test in the afternoon that would determine my assignment load for the next day. And I had a private Bible study with the reverend, and I really wasn't looking forward to the experience.

In the meantime, I was doing all my chores as well. I missed my phone, but I knew better than to ask for it.

Whenever I saw her, I couldn't stop looking at Patricia. There was no mark on her, yet I knew that her dress was hiding all the bruises she had after that beating. She was also very subdued and somewhat slow. She was clearly in pain, emotional as well as physical. The sight of her, so cowed and hunched over, filled me with fury.

Mrs. Bradford is a monster.

"Samantha, come here," Mrs. Bradford called me from the living room, as if she'd heard my thoughts.

I braced myself for what was to come. "Yes?" I asked, looking to the floor.

I hated this act, but after what had happened the other night, I found it necessary. I had to change my ways if I were to have any chance of destroying them from within.

She handed me my phone back.

I looked at her in confusion. "My three days aren't over," I said, not really sure why since I knew they basically were or would be this evening. Part of me knew I shouldn't argue with her to continue my punishment, but I decided that this was a necessary risk. I was playing a role, after all.

"I decided that your punishment is over," she said ever so generously. "Nevertheless, remember that the phone can be taken away from you for good if you continue to give out more of our private information."

There was so much I wanted to say to that, but I bit my tongue. "Understood," I replied, putting the phone in my pocket.

Without being told I was dismissed, I returned to my place in the kitchen and continued working. I couldn't wait for some alone time. I'd added what happened to Patricia to my note for the social worker, but I also realized that I needed to formulate a plan for how to run away if I had to.

I really wanted to wait for Dad to get me out of here legally, but if the situation became unbearable, I had to get the hell out before it was too late.

That was why I searched local maps on my phone before bedtime. I wanted to see exactly where I was.

I'm in the middle of nowhere, I thought glumly. Then

again, the Bradfords had clearly chosen wisely, needing privacy for what they were doing.

This farm was completely isolated, miles away from the nearest town. We only left on Sundays for church, which wasn't even in the town exactly, but just outside of town. There was nothing around the farm apart from that single highway. And that was troubling. Especially considering I didn't know how to drive a car. Dad never got a chance to start teaching me.

More to the point, if I stole a car, the cops would simply find me that much quicker.

So a car wasn't going to be much help. I needed a different plan. A better plan. One that had a chance of working.

20

JESSE

After Sam slipped the code word into our conversation and sent that undoubtedly unhappy text, I doubled my efforts to get her out of there.

I showed the text to Peter so he could have some proof she was being mistreated. He said we could definitely use the fact that religious practices that weren't her own were being forced on her to try to get her out or at least move her someplace else.

I completely freaked out when I couldn't reach her afterward. I wanted to cheer her up a little, show her things were moving forward, that I was doing my best alongside Peter to get her back. The phone rang and rang, and she never answered. I also texted and asked what was happening, and I got no reply.

Of course, I was worried that she'd gotten in trouble for reaching out to me. If those people were such religious freaks, then maybe they treated that as a challenge of authority. I'd dealt with people like that in the past, and they were always real pieces of work.

And then Sam's phone didn't even ring out: it was completely turned off. I didn't like that one bit. If I knew where she was, I would instantly drive there to make sure she was all right. She'd told me a farm and the name Bradford, but their address was unlisted.

When I contacted Social Services for the address, they refused to give it to me, claiming it was for Sam's protection. It was totally infuriating.

Although I hated it, I went to the CPS. The social worker responsible for Sam's case, Julianna Higgins, narrowed her eyes as soon as I entered her office. It was obvious she was preparing herself for a fight.

"I need your help. My daughter hasn't checked in for three days, and I'm worried." I explained why that was alarming, and I showed her the last message I got from Sam.

"Mr. Cotton, I assure you that your daughter is living with the best family in the county."

"What about the fact they're forcing her to learn from the Bible textbooks?" I challenged.

"All those books are approved by the Department of Education."

"I want to see her," I insisted. "There's clearly something troubling her."

"You know that's not possible," she said in a dismissive tone.

I took a deep breath the way Dr. Sheldon had taught me, so I wouldn't explode. "I know I've lost custody, but what about some visitation rights?"

"That's not up to us."

"Then who is it up to?"

"Only a judge can approve something like that."

The same judge who took Sam away from me in the first place. I gritted my teeth.

Thanking her for her time, I got out of there before I really lost my temper. The system was rigged. It was discriminatory against people like me. I had always believed that, and now I had proof.

But no way was I giving up. I knew Sam was in danger. So I went to see Peter again. I told him about my unsuccessful visit with the CPS.

"I just want to see her, make sure she's all right. Is that really too much to ask?" I stressed.

"No, it's not, but there are certain procedures and protocols in place we have to go through first," he explained.

"Sam would never willingly go radio silent," I insisted. She was like her mother in that regard. She constantly had something to say. Which was usually smart-ass, but I adored that about her.

Peter reassured me he would immediately start working on getting me visitation rights along with all the rest.

And then something else occurred to me. I'd always thought it was strange how quickly Sam had been placed with a foster family. And then I'd read online how that wasn't standard practice. I decided to mention that to Peter as well.

"It is a bit strange; normally kids get shuffled around through group homes a lot or even age out before placement," he said, looking untroubled. "Your daughter got lucky."

I frowned at his choice of words. "I don't believe in luck." Especially in that kind of luck.

I wasn't trying to be a pessimist, but I felt like something fishy was going on here. And I couldn't shake that feeling no matter what.

Sam had told me that besides her, three other girls were living with that family. Was that a coincidence, or were they specifically asking for girls? There was a chance I was paranoid. At the same time, while at war, I'd seen the very worst of humankind, and that made me suspect everything.

Although it seemed like everyone involved spoke of the reverend as though he were a saint, I knew he was just a man, like all the rest, and that meant secrets and darkness; they were inevitable: it was just a matter of discovering what kind.

I couldn't stop thinking about it during my next session with Dr. Sheldon, and she noticed how distracted I was.

"Tell me what's on your mind."

By then I had decided to trust her completely and share everything, without holding back. I'd also realized it was the best way to get Sam back, anyway. Only by being honest with my therapist could I be honest with myself. And that was the only way to heal my crazy head.

"I'm worried about Sam."

"Still no word from her?"

"Nothing. And after the last things she wrote to me, how she sounded the last time we spoke, I'm troubled. I really need to find her."

"I understand how you feel; it's natural to worry as a parent," she said carefully. "However, I have to advise you against trying to find her. She was placed in a foster house for a reason. And if you want to get her back, like I know you do, you mustn't make matters worse."

"It's not my intention to make matters worse," I said, defending myself. "I just need to know that she's safe, because this is very out of character. Plus, she used our code word to alert me to the fact she's in trouble."

Although I knew Dr. Sheldon was right, I still felt like she was telling me to do nothing, and I couldn't do that. So when I got home, I fired up my laptop and tried to find my daughter. The problem was I only had a few pieces of information. I knew their name was Bradford and the husband was a reverend. I hoped that could narrow my search somehow, so I tried googling. I read all kinds of articles until my eyes started to go blurry. Even that didn't stop me from continuing.

Eventually, I stumbled upon Reverend Gareth Bradford and his church. The article mentioned his youth program and fosterage program.

Is that him? It has to be.

Feeling encouraged, I started googling again. Unfortunately, the man had no social media presence. Neither did I, so I really didn't find that odd. It was simply unfortunate considering that it could help me a great deal if he was sharing details of his life on X or something.

I continued searching and found a news story of two runaway girls, who were presumed missing. It was heartbreaking, of course, but all by itself that wouldn't be something so strange. Kids ran away from their homes all the time. What caught my attention was the fact the reverend and his wife had been fostering those girls. Tanya Smith and Maria Taylor had run away from the Bradfords. One of the girls was eighteen; the other was seventeen, a few months shy of turning eighteen.

Is there a link?

Since that first report, I found nothing else about it.

Clearly, the case went cold. The police stopped investigating.

That didn't sit well with me. Did the girls run away because they didn't like living with the Bradfords, or did something else happen to them?

The Bradfords would definitely lose their power over the girls in that time period, so if they wanted to leave, they couldn't stop them, I speculated. If the situation in that house wasn't that great, no wonder they chose to run away.

But then, I thought, why run away in the first place? Once that girl turned eighteen, she had to leave the foster house all the same. I was definitely missing something.

While I was looking into this mystery, I received a text.

> Sorry for the radio silence. I was busy with chores and studying.

I frowned, confused. Again, I thought, *Am I missing something?*

> Are you all right?

I asked directly in reply, needing to hear Sam say one way or the other so I would know how to proceed.

> I'm busy, Dad. I don't want to fall behind with my studies.

Her reply troubled me even more because that was very definitely not what I asked.

Saving the articles about the reverend, I grabbed my phone and went to see Billy. I wanted his opinion. Was I losing my mind, or was something else going on here? I didn't know. All I knew was that I couldn't track her down and simply go and visit Sam without permission from the proper authorities. Dr. Sheldon was right about that.

And I found that Billy agreed with her. "That would definitely screw things up, for both of you."

"Would you go instead of me? Or maybe Emily could?" I asked, in desperation.

"You know we both will," Emily reassured me.

"We don't know where she is," Billy pointed out.

"I think I have an idea how to fix that." I couldn't believe something like that hadn't occurred to me before. Sam wasn't a little girl. She would know where she was.

> Can you write me your address? I want to send you a few gifts from me, Billy and Emily.

I sent to Sam, on a flick of inspiration.

> That's not necessary, Dad. I have everything I need here.

Why was she acting like this? Why was she resisting me, fighting me even? I couldn't understand what was going on.

> I know I don't have to. I want to.

I didn't have to wait long for her reply.

I smiled, showing the text to Billy. "We have it."

21

SAMANTHA

The loud bang of the door smacking against the wall woke me up from sleep, pushing me back to grim reality.

I have to stop waking up like this, I thought as Mrs. Bradford slammed the lights on and stormed into the room.

Grace and I shared a glance, as though silently asking for whom the wicked witch of the west came, but it became obvious as she stopped in front of my bed.

What did I do now? It was true that I'd texted Dad, but I'd made sure not to write anything that could trigger my jailer. Apparently, I was wrong. She was well and truly triggered.

To my chagrin, the reverend stormed into the room as well.

At that point, Grace hid under her covers.

The reverend and his wife loomed over me like some ragged, ominous birds of ill omen. Vultures ready to devour me.

"You wicked, wicked girl," Mrs. Bradford practically seethed. "You dared to disobey us yet again."

"I didn't," I countered, yet it was like speaking to a wall; their minds were already made up.

Perhaps this was all just an excuse so they could punish me, keep me on my toes.

"As punishment for your disobedient behavior, the phone will be permanently taken away from you," the reverend declared.

I looked at them wide-eyed. "What? It's mine. You can't do that." I couldn't believe this. I couldn't lose my phone, not permanently. That was all I had left. It would be the death of me at this place. Not to mention what it would do to my dad if he couldn't reach me.

"We can," Mrs. Bradford said with obvious satisfaction. She reached for the phone, and I reached to grab it. Unfortunately, she managed to snatch it from my hand just as my fingers curled round it.

I wanted to wipe that smirk from her face with my fist.

"You will be fasting on bread and water alone," she continued, then glanced at Grace, as though warning her not to give me anything else to eat, "so you can contemplate your actions."

"That's not fair. What did I do?" It was disorienting, this whole awful scene. My mind was spiraling, freaking out.

Mrs. Bradford waved my phone in the air. "I learned what you did after tonight's check-in."

Tonight's check-in, she said that as though that were the most normal thing in the world. *Did Grace rat me out?*

"What? I spoke with Dad, nothing else," I said sharply, defending myself. "I didn't say anything I wasn't supposed to," I added in a rush. It was true. He asked me if I was all right, and I lied.

They both narrowed their eyes. It was obvious they didn't agree with me.

"Nothing you're not supposed to?" she repeated incredulously. "It's infuriating you dared to give our address to some stranger."

Some stranger? Dad was no stranger, at least not to me.

"Why?" I asked. Why were they so angry with me? It didn't make any sense. Then again, few things did make sense in this house.

"You broke the rules, and you dare to ask why?" Mrs. Bradford yelled in my face.

"I know all your rules." *It wasn't like I had any choice. It was either learn them or end up grounded.* "And this wasn't one of them," I pointed out as rationally as I could. It wasn't my intention to challenge their authority, simply to reason with them.

By the look of it, I was failing miserably. Since I didn't like how they both continued to loom over me, I changed positions ever so slightly.

Mrs. Bradford looked ready to explode. "You dare to speak back to us?"

Before I could say anything else, she slapped me hard across the face. My whole left side started to tingle.

She tried to slap me again, yet although the first slap had startled me because I hadn't expected it, my initial shock quickly wore off, and my training kicked in, and I managed to catch her hand in time. She couldn't shake my iron grip on her wrist. I squeezed, wanting her to know I too could hurt her if I chose to. I was beyond furious. I didn't seem to have much choice about living in this place, but I wasn't going to tolerate them tormenting me, especially when I hadn't done anything wrong.

"Do not try to do that again," I warned, looking her straight in the eye.

She started to struggle, wearing a strange expression on her face. It was obvious she wasn't used to someone defying her.

While Mrs. Bradford and I shared our staring contest, the reverend acted. Without saying a single word, he back-handed me so hard I fell back onto the bed.

I was completely disoriented for a moment. I'd suspected he was strong, but I definitely didn't expect he was that strong. Unfortunately, something was telling me he'd actually held back on his power.

"If you don't mind your mother, I will have to intervene," he threatened. "And I have a switch with your name on it, girl."

The windows shook ever so slightly at the intensity of his words.

Mrs. Bradford wore a self-satisfied smile as she massaged her wrist. She was pleased he'd hurt me while defending her. They were both sick and twisted to the core.

"Did I make myself clear?" he challenged.

For a man of faith, for a person who was supposed to spread love, his eyes were full of hate, and something else, something even darker.

I had no doubt in my mind he could kill me if he wanted to. It was that kind of stare. And since he looked at me expectantly, as though waiting for a reply, I gave the slightest of nods.

My head was reeling, and not simply because of the impact of that punch.

If he didn't like children, then why foster in the first

place? Was it because of the image of a pastor, as a man to be held in high esteem by others?

With that message delivered, they left the room.

I would never be able to forget the grin on her face as Mrs. Bradford locked the door behind her. *She actually enjoyed this nightmare of violence and terror.*

My whole face was throbbing. It went nicely with the fury I was feeling. That wasn't all. Each time I thought about the reverend, what he said, how he looked at me, I felt fear, deep and primal. And I hated it. I hated that man with every fiber of my being.

I wasn't bleeding, but I was sure I would have a nice shiner tomorrow, especially since I wouldn't treat it in any way. I wanted everyone to see what he'd dared to do to me. And if I was lucky, the social worker would see it too.

The dam was broken. They'd hurt me physically. And I knew things would only get worse. My probation period, so to speak, was over. To them I was no different than the other girls. That realization scared me: there was nothing left to protect me at all.

I looked in Grace's direction. She'd remained perfectly silent, absolutely still, as all that went down. It was obvious she had gone through something like this before and had therefore learned not to draw attention to herself. That was troubling.

Even more troubling was the fact that they'd taken my phone away for good. That was a disaster because now I was completely cut off from everyone I knew. *What will Dad do once he realizes he can't reach me? Will he think I'm doing that to him on purpose?* I hoped he knew me better than that.

"I can't believe this," I muttered.

"I told you that you need to fall in line," Grace said.

Fall in line? Never. I glared at her. "You still think this is your home?" I countered. Although I knew none of this was her fault, she still allowed all of it to happen, without saying a single word, and that was just wrong. If things were reversed, I would protest, complain, and stand up to them for her. But hey, that was me. Apparently, we didn't all think alike.

"You need to be more careful," she warned. "The reverend has no limits."

"What's that supposed to mean?" I asked.

"The way you're behaving, you'll learn soon enough," she replied before turning to the other side as though to return to sleep.

I rolled my eyes. I was so over her "useful bits of advice." If she didn't have the nerve to tell me everything straight, I wished she wouldn't bother at all.

I had to discover exactly what was going on. And if Grace, Chloe and Patricia were too afraid to speak with me, then that simply meant I would have to discover the truth on my own. In a way, I preferred it that way. The stark reality was that I only had myself to rely on in this place.

I needed to be able to snoop around, but first I would have to be able to leave my room since Mrs. Bradford made it a habit of locking us up at night. So in the next couple of days, being extra careful not to get caught, I collected pieces of wire and hairpins and made some lockpick tools.

Dad had taught me how to make a lockpick out of practically anything. Those were a fun couple of months when he would lock me in a room, leaving various objects behind, forcing me to be creative to get myself out of there – sometimes working against a timer he'd set for me. At times, it would frustrate me, especially if I was hungry, but right now I was extremely grateful for his lessons.

I planned on visiting all the locked rooms in the restricted area to learn the Bradfords' secrets. I was certain they had plenty of them. Although I knew that finally discovering more about what was going on would be helpful and that such knowledge could be used as leverage, I couldn't deny that part of me was scared.

Do I really want to learn their darkest secrets? I wondered.

I already knew that they wore masks of kindness and piety when interacting with other people, but were completely different around the house when no one else was there. Was it possible there were a few masks left on still that they would only take off behind locked doors?

I was about to find out. Because no amount of fear would stop me from doing what I had to. I was desperate to go back home.

All my life, Dad had prepared me for fighting monsters one day.

And that was exactly what I planned on doing now.

22

SAMANTHA

Mrs. Bradford was in a bad mood, which meant we all kept our heads down, doing our chores in silence, making sure everything looked perfect.

I hated that I had started behaving like the other girls, walking on eggshells around the Bradfords so as not to enrage them, like they were our masters or something.

I fantasized about using their toothbrushes to scrub the toilet and about spitting in their morning coffee. Of course, I didn't do any of those things. I didn't dare.

Besides, such submissive behavior was necessary because I needed to be free to roam around while planning a bullet-proof escape. I knew I had only one shot at escaping. And there was no way in hell I was staying here any longer than necessary.

I was worried about what my escape would do to my father because I knew there would be consequences for him. Still, it had to be done. Of course, he might turn up to rescue me before I got out, but I couldn't count on that. He would have the law after him if he tried, and maybe he wanted to use legal channels to get me back. I wasn't sure I could wait that long though.

There was one more thing that worried me deeply at the moment. And that was when the social worker didn't come to check up on me. The visit was way overdue, and I feared she'd forgotten about me.

Maybe she'd forgotten me on purpose. I sensed she didn't like me. I'd argued with her, but that wasn't my fault. Her attitude annoyed me to no end. *And now she's punishing me*, I realized.

Since I couldn't outright ask Mrs. Bradford why my social worker wasn't coming, I decided on an idea of how to extract that information out of her in another way.

I asked Chloe to teach me how to make cookies. I knew how to cook, but I'd never learned to bake. My mom had died before she could teach me.

Part of me expected Chloe would refuse, but she agreed. The cookies I had in mind were pretty plain because Mrs. Bradford was of the mind chocolate was the devil's food; all the same, they would serve their purpose.

As expected, Mrs. Bradford came to the kitchen to investigate. "What is that smell?" she demanded.

I forced a smile. "Chloe taught me how to bake those cookies you like so much," I explained, offering her the plate. The timing was perfect. I'd just got them out of the oven. They turned out great.

It was obvious my behavior took her by surprise, and she eyed the cookies suspiciously before accepting one.

She tasted it. "You need more sugar," she observed.

"I'll remember that," I replied as though grateful for her feedback.

"You're finally behaving like a young lady should."

Perhaps in her mind it was a compliment, but to me it just meant my act was working.

"I was thinking of making them again for my social worker to show how well adjusted I've become," I said, looking downward, thinking that would be a nice touch.

"I wouldn't hold my breath," she commented. "They don't like coming out this far away from their offices."

I could definitely understand that. Who would want to drive to the middle of nowhere to see if some brat was all right? To my chagrin, that brat was me.

"And they're constantly behind on the check-ups anyway, thanks to understaffing," she said, actually being helpful for once.

Instead of showing how I really felt about her revelation, I sighed with relief. I intentionally overdid it to make sure she would notice. "That's good to hear, Mrs. Bradford. I don't like all their nosy questions," I offered, making a face, trying to mimic her usual disdain.

To be fair, what I said wasn't technically a lie. The people from the Child Protective Service had made my life miserable. And then they'd dumped me with an abusive family, so I wasn't feeling protected at all. All the same, I was deeply rattled and disappointed beyond words. I didn't know when or even if the social worker would come back, so that meant I definitely couldn't give her my note.

Dad had told me not to trust the government people, and he was right. Come to think of it, it was to be expected that I couldn't count on them to help me, let alone save me, and it was foolish of me to have even entertained that idea for a nanosecond. They were useless. They only knew how to destroy. They threw me into this mess, and now they were nowhere to be seen to get me out.

And the most tragic part was that everyone called my father crazy and paranoid. The way it looked to me, though, he was right about everything.

Mrs. Bradford laughed. "You noted that. Good," she said almost approvingly. "They are terribly nosy." Then she looked at Chloe as though finally noticing her. "Clean this mess up immediately." She grabbed another cookie before leaving the kitchen.

Chloe looked at me sympathetically before getting to work.

It was all for nothing, I thought with despair. Then again, perhaps it was better to know they weren't coming than to sit around holding onto hope like an idiot. This way I could focus on getting myself out. I was nothing if not adaptable. Thanks to my parents, I wouldn't allow myself to succumb to the despair I was feeling.

I wondered if the postman or a courier came here on a regular basis. *Maybe I could sneak into their vehicle.* Then again, control freaks like the Bradfords wouldn't allow someone to regularly come to their home.

They need privacy for what they're doing.

Now it made perfect sense why all the girls were locked up when I arrived. The Bradfords didn't want the social worker to see anything was amiss. All the signs were there; I just hadn't known I needed to look for them back then.

Maybe I could find another way to get my letter to Dad so he could use it to get me out.

If all else fails, I'll simply run and hope for the best, I thought glumly.

That was definitely the last resort, although I was confident about my odds if that scenario happened. I had skills, and I could survive in the wild for a few days even if I had no food or water with me. I'd just need to get far enough away from the house before anyone noticed I was gone.

The problem was that surviving wasn't enough. I had to be saved as well. For that to happen, I had to reach a place with a distinct landmark or an actual address in a town close by so that my father or Billy could come and pick me up.

I shivered. There was no telling what the Bradfords would do to me if I tried to run away and failed. I couldn't even imagine it. At the same time that terror was a huge motivator not to screw things up.

The Bradfords could never know about my true intentions. Until it was too late, of course.

I can't do anything without my phone, I realized in a bolt of shock. I had to get it back: without it, I wouldn't be able to reach Dad.

How to get it back? I knew by now that the Bradfords weren't the type of people who would change their minds so easily, or at all. That left me with only one solution. I would have to steal it back. The problem with that was that I had no idea where Mrs. Bradford had hidden it.

I didn't allow that to discourage me. During my night-time explorations around the house, in search of their secrets, I would look for my phone as well.

I needed to gather as much evidence against the Bradfords as possible because that was the only way the government people would believe me that something awful was happening inside this house.

What if my word against theirs isn't enough? I had an overwhelming moment of doubt. *It will have to be because I will have proof on my side.* Besides, I hoped that once the other girls saw how the Bradfords were going down, they would confirm everything I said about them.

I'm getting ahead of myself, I realized. There was no use in thinking about the tenth step if I didn't make the nine before it.

One step at a time.

Once they sent us to bed, I would wait for the whole house to fall asleep before picking the lock on my room, and then I would start looking about, see what useful things I could uncover about my captors. I was certain there was plenty that they didn't want anyone to see.

Their level of secretiveness, I realized, and the fact they were bad people could go in my favor. *I'll be their downfall; it was just that they didn't know it yet.* Dad would be so proud of me when I managed to get myself out of here.

That thought cheered me up because I'd really sunk low mentally for a moment. Losing my phone did that to me.

Surrendering and becoming like the other girls just wasn't an option. I'd always bounce back quickly because I had to. Perhaps others could be bullied into submission, but I'd been raised in a different way. I knew how to fight, shoot, and hunt. And I would use any skill necessary to not only leave this place, but also to completely destroy the Bradfords in the process.

I had to set Grace, Chloe, and Patricia free as well. They didn't deserve to stay in this prison either.

The only people who did deserve to be in prison, for tormenting a bunch of innocent kids, were the reverend and his dear wife.

23

SAMANTHA

That night, I was determined to continue my search. But I didn't get a chance because just as I planned on sneaking out, I heard a noise that forced me to run back to bed.

Mrs. Bradford came to the room. She was quiet, clearly so I wouldn't wake up. That was precisely why I pretended I was asleep.

Grace looked beyond pale in the dim light, and I could see that she was shaking all over. Mrs. Bradford came over and summoned her out of her bed. The two of them moved toward the door, although it was obvious Grace wasn't willing. She was afraid.

"Where are you taking her?" I asked, jumping out of bed and moving toward them.

Grace shook her head, a terrified look on her face.

Mrs. Bradford shoved me back by my face. "Get back to bed, or I'll be back with the spoon," she growled, giving me a menacing look.

"But—" I started to protest.

"I'll be okay," Grace whispered, but she didn't sound confident as she was yanked from the room.

I heard the lock click as the door was pulled shut.

I lay on my bed, fretting over her, wondering what was going on. Was she okay? Were they hurting her? Why couldn't I hear anything? A million questions ran through my head as the hours passed. Grace returned a couple of hours later. She leaned on Mrs. Bradford as she walked back to the bed. She threw up in her trash bin before curling into bed, crying. Then Mrs. Bradford left quietly.

I wondered if this had happened before, and I'd missed it. I moved over to Grace to check on her. "Are you okay?" I whispered.

Grace was silently crying and shook her head. "Leave me alone," she murmured.

"But... what happened? Where did they take you? What's going on?" I looked her over, and I couldn't see any marks on her, but that didn't mean anything. She was under her blanket now, and all I could see were her fingers and her face.

"Just leave me be, please," she sobbed softly.

I moved back to my bed, doing as she asked for the moment. I didn't know exactly where Grace had been taken, but it was obvious something bad had happened to her. Listening to her pitiful sobs, I came up with all kinds of possibilities, each worse than the last, making my heart beat like crazy.

"Grace, please, is there anything I can do?" I asked after another ten minutes of her softly crying.

She ignored me, or maybe she hadn't heard me ask over her own sobs. She just curled tighter into a ball on her bed beneath her blanket.

Watching her, seeing her hurting so much was killing me. "Are you hurt?" I asked softly, trying again. I hoped that at last she would tell me what they were doing to her. It felt like there was nothing I could do about it, but I was desperate enough to believe that together we could find a solution.

There was only silence in return.

"Grace, please talk to me. You know you can tell me anything," I tried again. "Did she hurt you? What did she do to you? Is she trying to make you sick for some reason?" I pressed, hoping I wasn't going too far too fast. I wanted her to speak, not close off like she'd always done before.

To my utmost horror, she started crying harder.

"I'm sorry for whatever happened to you."

Nothing.

"Please tell me what's going on; maybe I can help," I made sure my words were barely louder than a whisper so the warden of this prison wouldn't know we were breaking rules by talking.

Her sobs subsided, and she sniffled a little bit. "You'll find out soon enough. And there's nothing you can do about it, just endure," she said in a strange, whispering voice totally devoid of emotion.

I didn't press further. I knew her enough by now to tell that she didn't plan on saying anything else.

All the same, I wasn't done talking. "Have you ever tried to leave this place?" I asked.

I knew I was taking a huge risk. I already suspected Grace reported me to the Bradfords each time I did something wrong, so there was a good chance she would report this line of questioning as well. However, tonight I felt confident she would actually speak with me and not simply act as their agent. Perhaps the old me would hold that against her, but now, looking at her like this, I believed I understood. She'd been with them the longest, they were obviously hurting her, and she was afraid.

Maybe I would act in a similar manner if roles were reversed. Especially if I lost all hope, as she has.

Grace didn't reply. The silence stretched long between us.

Despite my racing heart, I'd started to doze off by the time she finally started speaking.

"I've tried to run away two times in the last seven years," she said.

I was relieved she sounded like herself again. Sad, defeated, but still her.

Part of me was really surprised to hear that because she'd always struck me as being the most obedient one, almost broken on the wheel of her need to do what was asked of her. I felt guilty for thinking something so horrible, yet it was true. At times I truly believed the Bradfords had managed to break her spirit and eradicate any kind of self-respect or defiance from her.

That can still be true, I noted.

"But they managed to find me," she said with a sob. "They'd hunt me down, then drag me back."

"I'm sorry," I said, and I meant it. "What happened once they brought you back? Why did you not try again?"

I didn't think she was going to answer, but after a couple of minutes, she said, "I was beaten so hard I had difficulty breathing at times." Her voice was monotone, as though she had distanced herself from what happened.

My heart pounded as I lay there, trying to imagine such a

thing. I thought she was finished, but after another minute she began to speak again.

"I had nothing to eat save for bread and water. They made me live in the barn for a month." She paused, and I made myself wait, giving her space to speak. "They took my shoes away from me. For almost half a year. Even when I had to do the chores outside, I had to walk barefoot."

They starved her, and they degraded her, making her live with animals in the cold. Although it sounded weird, the part about not having shoes seemed like the worst, cruelest punishment to me. It meant she couldn't try to run away again. Nobody could walk barefoot from here to another town. Even with shoes on, that journey would be extremely hard. The Bradfords knew exactly what they were doing. *Monsters.*

"My roommate at the time was also beaten as a punishment for not stopping me. I had to watch the whole thing as Tanya cried and begged for mercy. Mercy, they didn't have an ounce of it." She wiped her nose. "We were friends, and she wouldn't talk to me after that."

That was so sad. And her story filled me with pure fury toward the Bradfords. If I hated them before, it was nothing compared to what I was feeling now.

"What happened to her?" I asked. No Tanya lived in this house anymore. So I wondered if she'd aged out or had been transferred someplace else. If she managed to leave this house, then that gave me hope. Then again, if she'd reported the Bradfords for what they'd done, how come they were still allowed to foster?

"If you try to leave this place, I will have to take the same punishment. They will do to me everything they did to her, probably more," Grace warned without answering my question.

So Grace didn't want to tell me the whole story. She was still hiding things from me, and that was downright infuriating and frustrating too.

"There is a very simple solution to avoid that, Grace. I won't get caught."

"The reverend has connections. You will get caught."

Connections? What does that mean? I wondered. *Does he have helpers outside this farm? Is he working with the sheriff's department?* That was a truly disturbing thought.

"You can come with me," I offered.

In ideal circumstances, I would take Chloe and Patricia as well, but I worried they were too young to make the journey. It would be better to leave them behind and bring help to rescue them. Now that I knew the police were probably compromised, I would go straight to Dad and get him to bring his friends to take the girls from the Bradfords' clutches.

To my surprise, Grace started crying harder. She was so loud I worried Mrs. Bradford would march into our room to punish her. The poor girl didn't look like she could endure any more punishment tonight.

"I don't have the strength to fight back," she confessed. "Not anymore. They took everything from me."

"Don't say that. You're young, and you're strong, whether you see it or not," I said, desperate to encourage her.

"Thank you for saying that, even though it's not true," she replied. "I won't run, but I won't stop you from trying to either."

"That is very brave of you, Grace," I said.

I understood what her offer entailed. She was prepared

to receive punishment for me and still say nothing, do nothing. That meant everything to me, and it strengthened my resolve to not only get the hell out of here and free the other girls, but completely ruin the Bradfords in the process while I was at it.

There was no other way. They had to be stopped permanently.

"Go to sleep, Samantha," she said, sounding beyond tired and old.

I didn't say anything else, leaving her to rest.

I couldn't sleep. Not now. I had so much plotting to do.

24

SAMANTHA

I was standing by the sink, eating, because I wasn't allowed to sit down while having breakfast as a punishment for spilling the milk, when Mrs. Bradford stormed into the kitchen. The reverend was right on her trail, looking like an animal stalking his prey. They acted as though they weren't even aware I was there, too consumed with their personal drama. I didn't move.

"You went too far last night," she reprimanded.

He flinched. "I wouldn't have to do that if you just did what I asked," he growled.

They both looked pretty angry at one another. Part of me really wished this would turn ugly, with all kinds of kitchen objects flying about.

Sadly, I didn't have my phone to video what was playing out before me. It would be a nice thing to present to the social worker. *If that woman ever resurfaces again.* Then again, I could always post it on social media. If I just had my freaking phone.

"Of course, this is my fault," Mrs. Bradford cried with an

exaggerated wave of her hands. "I'm to blame for everything, always," she shouted before rushing through the kitchen door to the backyard.

Of course, he went right after her.

He always did that. Whenever they had an argument, and she tried to get away from him, he wouldn't allow her. Not that I felt sorry for her. They were both monsters in my book.

Unlike the other girls, who were never anywhere to be seen when the Bradfords argued, I decided to do the opposite. I neared the door so I could eavesdrop. I wanted to know what this fight was about in case it could be used against them.

"It is your fault. You're not giving me what I want," the reverend argued.

His voice was so loud I didn't even have to bother to hide behind the door, but if I wanted to hear Mrs. Bradford's replies, I would have to stay close and risk getting caught.

"You make it sound as though it's on purpose," she defended.

"God cursed you with a barren womb that prevents me from having daughters of my own," he accused.

I raised my eyebrows. I always wondered why those two fostered, and now I knew. They couldn't have children of their own, so they tried to fill that void with orphans. Not that I was an orphan. I had been stolen from my father. I stashed that knowledge away.

"The fertility treatment didn't work," she snapped. "And you know that's not my fault."

"God is punishing you. He is punishing us for your disobedience."

"You know exactly what I do for you, the sacrifices I make," she defended. "You don't need to be so cruel."

"If you were a better wife to me, then God would bless us with daughters of our own," he said with such conviction that I could picture his exact expression. I hated that I could do that.

"I agree with you, my dear husband," she said in a tone I could only characterize as mocking. "God clearly doesn't want us to have children no matter how much you torment me."

"It is my duty as a husband, your master, to keep you on the path of righteousness," he said, now sounding as though he were in the middle of one of his sermons.

"And it is my duty to point out that this is happening not because of my wickedness, but your own," she argued.

I raised my eyebrows. I'd never heard her speak to him like that before. He'd clearly hit a nerve during this fight.

Since the situation was starting to really heat up, I dared to look through the small window.

I watched as the reverend grabbed her by the arm. "How dare you speak to your husband in such a manner."

"Someone has to," she said defiantly, her chin tilted. "Nobody is infallible, not even you. And your hubris is a sin against God."

He slapped her with his free hand, and she whimpered, her spirit gone in that flash of violence. "I will make sure you never speak to me again in such a manner," he boomed.

I barely had a second to move out of the way as the reverend dragged his wife inside.

Once again, I was completely invisible to them, which was a blessing. I wouldn't want the reverend shifting his attention from his wife to me. Perhaps it was cruel of me, but better her than me. Better her than Grace, Chloe, or Patricia.

"No, let go of me." Mrs. Bradford struggled as he took her upstairs.

"Silence," he warned, slapping her again.

I knew what this meant even before the beating started. The whole house was filled with the sound of his terrible rage as he hit her with his belt, and she sobbed.

The way Patricia had sobbed as Mrs. Bradford beat her the other night.

I remained frozen at the bottom of the stairs, looking upward, waiting for the reverend to finish "educating" his wife, because I knew that in his distorted mind this was a lesson. As he beat her, he recited Bible verses designed to put her firmly back in her place. Mrs. Bradford continued to cry and beg for him to stop.

At some point, Grace came to stand beside me. We exchanged a look. Her look was saying, *I told you so. Never cross him.*

Mine remained defiant. It was all for show, though. I was deeply rattled. If he could beat his wife this savagely, the wife he'd once promised to love, cherish and protect, then the rest of us were doomed. We had nothing to hope for.

After a few moments, Grace went to the living room and started reading the Bible. I knew she thought that her piety offered some kind of shield around here, but it really wasn't. I was aware that once the reverend left his wife alone, he would start bullying one of us, if not all.

And I am at the top of his shit list. I gulped at that.

Perhaps I should find something to do as well. Then again, why bother? Nothing could save me. I hated how powerless I felt. I was trapped in a house in the middle of nowhere with a complete monster. My brain almost refused to accept this as reality. At the same time, some primal part of my psyche was urging me to just start running, without looking back.

But what would that accomplish? If any of us tried to run away, the police would bring us back, I realized. Grace had tried to tell me that, but I wasn't listening. The authorities all believed the reverend was the best human being in the county because they never witnessed this savage side of him. That was why they were all helping him to keep us trapped even if they weren't aware of it.

I felt angry at the whole world. I was angry at the Bradfords for existing. I was angry at the stupid social worker who placed me here. I was angry at the sheriff and the police in general because they were too blind to see what was going on around here. And I was angry at Dad because if he was all right in the head and hadn't tried to kill himself, then I wouldn't have ended up here in the first place.

And then I forced myself to stop. This was solving nothing. So instead of succumbing to all those negative emotions like fear, anger and frustration, I allowed them to fuel my resolve, and I actively started thinking about finding a way out.

I needed to find a way to communicate with the outside world without leaving any record of it. Confronted with this scenario in which I was stuck, it was becoming more and more obvious I couldn't deal with these people on my own. I needed help. And I could only do that if I managed to get my phone back. And then find a way to send my message without the Bradfords being any the wiser. Because if they had no proof I'd done something wrong, they couldn't punish me for it. It was as easy as that. It was as difficult as that.

With my mind set, I finally forced my feet to move. I went to my room and tried to tune out the sounds of another human being's agony as I did my mindless homework.

I couldn't believe this was my new reality.

Despite the eventful day, the nighttime schedule remained the same.

Mrs. Bradford, limping, her face puffy and bruised, came and took Grace away. Grace had an expression of pure panic on her face.

This time, I snuck out after them.

I followed in silence as Grace was taken to one of those forbidden, locked rooms.

Why had she been brought here? What the hell was going on behind this locked door?

25

SAMANTHA

I didn't manage to peek into the room Grace was being taken to night after night. It was beyond frustrating.

I realized that the only time I saw her sleeping in her bed throughout the entire night was when she was suffering from menstrual cramps. I wondered if those two things were related. *I really hope not.*

I wasn't so young or naive to be oblivious to the fact that all this could have a sexual connotation. Nonetheless, I hoped like hell that wasn't the case.

I was determined, though, that I would find out. It was just a matter of time. And until then I had to continue to keep my head down and not cause problems.

Mrs. Bradford tried to goad me to snap at her by commenting on how I'd changed my tune as of late, how I'd become tame as a lamb, but I didn't fall for it.

"Are you reading the words of our Lord and savior or simply pretending?" the reverend asked me, looking over my head.

I had been so lost in my thoughts that I didn't realize he

had entered the room. I couldn't allow myself to space out like that. I had to always be on guard.

"I'm reading," I said without looking up at him.

"Don't lie to me!" he shouted, and the suddenness of it made me jump.

"I would never lie. It's just that I don't understand this particular paragraph. And I hoped that by reading it a couple of times, it would come to me," I rushed to explain, hoping I didn't sound like too much of a smart-ass. I was going for timidness, which wasn't that difficult. That man made my skin crawl.

"Look at me, girl," he commanded.

I obeyed, still looking away a couple of times. I didn't like his eyes. They showed the truth now. The truth that made me wary, the truth that kept me up at night.

"I know what the problem is," he said, as though musing out loud. "You're not properly motivated to understand what you're reading."

It went without saying that he was completely right. I was irked he'd noticed. I hoped that at least during Bible studies I would have some free time to work on my plan, but as it turned out, I'd made a mistake. This was the most important subject in this house, and I should have treated it as such if I wanted to stay under the radar.

"I know precisely the way to fix that," he added with an evil grin. "From now on I will personally monitor not only your Bible studies but your academic progress in general."

I screamed inside my head. I didn't want to be singled out. I didn't want to spend time with him. But I also knew that saying no to him wasn't an option.

I was screwed.

Mrs. Bradford entered the room as though summoned telepathically.

"Samantha's education is my concern now," he informed her.

She made a face, clearly not pleased. In that one thing, we were in perfect agreement. "That's my duty," she said.

"And it still is. Samantha merely needs a little individual encouragement."

She looked at me, and I couldn't decipher what she was feeling at that moment, fury, irritation, hate, jealousy. The dynamic in the room was weird as hell. And whatever Mrs. Bradford's feelings were, I knew I would be the one punished for them.

"Very well," she said, storming away.

In the days that followed, I was subjected to a lot of surprise questions, especially on the Bible. However, the interrogations almost every time turned philosophical.

The reverend would question me about my thoughts on sin. He asked about a woman's place in the family. The duties of children. I constantly had the sense he was actually talking about the people in this house, including me.

His lectures turned increasingly uncomfortable when he started asking about sex. That subject slipped in quite unexpectedly, but I couldn't help but notice how he looked frighteningly curious about the subject.

Of course, I'd had the usual teenage conversations about sex with Hillie and my other friends, but they were more funny and a bit embarrassing than anything else, and my dad had done his awkward best to make sure I knew how to handle myself in different situations, but none of that had made me feel uncomfortable or freaked out. Not like now.

Not like how I was now being forced to discuss stuff I really didn't understand with this creepy, old man.

I couldn't make sense of half of what he was saying. On the one hand, women were always the temptresses. That was why we had to do everything in our power to hide our sexuality. That was especially true for young girls because their innocence was the strongest aphrodisiac since it reminded men of the Garden of Eden. On the other hand, women should always be utterly obedient and allow men to satisfy their desires. Of course, they would have to repent for it afterward, because not only had they sinned, they had encouraged men to be sinful too.

I really didn't want to listen to him, nor did I want to follow the logic of what he was saying. The glint in his eyes, the passion in his voice as he spoke, frightened me.

"And the Lord said to be faithful and increase in numbers. It's our duty to be joined and fill this earth with our offspring," he lectured me when I stated how all relations between an unmarried man and woman were a sin. I thought that would be an easy answer. I was wrong.

"A man who doesn't spread his seed," he intoned, as I tried not to show how queasy his words made me, "has failed to fulfill the most sacred duty to his God."

I was of the mind there were too many bad people on this planet as it was, but I held my tongue because each time I gave the wrong answer, he would punish me. Sometimes he would add more chores; other times he would hit me with something. The violence would always happen so fast that I didn't have time to react.

I came to see that there would never be right answers with the reverend. Even if I recited his own words from the previous day, he would find a way to twist them as if I'd made a mistake. Even if I quoted the Bible, he would find some other verse to rebuff it.

He enjoyed punishing me, and there was nothing I could do about it. I was forced to kneel in front of him when I gave my answers, and although I fantasized about hurting him, I never did. It felt like I'd forgotten all about my training in his presence. My confidence in myself, in my skills, in my hope that I would ever be able to leave that house started to waver.

And the more time I spent with him, the worse Mrs. Bradford acted toward me. There was nothing I could do about that either. My days consisted of trying to avoid as many landmines as possible, and still activating quite a few all the same. Explosions of rage and religious righteousness were going off all around me.

In their brutal war, I was the only one hurting. None of the girls offered any advice or even tried to console me. I had the sinking feeling they'd all been in my place at some point and were simply glad it was now someone else who was suffering instead of them.

I am turning into one of the girls, I thought with dread.

"No one who practices deceit shall dwell in my house; no one who utters lies shall continue before my eyes. I won't allow deceivers to serve in my house, and liars won't stay in my presence," the reverend recited.

I remained silent because that was expected of me until he asked a direct question. It was always better when he spoke, when he got almost feverishly consumed by his words than when the focus was on me.

"What does this verse mean to you, Samantha?"

It meant I was relieved at how this offered a nice change of pace from all the other creepy subjects he usually liked to inflict on me. That wasn't what I said, of course.

"We shouldn't lie?" I had no idea why my answer sounded like a question. Probably because I was starting to get accustomed to constantly being wrong. I doubted even the simplest things now.

"Lying lips are an abomination to the Lord," he said with a nod, which meant I'd given a satisfactory answer, for once. "So what do you think should be the punishment for those who indulge in such acts?"

"I don't know, but in the scripture, the punishment always fits the crime."

He narrowed his eyes. "So you believe your tongue should be ripped out for lying to me?"

"What?" I exclaimed. "I've never lied to you." I was quick to defend myself, reprimanding myself for falling into such an obvious trap. I should have known better.

"Samantha, you're doing it again," he said through gritted teeth. "You're merely pretending to be one of my good girls."

I panicked, sweating like hell. I was keeping all kinds of secrets, doing all kinds of forbidden things, so it was hard to determine what he was specifically talking about.

"I have no idea in what way I have displeased you, but I apologize for it. I am deeply sorry, I truly am," I recited, looking to the floor in front of me.

"Hmm, at times I really do not know what to think of you. I asked the Lord for guidance because you are a strange thing, Samantha. But you know that you have been doing wrong."

"What did I do, Reverend?" I asked, all innocent eyed.

"You have been looking at local maps."

"Yes," I replied because there was no other way. I had to tell the truth.

"Why?" he demanded.

"I want to know where I am," I replied simply.

"So you can run away like all the wicked girls do?" he boomed.

"No, of course not."

"Lies." He frowned, raising his Bible as though he was prepared to hit me with it.

"Grace told me what happens to runaways and their roommates. I would never run away," I said in one breath.

That stopped me from receiving the blow. The reverend smirked instead, putting the heavy book back onto his lap. "Grace is a very wise girl."

"I wish to be like her in every way."

"Why did you look at maps, Samantha?" he asked again. "Tell me the truth, girl."

I gulped before answering, "On Sunday, Mrs. Hollows complained the drought ruined all her family's crops. I simply wished to add the area into my prayers, to beg God for rain," I answered, hoping with all my might the lie would stick.

"Your lesson for today is over," he said after a long pause. "Leave me to pray."

That whole exchange was so bizarre I shook from head to toe. All the same, I sighed with relief for surviving unscathed.

The next morning, I woke up, only to find that my shoes were gone. That instantly filled me with dread. Of course, I knew what this meant. *Crap, crap, crap.* The reverend hadn't fallen for my false explanations.

I'd believed I was being extremely careful with my plans to escape, but unfortunately, the reverend was onto me. And this was proof.

I wouldn't be able to get away without my shoes.

Feeling like I didn't really have a choice, I went in search of Mrs. Bradford to ask her about my missing footwear.

"They were taken away from you," she said in her usual manner.

I suppressed an eye roll. *I already know that.*

"Why?" I pressed, acting confused and ignorant.

"Your shoes will be returned to you when the reverend is convinced you're not at risk of falling into error," she explained.

"What error?" I asked, because it would be suspicious if I didn't.

Mrs. Bradford gave me a look. "This conversation is over; go and do your chores," she ordered.

I nodded. "I'll do my best to convince the reverend and you that I've learned my lesson," I said meekly before going to the kitchen to help the others prepare breakfast.

My head was reeling at this turn of events. *Did Grace rat me out despite promising she wouldn't?* I couldn't rule that out.

No matter how the reverend knew about my plans, my predicament stayed the same. I couldn't walk for miles barefoot. So unless I found a way to steal a pair of shoes, ones that fit me, which wouldn't be easy, I was stuck here.

26

JESSE

There were still no new texts from Sam.

I called Billy to see if she had reached out to him. The answer was no, she hadn't. I waited for Hillie after school to see if any of her friends knew anything about Sam. I got a negative reply from all of them. That worried me deeply. There was no doubt in my mind Sam was in real danger.

To help Sam, I knew I had to learn as much as possible about the family she was staying with. To learn everything about that reverend character, which meant looking into the disappearance of those two girls as well.

I had tried before to research the disappearance of Tanya Smith and Maria Taylor, although there really wasn't much, at least not online or in the papers.

I decided to contact the news reporter who'd written the article about the girls, but when I reached him, he seemed extremely uncomfortable to share anything with me, especially when I asked if there was a suspicion the reverend was involved.

That was a mistake because he shut down completely, clearly afraid about something.

All the same, I showed what I'd found out to Billy, and he agreed that it was definitely worth looking into.

"I have a cousin living in that area," he told me. "I'll ask him if he knows Reverend Bradford, but you know you can't go there to get her. They'll lock you up, and you'll never see her again."

"I know, I know." I nodded. I didn't want to give them any reason to lock me up again. I needed to prove I could care for Sam, but in the meantime, I was terrified of what might be happening to her there. "Try to reach your cousin; maybe he can find a way to check on Sam?"

"I'll see what I can do." Billy nodded. "It might take a while; he's not real tech savvy and doesn't have a cell phone."

I still felt like that wasn't enough. My lawyer had encouraged me to go to the police, so although I hated asking for help, I swallowed my pride and went to see the sheriff.

Once again, I mentioned how Sam had suddenly stopped answering my calls after she complained about her foster parents. I showed him the article about the girls who'd vanished into thin air. I was confident I presented my case pretty well, and although that asshole hated my guts, I was convinced he would help, especially since I'd got nowhere with CPS. "Something fishy is going on in that house," I insisted.

The sheriff pushed the photocopy of the article away from him without bothering to look at it. "That's a pile of rubbish," he said sternly.

"You can't deny those girls went missing. There must be a reason."

"I know about those two, and they were troublemakers

from the start," he said with a deep frown. "The reverend did his best, but as we all know, you can't make a rotten apple good again no matter what garden you put it in."

"So what you're saying is that there was no reason for such behavior from those two girls, no provocation," I said, summing it up.

"Exactly. The reverend is a pillar of the community, and I won't allow you to tarnish his good name."

"Really? It's too big a coincidence, Sheriff," I insisted. "Those girls wouldn't just run away, especially considering one was already eighteen, so there was no reason she would have to. And my Sam wouldn't just stop speaking with me, or start ignoring her friends," I argued while trying to sound calm and reasonable when in reality I wanted to smack his head against the wooden table, hoping that would put some sense into him.

"You're thinking about this all wrong. There is nothing nefarious going on here," the sheriff insisted. "The reverend is simply too devoted to Jesus for most teens these days, so things like this happen. I caught his girls a few times, but no matter how much they begged, I knew they would thank me someday for returning them back to that safe, stable, right-eous environment."

Yeah, I'm sure those two disappeared girls were the most grateful, I grumbled to myself. I couldn't believe this man was so blind as to not see what was right in front of him.

"Even if that's true, it still doesn't make sense that Sam's not answering my calls or texts, or that she broke all contact with her friends. We both know teens live for their friends at that age," I challenged.

The sheriff waved his hand dismissively. "My daughter barely speaks with me, and we live in the same house. You're blowing things out of proportion. Your daughter is fine, more than fine. She's right where she's supposed to be."

I gritted my teeth. It was more than apparent I wouldn't be able to persuade this man that something bad was going on inside that house.

Part of me was worried that I could jeopardize my chances of regaining custody if they thought I was genuinely crazy. However, Sam's safety had to come first, so I wasn't giving up no matter the consequences.

Although I wasn't prepared to openly admit it, talking with Dr. Sheldon really helped me. She never dismissed anything I said, no matter how crazy it sounded. And she always guided me through the labyrinth of my thoughts and emotions.

"I know my daughter, Doc, and something is definitely wrong," I told her, letting all my frustrations out during our session. "I can feel it."

I showed her the article, and I called Sam in front of her so she could see I wasn't delusional.

"You may be right," she allowed. "The CPS as a system is imperfect. They are underfunded and understaffed, and some people can be corrupted. In such circumstances, mistakes can happen."

I knew it. I knew I wasn't crazy, and I was glad there was another person who believed me.

"I agree with you, Jesse. Something doesn't feel right, and I would rather help you to make sure she is all right, and be wrong, than do nothing."

"Thank you, Doc, that means a great deal to me."

It was reassuring that I had someone like Dr. Sheldon watching my back. Who knew, perhaps with her help, I could actually accomplish something.

Maybe she can call CPS for me and ask about Sam, ask to see her, I mused and then decided it wouldn't hurt to ask.

Dr. Sheldon hesitated for a moment, but then nodded. "I don't think it would be a breach for me to ask that CPS check on her for you. It's related to your own mental health that you are assured she's well."

Once I finished my session, I went to see Peter and ask if there was any progress regarding my case. To my chagrin, the judge had taken the next week and a half off, and we couldn't do anything without him. *Son of a bitch.*

"Did you hear from Sam?" my lawyer asked.

"No, nothing. And the sheriff won't do anything about it. He is a lazy fuck who's so incompetent he couldn't even tell something is wrong with his own ass," I fumed.

"You need to work with CPS; that is the only way," Peter insisted.

I groaned. "I have tried, but they won't listen to me."

"You must keep trying."

They all believed I'd gotten exactly what I deserved. That I wasn't fit to be a father, so now they refused to move a finger to help me get my daughter back. *They won't help even if it means putting Sam in danger, because they can't fathom she's in danger in the first place.*

Something crossed my mind. I couldn't beat the system; however, I could definitely try to use it in my favor.

"What about supervised visitations? Is that something you can arrange?" I asked, not daring to hope.

"Yeah, sure, but we have to wait for the judge to return. Even if he approves it, I can't guarantee you'll be able to see her for at least a month," he cautioned.

Fuck. I shook my head. That was too long. I needed to

see her now. All the same, I said, "Do it; set everything in motion."

I had to keep up the appearance that I was following the rules. In the meantime, I would find other ways to reach my daughter. Because I couldn't just sit around and do nothing.

At the same time, I felt like I was running out of options.

If I showed up unannounced at the address Sam gave me, it would cause a lot of problems for both of us. The Bradfords could call the cops on me, and then I wouldn't be able to help Sam, so I was determined to keep that option as a last resort.

Speaking of the sheriff, although I felt like I was going in circles, I decided to give that jumped-up asshole one more chance to act like a human being and do something good for a change.

"Please, Sheriff, help me," I pleaded. At this point, I wasn't too proud to beg. "You said you also have a daughter. Wouldn't you be worried if she vanished on you?"

"It's not the same situation, Mr. Cotton."

"I only want to know that she's okay. Can I see her for two minutes? You can have two deputies breathing down my neck the entire time, making sure I behave."

"I really don't understand your behavior, Mr. Cotton. However, I'll send one of my deputies to check up on her," he promised.

"Thank you," I replied, beyond grateful, relieved he was finally prepared to do something.

Although it wasn't exactly what I'd asked for, it was still better than nothing. At this stage, I would take it.

27

SAMANTHA

A very angry, irritated, almost nervous-looking Mrs. Bradford called me into the living room and then shoved the phone into my hand.

"Someone wants to speak with you," she said in a tone that promised all kinds of Old Testament retribution if I didn't play this right. Despite that, I was happy and prayed with all my heart that it was Dad.

"Hello?" I answered, playing it cool. In this house, it was never prudent to show true emotions. The reverend and his wife were masters of exploiting other people's feelings.

The reverend was sitting in his favorite chair, by the fireplace, without taking his eyes off me. In one hand he held his Bible, and around his waist was the leather belt he'd whipped me with a couple of days ago all because I'd gotten a bad grade on my test. I was sure I'd given all the right answers, just not the ones written in his stupid religious books.

My body instantly recoiled at the sight of that belt,

remembering how it felt. The pain was excruciating, and my back was far from properly healed yet.

During my training, I'd gotten pretty used to enduring pain. For example, I'd sprained my ankle and injured myself doing some exercises. But that wasn't the same. This was completely different. Especially when I couldn't fight back. That was the worst for me. Not the pain I had to endure but the powerlessness that accompanied it.

I didn't have to wonder why the reverend was sitting there. He clearly felt the need to add his silent presence onto the threats of his wife. He didn't have to bother. I didn't plan on saying anything I wasn't supposed to. I wasn't stupid. Besides, I planned on slipping a code to Dad, so the Bradfords would be none the wiser.

Not that the last code had done anything. I had hoped Dad would come to the rescue by now. And he hadn't.

What's the hold-up?

"Hi, Samantha," a woman's voice greeted me.

I barely stopped myself in time from showing how disappointed I was.

"It's Julianna Higgins here, from the CPS. I'm just doing a follow-up to see how you've settled in with the Bradfords," she practically recited.

This was what they called a follow-up, a freaking phone call? *Unbelievable.* Irritation quickly turned to anger: once again that woman had failed me. Now I couldn't slip my letter to her, and I definitely couldn't say anything against the Bradfords with them in the room with me like this. And not simply because she wouldn't believe me. Mrs. Bradford was looming over me like a bad omen. I could see her intent in her eyes. Although she was afraid that I might say the wrong thing, there was a part of her that relished the opportunity to punish me, and good, if only I would give her the chance.

"I'm settled just fine," I replied curtly.

It went in my favor for Mrs. Bradford to see I didn't want to do this thing. I was working really hard on fooling the masters of the house into believing that they had managed to break me, so I could continue snooping around, gathering evidence against them. And I hoped this would also allow them to drop their guard.

And return my freaking shoes to me.

Then the social worker asked me all kinds of dry and clinical questions about how I was feeling and my eating and sleeping habits.

When she asked if I was going to school, I almost growled, "I'm homeschooling." That still stung the most. I was forced to learn from those inaccurate books, so that every day I was left feeling like I was being indoctrinated against my will.

The questioning went on and on, and it showed me she was definitely going down a checklist.

I replied simply to all her questions like a good little girl. It rubbed me the wrong way that I was forced to lie and cover up everything I'd seen and experienced since coming to this damn farm. Unfortunately, I didn't have a choice.

Once the social worker got all the answers she needed, once all the boxes were checked, papers filled with nonsense she could file, and then pat herself on the back for a job well done, she asked to speak with Mrs. Bradford again, which meant she was done with me.

Is that it, for good? I wondered, dreading the answer.

The reverend looked hard at me for a few heartbeats more before leaving the room without a word.

Did he buy it?

Mrs. Bradford tapped me on the shoulder, silently telling me to leave too.

I nodded.

On my way out, I heard Mrs. Bradford, in her fake pleasant manner, praising my improvement.

I felt like shouting. I felt like disrupting their complacency in my pain and imprisonment. I felt like smashing down the doors and setting all of us girls free.

LATER THAT DAY, as I was in my room studying, Mrs. Bradford came in, holding my phone. It was ringing. It was Dad, I just knew it. And that knowledge almost brought tears to my eyes. I had to suppress them, quickly.

"This damn thing won't stop ringing," Mrs. Bradford complained.

I wondered why she didn't just put it on silent, but I was grateful that she hadn't. Maybe she didn't know how? She didn't have a cell phone of her own that I'd seen, only the house landline.

"You have one minute to get rid of him, and if you try anything, I will beat you so hard you will regret ever bringing this devil's device into my home."

I didn't care about her threats. I was too happy that she was actually allowing me to speak with Dad.

"Hi, Dad," I answered, trying to sound as normal as possible.

"Sam, thank God," he replied, with clear relief in his voice. "I've been so worried about you."

"You don't have to worry about me. I'm fine," I reassured him as brightly as I could.

"I heard the social worker did a check-up, so I had to call to see how it went."

"Yes, she called this morning. It went fine."

"Called? She didn't come to see you?" he asked, outraged.

Mrs. Bradford frowned, clearly not pleased I was sharing too much with him.

"It's standard procedure, Dad," I tried to convince him.

"Are you all right?"

"Right as rain," I replied immediately.

"From now on, answer yes or no to my questions, okay?" he said more quietly.

I knew Mrs. Bradford didn't catch that because she frowned again.

"Okay, Dad," I replied almost cheerfully.

"Is someone next to you, listening to our conversation?" he asked.

Mrs. Bradford took a step closer.

I pressed the phone more tightly against my ear. "Yes," I replied.

"Are you safe in that house?"

"No," I replied, although my tone was light, casual.

"The reverend?"

"Yes."

"Should I come and get you?"

I hesitated. My first instinct was to say yes. I desperately needed him to come and rescue me from these people. But in a split second, I realized I couldn't ask that of him. I feared he would get arrested if he came here, or worse. The reverend had connections, and he would make sure my dad was punished, to punish me. I couldn't allow that. So no matter how much it pained me, I said, "No."

Mrs. Bradford made a show of looking at her watch. I was running out of time.

"I don't understand, Sam. You say you're in danger, but don't want my help?"

"No," I repeated. And some of my frustrations seeped through. It couldn't be helped. I felt like this was an impossible situation for me. I wanted to tell him he could be in danger as well if he tried something, and didn't know how. We'd never created a code for something like that.

"You know, I have Bible studies every day, and I'm starting to really enjoy them," I said, not wanting Mrs. Bradford to become suspicious at how I was only replying with yes and no. "I know you're not religious, but it's become very important to me. And I've already written to you about how much I enjoy working in the gardens. As it turns out, I have a natural green thumb. I've learned so much in this short period of time."

Dad was silent; I could imagine him trying to figure out what was going on.

I nodded as though listening to something intently. "I'm grateful for everything."

"As long as you're happy, Sam, I am too," Dad said louder now so Mrs. Bradford could hear him.

I was relieved he was playing along. Mrs. Bradford would have figured out something was going on if we continued to speak like that.

"I'll be sending you that care package soon."

I wanted to curse him for mentioning that. I was still being punished for giving him the address. I really didn't want him reminding Mrs. Bradford about it so she could get angry with me all over again. And then I had an idea.

"Can you send that wild strawberry jam Emily makes? Mrs. Bradford is very fond of it," I added, feeling like that would be a nice touch. I figured if I convinced Mrs. Bradford that the fact my dad knew the address wasn't a big deal, then maybe I would get my shoes back. I wouldn't hold my breath I would get my phone back. Ever.

"Of course, and make sure to thank the reverend and his wife for taking such good care of you."

"I will."

"I have to say, I'm relieved all the initial friction has passed."

"Me too."

"I love you, kiddo."

"I love you too."

"Talk to you soon," he said with intent, and I understood why. He wanted whoever was listening to know this would be a recurring affair. He wasn't giving up, no matter what, and I was relieved.

Mrs. Bradford snatched the phone away from me. "That was tedious," she complained, putting my phone in her pocket and leaving me be once again.

This whole thing made me realize one thing. The only way I would be able to get out without my dad sacrificing his freedom or possibly his life was to join forces with my friends. I figured that the reverend and his wife wouldn't be so suspicious of Hillie or see another kid as a threat, especially another girl, which was why I decided I needed to use Hillie to get my message to Dad.

I needed him to understand what was going on, and how delicate this situation was. And that I was trying to protect him by stopping him from coming here. I hoped that if he knew what the true reality was, then he would find a way to get me out without putting himself in danger.

That night, as we went to bed, I spoke with Grace. I felt like I had to confide in someone so I wouldn't go crazy. "I talked to Dad today."

"I know, Mrs. Bradford complained about that all day," Grace said in her usual, dry manner.

"I realized he can't help me with this, not directly, but I think I found another way," I confessed.

She covered her ears with her hands. "Please don't tell me anything about your plans," she pleaded, looking pretty freaked out.

Her behavior was strange, even for her.

"What's wrong, Grace?" I asked with concern. "Did something happen?"

"Yes," she said meekly. "There's something I haven't told you."

"What?" I prompted. The room was silent for a long moment, and I braced myself for what she had to say.

"The two girls who tried to escape this place..." she started, and then her voice fell to a terrified whisper. "They are dead."

28

SAMANTHA

Dead? I rose in bed, my heart starting to beat like crazy. Although I felt like panic was pressing in on me from all sides, I still had to learn as much as possible about the two girls. "How do you know that, Grace?"

She went pale, shaking all over.

Is that shock? I wondered.

Grace shook her head as though repelling bad memories. "You can do whatever you want. But leave me out of everything."

It wasn't lost on me that she didn't answer my question. What was she hiding? "Grace..."

"Samantha, don't. I beg you." And with that, she tuned out as though to sleep.

I looked at her in utter confusion. She threw a bomb like that at me and then expected me to back off?

Learning that the two girls who tried to leave this place had died was deeply troubling.

At the same time, this bombshell wouldn't change my mind. I was leaving no matter what.

I COULDN'T STOP STRESSING about what Grace had said to me, about how the two girls who tried to escape were now dead. That revelation rattled me. There was no doubt in my mind those two things were related.

They were dead because they tried to escape.

Even so, I was trying not to jump to conclusions. There was an outside chance their deaths were an accident, not something that happened on purpose, as a direct consequence of their disobedience. Grace didn't say for sure, but I knew that if I pressed her, she wouldn't say more than she wanted to. Then again, she wouldn't be so disturbed by it if it was all purely coincidental.

I thought about Tanya, who I presumed must be one of the dead girls. Grace had told me that Tanya had been savagely beaten because Grace had tried to escape, and the other girl did nothing to stop her. So I guessed that Tanya had tried to escape next. I could see that happening. However scared Tanya must have been, living here was unbearable – anything was better than that. Which was precisely why I wanted to escape as well.

I was determined to uncover all the secrets in this place. I had no other choice. That was the only way to leave. *And not in a body bag.*

I continued to snoop around the house at night, trying to get into the locked rooms without being detected. It was slow work because I had to be extra careful. To make matters worse, I never had a whole night at my disposal because poor Grace was still being taken away, night after night, to that sinister locked room.

I chose to try to get into the sewing room first because it

was the only place in the house that belonged entirely to Mrs. Bradford. Not even the reverend was allowed inside. She even cleaned it herself so none of the girls would enter it either, which had always been fine by me.

My homemade lockpick worked like a charm, and I was inside in no time. I felt ready and fired up to see what this woman was hiding. It was hard walking around in the complete dark, but eventually my eyes adjusted. The light from the moon helped.

A desk with a sewing machine was in the corner. A huge table for cutting fabrics was in the center of the room, and lots of fabrics were stashed on the shelves from top to bottom on the right-hand wall.

I put my hand between the fabrics, hoping she was hiding something there. She wasn't. I looked under the table and only found discarded scraps of fabric. Next, I went to the desk and very carefully opened the drawers. I found sewing thread, needles and scissors.

But the drawer at the bottom was full of documents, so I grabbed a handful of the papers, then walked over to the window to look at them more closely.

One particular paper drew my attention. It was a medical report that belonged to one Evangeline Bradford. I was surprised to learn she was thirty-seven years old. I'd believed she was younger than that.

Her wickedness keeps her young, like all witches, I joked to myself, even though nothing was funny in this scenario.

I started reading through it, wanting to know what was wrong with her.

"No way," I murmured under my breath, in total disbelief.

Although I couldn't understand all the medical terms, it

appeared that Mrs. Bradford had got herself sterilized ten years ago. And I was sure she must have done that behind her husband's back. He wouldn't pester her for a child if he knew the facts. Each month when she started to bleed again, he had what amounted to a complete mental breakdown. In his mind he was doing everything in his power, which could only mean she was to blame.

He'd got that much right.

Oh my God, this is huge.

I decided to keep that medical report because it could be the secret weapon I'd been hoping for. I wondered if I could blackmail Mrs. Bradford with it. I was sure she would do anything to prevent me from showing it to her husband. *Maybe even let me go,* I mused.

Let us go, I corrected. There was no way I was leaving without the other girls. We had to leave this house of horrors together.

Is this a big enough weapon to accomplish something like that? I decided that it was. The reverend would go crazy if he ever found out his wife couldn't have children because she'd deliberately made it so.

Stashing that valuable piece of information in my dress, underneath my left armpit, I left the sewing room and locked it up again. Checking the time, I knew I'd run out of time and had to return to bed if I was to avoid detection.

The next night was a complete waste of time. I was disappointed to discover that the next three rooms I visited were near-empty bedrooms. If I hadn't seen how all the doors were only unlockable from the outside, I would've considered the night a write-off. *But now I knew that those rooms were like prison cells.*

I found that interesting, in a disturbing, horrifying way.

At the same time, I was saddened I hadn't found any more useful information.

I knew I was pushing it, constantly sneaking around, but I couldn't stop now, so I went to investigate the last room in the forbidden area. It was the room Grace was forced to go to almost every night. I knew this was my only chance to check it; she wasn't there tonight.

It took me no time to unlock it. I had really become an expert. I rushed inside and stood still for a moment, confused at what I was seeing.

The whole room was decorated completely differently from the rest of the house. Everything was vibrant and full of colors. At first, a honeymoon suite came to mind. But then I started to see it as something else much less romantic. One piece of furniture dominated the space. It was a huge king-size bed in the shape of a heart. A professional-looking camera was pointed right at the bed.

To the right was a rack with clothes. If they could even be called clothes in the first place. They looked like something porn stars would wear, but they were all freakishly small, child sized.

I felt sick to my stomach. That sick bastard was making Grace wear sexy lingerie; he was forcing her to pose for him so he could take pictures.

I had a horrible feeling that wasn't all Grace was being used for. Whatever it was, it would explain why Grace looked so sickened each time Mrs. Bradford returned her to our room. I understood now why she threw up, why she hated herself and her life.

Then another horrendous thought came to mind, and I felt like throwing up too. Grace wasn't the only girl in this house this was happening to. I'd heard Patricia cry countless times during the night. I remembered seeing Chloe hurt and wondering when she'd gotten beaten up.

The girls in this house were being used as "models" in these horrible, sexualized shoots. The look in their eyes and the way they acted around the reverend made perfect sense now. They weren't afraid of him simply because of the beatings. They were afraid because they didn't want to end up in this room.

Patricia was autistic, for crying out loud, yet he had no mercy toward her either. He was a sick, sick man. And Mrs. Bradford allowed all of it to happen.

All kinds of images filled my head, images I couldn't stop. I started shaking all over. I had to get out of there.

Making sure I hadn't disturbed anything, so they wouldn't know I'd been there, that I'd learned the truth, I left the pedophile's den and locked the door. Although every part of my being wanted to run away as fast as possible, even without shoes on my feet, I forced myself to return to bed.

My head was spinning from this discovery. The reverend and his wife were even worse monsters than I originally thought. She took the girls to that room in the middle of the night; the girls were forced to wear those clothes and do God only knew what else in front of the camera, in front of him. I rushed down the corridor to the nearest bathroom, where I threw up as the terrible realization hit me.

The reverend was a pedophile. He was engaged in creating child pornography. He was an abuser, and his wife was complicit. I knew that was true with my entire being. Now it all made sense, especially the "personal" Bible studies sessions in which he would ask me about sex.

He's grooming me, I thought with horror as I washed my face in the sink. *Or at least trying to.*

"You'll find out soon enough," Grace had warned me one night.

Oh my God. I was next. They were trying to break me, physically, mentally, emotionally, so that they could prep me for that vile room.

I started shaking uncontrollably. I couldn't stop thinking about that room. I had finally discovered their secret, but right now I really wished I hadn't.

29

JESSE

The sheriff was a lying motherfucker. A total piece of shit. He never sent a deputy to the farm to check up on my Sam and make sure she was all right. That was the final proof that he didn't give a shit about me or my daughter, and that I couldn't count on him for anything.

To make matters worse, the social worker looked almost victorious when she threw in my face that Sam was thriving at that farm, telling me in a condescending manner how she'd done a follow-up and that my daughter was better off without me.

I highly doubted that; I was sure that Sam would have only said what the other woman wanted to hear. What she was forced to say.

She was in danger, but for some reason she didn't want my help. I still couldn't get my head wrapped around that. Then again, maybe I was looking at it from the wrong perspective. She was very mature for her age, but even so, she was still a child. And if she was afraid, if she was threatened in any way, she wouldn't tell me everything, clearly thinking she was protecting me either from the truth or from more trouble befalling me.

She undoubtedly wanted me to stay away so I wouldn't act like a hothead and go there to kill the bastard and his wife. Thanks to therapy, I was able to put all those pieces together and consider them rationally. Nonetheless, I was determined to learn what the hell was going on and get Sam out of there.

I have to be smart about it, I told myself, exactly at the same time as I knew being smart wasn't my strongest suit.

At first, Sam's behavior really hurt me, but when I stopped to think about it, I realized that my daughter was way smarter than I was. Everything she was doing was in order to stay safe. And I should follow her lead. Because if I got myself arrested, then I wouldn't be able to help her. I would be damning her to live in that house forever, and that was something I couldn't allow.

Seeing how nobody was taking me seriously, I decided to take matters into my own hands, sort of.

I wasn't talking about storming that farm, getting my daughter back with guns blasting. I was keeping that as plan B. Plan A was slightly more subtle.

I found out who'd worked on the case of the disappeared girls, Detective Mathew Overton, and I paid him a visit. Although he worked in the sheriff's department, I could only hope he was a lesser dick than his boss.

I walked into his office without bothering to make an appointment. I wanted to catch him off guard. And I definitely didn't want to give him an opportunity to say no to me.

Detective Overton was six feet tall and had a blond crew cut. Checking the photograph on the wall behind his desk, I realized he had a military background. I liked that.

After a short conversation, we discovered that we'd served at the same time at the same place for a brief moment before he was shipped someplace else.

Establishing a connection, as Dr. Sheldon would say, I introduced myself and then explained my concerns about my daughter's safety while she stayed with the reverend and his wife. As evidence, I presented a few texts I'd had from Sam.

"I hope there's a way you can help me, Detective," I concluded. "Or maybe I can help you," I added as an afterthought. "I just want my daughter safe."

The detective stayed silent for a moment. "I wish I had something good to tell you, Mr. Cotton, but I encountered a lot of resistance trying to investigate the disappearance of Tanya and Maria," he said eventually, clearly deciding to trust me.

"That's because of the reverend," I guessed. "The man is well connected. I've also noticed that most people believe he's some kind of saint or something."

"Exactly," he agreed. "Which made my job very difficult, impossible even."

"Do you have any theories on what happened to those girls?"

"The reverend and his wife were the only two local people who interacted with them. And their version of events was that the girls snuck out during the night, never to be seen again," he explained.

"Did you believe them?"

"I'm not a trusting man. I can't be, in my line of work."

I thought about that for a moment. "Do you think they ran away or that something happened to them before they had a chance to escape?" I asked. That was my way of asking if he thought the reverend killed them.

Sam had told me that Reverend Bradford was a dangerous man. In my mind that meant he was capable of killing. It gutted me inside that I was leaving my daughter with a potential killer. Nevertheless, I trusted that she would be able to take care of herself long enough for me to get her out, the right way.

"I think I'll keep my opinions about that to myself," the detective replied.

I got the strong feeling he was suspicious of the reverend, yet he was reluctant to share much because of the pastor's powerful connections. After the way the sheriff had fucked me over, I was of the opinion he was the reverend's friend as well. That made my job more difficult yet not impossible.

"I'll tell you one thing, though," the detective continued. "Despite the whole county protecting the Bradfords, I couldn't verify their story. They said both girls left in the middle of the night and then found someone to drive them to town. I checked all the security cameras available on the highways and at the bus and train stations in all the towns in the radius of the farm. And I found no traces of them."

"As though they vanished into thin air?" I guessed.

He nodded. "I couldn't find even a shred of evidence that they'd actually left the farm. There was nothing to show that they'd run away."

"So did you find anything to suggest they are buried in the ground?" I said reluctantly.

"I considered that, but as I said, there is no evidence."

If there's no body, there's no crime, that was the phrase that came to mind.

The more I learned about the fate of these two young women, the more restless I felt. This was wrong. Sam shouldn't be placed with those people. They were clearly rotten to the core. Even if they'd done nothing to those missing girls, something shady was going on inside that house. I had to get Sam out.

"You still suspected it?"

"It's my job."

I was sure that was the case, but I had a sinking feeling that Detective Overton suspected the reverend and his wife had done something to those girls.

"Something is definitely happening on that farm," I insisted. "My daughter is not safe there. She couldn't go into details when I spoke with her, since one of the Bradfords was beside her making sure she behaved, but they're not good people. Far from it. I'm certain all means of communication are being tightly monitored. The last time she complained about them, I couldn't reach her for days."

My words seemed to spark something within him. "What's your daughter's name again?" he asked.

"Samantha Cotton, but we all call her Sam."

"I have an idea."

"What?" I asked with interest.

"I'll go to the Bradfords' farm first thing in the morning to ask some follow-up questions about the case. I'll make it look like it's just a routine interview. While I'm there, I'll speak with your daughter. Hopefully, she'll have something I can use against the Bradfords to get a warrant to search the house."

I was so grateful that someone was finally willing to help me and not treat me as though I were a madman. "Thank you so much, Detective. You're the first person from the government I've encountered who's willing to help. I was starting to get pretty desperate."

"I feel like this might be what I need to reopen those cases," he offered.

"Be sure to compliment Sam's red hair, call it a fire elemental," I told him. "That way she'll know I sent you, that you're trustworthy."

"I'll do that," he said with a nod as he shook my hand.

Finally feeling like there was a shred of hope, I called Dr. Sheldon once I left his office.

"Has something happened?" she asked, sounding concerned. "Have you had an episode? Do we need to schedule an emergency session?"

I almost smiled. Although I knew her concern was strictly professional, it was still nice to hear. I had encountered so many jaded people in my life that Dr. Sheldon was like a breath of fresh air.

"I'm fine. Actually, I'm better than fine after speaking with Detective Overton. That's why I'm calling to share the good news."

"What's the good news?" she asked, and I suddenly wondered if I was jumping the gun, celebrating too soon.

"He's going to help. And I'm finally feeling like I'm one step closer to getting Sam back."

"That is good news," she agreed. "What will he actually do?"

I told her about my conversation with the detective.

"When is he going to the farm?"

"He said first thing in the morning."

"Keep me posted."

"Will do."

Once I ended that conversation, I left the police station. I went to work, but I couldn't stop thinking about Sam, counting the hours until Detective Overton would have his eyes on my daughter. He'd be able to talk to her, to see for himself if she was being mistreated in any way.

I tried to picture what I would do if I learned the reverend had done something awful to her. The old me, the PTSD trigger-happy and violently angry man would storm, there and cause havoc. I realized that the therapy version of me wanted to do the very same thing. And I was perfectly all right with that.

Nobody messes with my family. I would teach the reverend that fucking lesson no matter the consequences.

30

SAMANTHA

The Bradfords were pornographers, abusers and potentially murderers. That knowledge shook me to the core and paralyzed me.

I kept my head low and did everything that was expected of me, but now I lived in a state of pure panic because I knew that every mistake had much more severe consequences than I'd initially thought. The knowledge I could end up in that room and learn firsthand what was happening in there brought tears to my eyes. I'd never felt so powerless in my life. I didn't know what to do.

And then I forced myself to stop thinking like that. I thought of Dad and what he'd taught me. This kind of situation was precisely what he'd been training me for, so it was time for me to really prove myself. Prove it wasn't all for nothing. I couldn't succumb to fear. Although I now had this knowledge, there was nothing I could do with it. I had no means to share that with anyone in the outside world.

Then, quite unexpectedly, something bizarre happened. I woke up to find my phone back. I felt like kissing it as I held it tightly against my chest. I still had no shoes, but I wasn't going to look a gift horse in the mouth.

"It's a trap," Grace said over her shoulder as she left the room, preparing for her chores.

Even if that was the case, I didn't mind. I finally had a way to send my message out and create a plan with the people on the outside that would guarantee my rescue. I had no more illusions. I'd been kidnapped, plain and simple. The Bradfords wouldn't give me up so easily, not after spending so much time and energy to mold me into something that would serve their needs.

I got my most valued item back. So, apparently, I had played my part to perfection. *Or maybe they just want me to think that, lower my guard, make a mistake.* I couldn't disregard Grace's warning. I would be careful.

It also occurred to me that getting my phone back had nothing to do with me. At least not directly. Perhaps after my last conversation with Dad, the Bradfords realized they needed to pacify him so he wouldn't storm in here.

The Bradfords knew who I was, and they knew who my dad was, so if they were wary, I was glad because they definitely should be. And I would find a way to use everything to my advantage, even if it was meant as a tool of control on their part, even though it was offered as a trap.

I texted Dad, Billy, and all my friends. I kept it simple and neutral so my words wouldn't cause any red flags.

Of course, Mrs. Bradford did her usual song and dance routine and made sure to warn me my ability to use my phone was all just a display of their good faith, generosity, and Christian values. However, it would all be taken away again if I fell out of line.

I nodded like a good little girl, then did all my chores

without complaint before I settled down to my studies. I couldn't look at those two evil creatures anymore. They were utterly disgusting, pretending to be so good and moral, when in reality they were the opposite.

Each time I closed my eyes, I saw that room. It filled me with rage. It motivated me to destroy them. I couldn't allow them to keep tormenting and exploiting Grace, Chloe, Patricia, or me.

While I was having a break, meaning I was supposed to be studying and wasn't, I got a text from Hillie.

Princess Astari Quest?

I made a face. I wasn't in the mood for games, especially one we used to play when we were kids. Then again, I could use a distraction from this life at least for a few minutes.

I texted back, logging into the game.

Sure.

As soon as I was online, Hillie texted me inside the game.

"Guess what? We can chat during games, and there will be no records of it anywhere," she wrote, ending with a smiley face.

I was ecstatic to hear that. "How did you know I can't talk normally?" I had to ask.

"I spoke with your dad, and then I remembered this game."

I smiled. "Hillie, you're a genius."

"I know. How are you?"

"So-so."

"We'll find a way to get you out."

"I know."

But before we could say anything else to each other, I heard someone approaching, so I exited the game immediately, put the phone down, then returned to my studies.

It was so fortunate that now I had a way to speak with my friend, with Dad, without the Bradfords being the wiser. But it still wasn't easy to talk about all the specifics, and that was because I was constantly being watched.

Between the Bradfords and my chores and studies, I didn't have much alone time to chat with Hillie. My phone was still confiscated a couple of times a day for inspection, which made matters even harder. And I couldn't trust the other girls not to rat on me. I knew they were scared, and that was why I didn't hold it against them. I simply made sure not to put them in that situation in the first place.

Being extra careful had its problems. It was extremely difficult to find a specific time when Hillie and I were online at the same time. We had to keep it random because I was worried if I tried to set a specific date and time, the Bradfords would find out, uncover my secret communications, and then it would be all for nothing.

I managed to steal a few moments to complain to Hillie as I was supposed to shower.

"This is a horror show. I have so much to tell you, but I have to be careful."

"Of course. And don't worry, whatever you tell me, I'll forward it to your dad," she reassured me.

But I had to stop there yet again because I could hear Mrs. Bradford warning me to hurry up because she needed me for something before bedtime.

THEN THE NEXT day I couldn't steal a moment to write to Hillie. I felt like I was constantly in the kitchen, either cleaning or cooking.

Mrs. Bradford was pleased I was so handy in the kitchen, and took advantage of my culinary skills all the time. She had the audacity to tell me that it was good fortune for her that my mother had died, forcing me to learn how to cook. God took my mother away so I would become all that I was supposed to become, meaning Mrs. Bradford's slave.

I barely stopped myself from jumping on her and hitting her, showing her how it was my good fortune that my father had taught me how to fight for specifically that reason, to teach bad people some decent manners. I held my tongue, knowing that any outburst from me would only negate everything I had managed to accomplish so far.

I finally had a way to do something, so it would be extremely foolish to jeopardize that. It was true I had that medical document I could use against her, but I was determined to save that secret weapon for the right opportunity.

Just as I was stressing about all that, I noticed the Bradfords become nervous all of a sudden, and when they got nervous, it meant the whole house went on red alert.

"We have a visitor," she announced. "And you all know what that means."

"Behave," the reverend boomed.

A few minutes later a car stopped in front of the house, and Mrs. Bradford, wearing that fake smile of hers, opened the door. The reverend took a seat at his favorite place in the living room, in his throne-like chair, next to the fireplace, pretending he was reading his Bible.

We were sent upstairs.

I peeked through the window to see a man around my dad's age with short blond hair exit the car. "Do you know who that is?" I asked Grace.

Grace looked beyond concerned, coming to stand next to me. "He's a detective. I think he's the one who came to investigate when Tanya and Maria disappeared."

Why does she look like that? I wondered. *Isn't a visit from a cop a good thing?*

"The reverend hates him," she added.

I could understand that. Especially since he had something to hide.

It was frustrating I couldn't hear what was happening downstairs between the detective and the Bradfords. Why had he come here? Had he discovered something? Was he here to make arrests? I banished that last thought because I knew it would never happen. At least not like this. If the detective came to arrest the reverend, he wouldn't come alone. Law officers always did things in packs.

"Girls, please come downstairs," Mrs. Bradford called out.

My heart started beating like crazy. I had no idea why we were being summoned downstairs, but was still glad we were.

The four of us politely greeted the detective, and without saying anything else, we went to stand next to the reverend's chair.

Mrs. Bradford was standing on his right; we were on his left. We must have looked like we were his bodyguards. The detective sat alone on the couch.

So this is the cop who's been snooping around, I mused.

He clearly wasn't that good at his job if he hadn't learned the truth yet.

I sensed a special kind of energy in the air. We were waiting for something to happen. It became obvious to me that the girls hoped this cop showing up would be the pair's downfall. At the same time, it was clear they would do everything in their power to protect the Bradfords because they were so afraid of retribution. They were afraid of that room the reverend kept locked away from the world.

I couldn't stop my head from spinning. I so desperately wanted to use this encounter to my advantage but didn't know how. I wanted to take him, show him the locked room with the heart-shaped bed so he could arrest the reverend for child pornography, but I too was afraid. I felt unable to open my mouth to speak, let alone move.

What if the Bradfords prevent me from doing anything? What if we go there and all those things are gone?

This was my shot; I was aware of that. The problem was I didn't know how to use it. I could feel the letter, with all the gory details about this place, pressed against my heart. I had decided to bring it with me, even though I knew the chances of me getting it to him, with all these people around us, were slim to none.

"I apologize again for disrupting your day, but this had to be done," the detective said. "It's just routine, I reassure you."

I suppressed a groan. So he wasn't here to actually do anything useful; he simply wanted to check some boxes so he could say he did his job. *How typical.*

"We understand, Detective," the reverend said, his voice all syrupy and generous. "You can ask us whatever you like. My girls are here to cooperate as well."

The detective took out a pen and notepad. "I don't remember seeing you here before," he said.

It took me a moment to realize he was talking to me.

"This is our newest foster daughter, Samantha," Mrs. Bradford said to introduce me.

Apparently, I wasn't even allowed to say my own name.

"You have very interesting hair, Sam," he asked before adding jokingly, "Are you a reincarnation of some fire elemental?"

His words stunned me. There was only one person in this world who called me fire elemental, and that was my mother. How could he know her special name for me?

"We don't want to keep you any longer than necessary, Detective," the reverend said, clearly very displeased that the other man was trying to interact with me.

Why was he trying to interact with me? Was it a coincidence, or did this mean something? He still looked at me intently. Was it possible Dad sent him? What if this was a message to me so I would know he was on our side?

There was a chance I was making things up, but what if I wasn't?

"Of course," the detective refocused on the reverend and launched himself into that professional, detective mode.

The detective asked the Bradfords about the last day that they'd seen the two missing girls. By the way Mrs. Bradford was describing it, I knew she was lying through her teeth. And the reverend was no better. I knew things definitely went down differently on that day. There was no way he'd been preparing for his sermon all day, while she made some dresses, and the girls were left to their own devices working in the sunny garden. Something so ordinary and pleasant like that was impossible in this house. Not with those two control freaks at the helm.

Of course, the other girls agreed with everything the pair said. It was infuriating how they all faked ignorance.

"Does anyone have anything to add?" the detective asked.

I got the impression he was stalling, but why would he do that?

"Tanya and Maria never left the secret room," Patricia said, taking everyone by surprise with her voice as clear and direct as a newsreader's.

I almost jumped. Did Patricia see something?

"What room?" the detective asked.

"Patricia," Mrs. Bradford snapped, "you know better than to bother people with your stories. Forgive her, Detective, our Patricia is special, you know."

"Autistic," the reverend added, as though he was saying a dirty word.

"They never left the secret room," Patricia insisted, speaking louder now.

"Stop lying, Patricia," Mrs. Bradford said more sternly.

"The child tells stories to soothe herself," the reverend tried to explain; however, it was obvious the detective was on the fence about whom to believe.

"I'm not lying!" Patricia yelled, running to the detective and hugging his leg. "Please, sir, I don't want to go to that room anymore; it hurts." She started to cry as she clung to him for dear life.

As if on cue, Grace and Chloe both started crying as well.

"Please help us," Grace said softly.

"We don't want to stay here anymore," Chloe added, starting to walk toward the detective.

I could only stare at the people around me. I hadn't imagined for a minute that something like this might happen.

Mrs. Bradford looked horrified, scared by this unexpected turn of events. The only one looking exactly the same as before was the reverend. He sat in his chair as though he didn't have a care in the world.

"What is going on here?" the detective demanded, with all the authority he possessed.

The reverend sighed. "I really hoped it wouldn't come to this. I need to show you something." He got up and swiftly walked to the desk, getting something from the drawer.

I saw it a millisecond too late.

The reverend pulled out a gun and shot the detective straight in the head.

With poor Patricia still wrapped around his limbs, Detective Overton slumped forward in his chair.

31

SAMANTHA

The detective died right in front of our eyes.

I'd never seen a dead body before. At least, not a human one. I'd hunted with Dad all the time, but this was different. The detective came here, clearly, to help, and now he was gone. In one minute, he was living, breathing, speaking; in the next, he wasn't.

It was insane how everything could change in a split second. Unfortunately, I had already been in this situation. One single bullet had changed my life before. The one fired by my father's gun.

And now I was sure that this bullet would change my life once again. There was a long, weird moment in which no one in the room moved.

Then chaos ensued.

Everyone started screaming, me included until I forced myself to stop.

Patricia was covered in blood since she was the closest. Feeling all that gore on her, in her hair and on her clothes and her face, made her freak out like never before.

Although she was crying and in shock, Chloe rushed to move Patricia away from the detective's leg, but Patricia simply wouldn't let go.

Grace was completely frozen in place. Her expression made it clear that she believed the reverend was now going to kill us all, and she was making peace with that awful fate, silently praying, her lips moving in a rush to get her words out as tears poured down her face.

Mrs. Bradford covered her mouth with her hands. She didn't make a sound. She just looked at the dead detective before staring at her husband.

While all that was happening, there was only one thought in my head. *I can't be here.* I didn't belong here.

I wanted to make a run for it while everybody was distracted. There was just one tiny problem with that. I couldn't make my legs move. I felt like I had huge weights on them. Not to mention I still had no shoes.

Maybe I could take the detective's shoes, his car too.

Even if I had my own shoes on, I couldn't simply run away. And not because I knew the reverend would hunt me down and kill me. But because I couldn't leave these girls with such a monster.

"Shut the fuck up," the reverend boomed. "I can't think with all of you wailing like a bunch of pathetic bitches."

I'd never heard him swear before. Then again, this was the first time I'd seen him kill a man. *Will it be the last? Who will be next?*

The noise dimmed. Only Patricia was sobbing, yet even she was quieter now. Chloe was still trying to move her away.

What a bloody mess.

I wished I could call the police. Not even the sheriff

could ignore a dead body on the couch, but my phone was in my bedroom. And there was no way I could go and get it undetected.

"What the hell have you done?" Mrs. Bradford demanded, clearly coming to herself.

"What I had to," he snapped. "If you'd trained this one better" – he pointed the gun at Patricia – "then none of this would have happened."

"Of course, this is all my fault," she countered.

Was she really arguing with an armed man? A man who'd just shot a detective? Not a smart move; then again, I wasn't rushing to point that out.

"Stop," he shouted, waving his gun even more erratically.

"What are we going to do, Gareth?" Mrs. Bradford asked more softly now.

He scratched his head then, looking at the detective, at all of us. It was obvious he was calculating what to do with us. The best course of action would be to kill us all, but he couldn't do that. That many missing persons would definitely raise a few eyebrows. Not even he could get away with killing that many people at once. At least I hoped not.

"I have an idea. Move," he commanded us as he pointed the gun toward the hallway.

Nobody moved.

"Come on, Patricia." Chloe tried to coax her, but she wouldn't budge.

"I said move," he snapped, grabbing Patricia, picking her up, dragging her up to her feet.

We all knew that Patricia really didn't like to be touched, especially not by him, and now we all watched as she completely freaked out.

"I will kill you if you don't stop challenging me," he threatened.

Chloe wrapped her arms around the other girl from behind. "Everything is going to be all right, Pat; let's just go," she said in a soothing voice.

I was impressed she could manage that considering the situation. Considering tears were still streaming down her face.

The reverend ushered us out of the living room, and to my horror, he opened the heavy wooden basement door. "Get in, all of you, now," he commanded.

He didn't even bother to turn on the lights as we started descending the stairs.

"I don't want to hear a sound from you. Is that understood?" Then he simply slammed the door shut.

"Please don't leave us here," Chloe begged.

"We won't tell anyone, I swear," Grace added. She grabbed my hand. "He's going to kill us all," she said in panic.

"He already would have if that was the plan," I tried to reassure her.

The whole place reeked of mold and something else, something more unpleasantly pungent. It was very cold, and the lack of light really bothered me. I was never afraid of the dark before, but after all that had happened today, I was starting to reconsider.

A little while later, the door swung open again. I stood where I was, but the other girls went to the steps as though rushing to their freedom.

The reverend appeared, holding the dead body of the detective over his shoulders. Without a word and quite uncermoniously, he threw him inside. The body started tumbling down the stairs, making the girls scream in panic.

The door closed again. Despite all the noise of fear and distress, I heard a very distinct sound.

It was that of the basement door being locked.

He had no intention of letting us out, at least not anytime soon.

"Oh my God, oh my God," Patricia gulped as she completely freaked out once again.

Chloe tried to comfort her. At the moment, it was an impossible task.

I had to do something about this darkness. I neared one of the windows and started ripping away the newspapers they were covered with.

"What are you doing?" Grace demanded.

Trying to keep myself together no matter how hard it is. "We need light."

Grace nodded and immediately set to work helping me uncover all the other windows.

It was better, only not by much. This was a screwed-up situation, and to be perfectly honest, I didn't see a way out.

"Samantha, I'm really afraid," Grace added.

"I know."

"You have a plan, right?"

No, not really. "I'll think of something."

"Do you have an idea how to convince him not to kill us?"

No, not really. "He won't kill us."

Chloe and Patricia huddled underneath one of the windows, moving as far away from the dead body as possible, while Grace followed me around as I used the light that was coming from the windows to start looking about. On one of the shelves, in a storage box, I found a flashlight. I grabbed it, hoping it still worked. It did. It was time to investigate our prison further.

The first thing was to work out where that smell was coming from. It was so strong, so repulsive that it made me sick to my stomach. I knew the smell wasn't from the detective. He had just died. So it had to be something else.

"What are you looking for?" Grace asked.

"I'll know when I see it," I replied vaguely. I hoped I would find something that could help us get out of there. Maybe even a weapon. Then again, the reverend had a gun. There wasn't much that could beat that, since there was no chance the reverend had stashed a rocket launcher or a tank down here.

I started searching through all the corners. I was hoping there was a second room or a secret passage. A man like the reverend had to have another secret room, right?

I stopped in my tracks and screamed before I could stop myself.

I'd found the source of the stench.

32

SAMANTHA

The two missing girls weren't missing anymore. Tanya and Maria were decaying in a blocked-off, far corner of the basement. I had no idea how they'd died, but it was evident the reverend had murdered them. He couldn't allow them to escape, share what they knew about him, about this place, so he'd silenced them for good.

"What's wrong?" Grace rushed toward me.

I stopped her with my hand. Turned the flashlight off. "Don't come over here," I warned.

She didn't listen to me. She looked over my shoulder. "What's that in the corner?" she asked, although, by the sound of her voice, it was obvious she suspected.

"You were right," I said as I dragged her away. "Tanya and Maria are dead."

"Oh no! He's definitely going to kill us all," she cried with a trace of hysteria in her voice, alerting the smaller girls.

"Pull yourself together," I snapped. We couldn't afford to lose the plot; it wouldn't help us one bit.

Bracing myself, I went toward the detective. Had the

reverend remembered to take his gun away from him? I hoped like hell that in all the confusion, he'd overlooked a few essential things.

I hesitated, not wanting to touch him. But then I told myself that this was no time to be squeamish. I was used to killing, skinning, and gutting wild animals. In comparison to that, searching a few pockets should be a walk in the park.

Think of it as a dead rabbit. Nothing else, I instructed myself firmly.

I tried not to think about what I was doing as I went for his holster. It was empty. The clips with extra ammunition and the handcuffs were gone as well. I cursed loudly because there was nothing stopping me from doing so. Feeling desperate, I searched all his pockets.

"Why are you doing that?" Grace asked.

"Perhaps he has something we can use." *Is it too much to ask for a Swiss Army knife?*

In a moment of inspiration, I checked his shoes. He didn't have a second gun hidden around his ankle. *I guess that only happens in movies.*

Regrettably, I found nothing at all on him. Clearly, the Bradfords had confiscated all his belongings, phone, wallet, keys, and badge, before dumping him in here with us. They weren't stupid.

Still, I refused to give up. There had to be something here that could help us. Something we could use as a distraction to get us out of there.

I started searching the basement again, avoiding that one corner that held the burial site of the two girls. Not that they were buried, simply dumped there as though they were nothing, left for maggots and time to decay.

My stomach became queasy again, so I made myself stop thinking about it.

Eventually, I had to halt my search because there was nothing down here, only junk. This place was a tomb, nothing else. I felt like screaming out my anguish and frustrations at the top of my lungs.

The minutes turned to hours as we stayed there in that cold, moldy basement that hosted three dead bodies.

We were deep into the night when at last we heard the door being unlocked.

I squinted as the light broke in from the open door. Grace and I shared a look.

The reverend appeared in the light like a ghoul from all our worst nightmares.

The other girls started crying.

I was very much afraid of dying, but I refused to cry.

"Come with me, my beloved girls," he intoned. "We must pray and ask God for forgiveness that He might wash away your sins."

Very reluctantly, going around the dead body of the detective, which was still in a heap at the base of the stairs, one by one we left the basement.

It didn't surprise me that in his mind it was all our fault. He'd had to kill the detective because Patricia, then all the rest, had dared to tell the truth.

We were forced to return to the living room. It was completely clean. The room reeked of bleach and other cleaning products, but there wasn't a speck of blood anywhere. The couch was damp yet spotless. Mrs. Bradford must have cleaned it all herself. She looked rattled, her eyes darting about in fear and panic.

The reverend forced us to kneel around him in a semi-circle as he stood by the fireplace, reading from the Bible.

I was terrified of what might come next. At the same time, I was relieved not to be in that dark basement anymore. The rot and decay were still very much present in my nostrils.

I dared to open my eyes and glance at Mrs. Bradford during the prayer. She had a blissful smile on her face, yet her eyes were full of terror.

Can I use that?

For what seemed like hours, the reverend read feverishly from the Bible; his aim was that we should atone for "our" sins.

After he was finally done, it was difficult for me to get back up on my feet. I couldn't feel my knees or the muscles in my legs after kneeling so long on the hard wooden floor.

He ordered Mrs. Bradford to take us back to our rooms.

Without wasting time, as though we were all afraid that he would change his mind and start shooting wildly at us, Mrs. Bradford included, we returned meekly to our rooms, and she locked us in.

I was actually relieved I was behind a locked door. No matter if that was a false sense of safety, it still felt better than being downstairs in the basement, with those dead bodies. I shivered thinking about it.

Despite the hunger, shock, and fear, I managed to fall asleep.

But I felt like I slept only a couple of moments before Mrs. Bradford strode in to wake us up. By the way she was acting, it was clear that we were expected to pretend yesterday didn't happen at all.

The other girls accepted the game of deceit immediately.

And I understood why. It was better, safer, to return to how things were before and not dwell on the fact that Reverend Bradford had actually killed someone in front of us. That he could potentially kill all of us. I did the same, seeing merit in their approach to the bizarre situation we were trapped in.

Our schedules returned to normal. We did our chores – I did them barefoot; I hadn't dared take the dead detective's boots after all – and we studied, with both the Bradfords quizzing us at regular intervals throughout the day.

To be honest, I was shocked when I found my phone still sitting on the desk in my room, right where I'd left it. I wondered if that was an oversight or if the Bradfords were truly that confident that I wouldn't call the police on them.

And I didn't call the police, but only because I'd learned by now not to trust them. And although I was sure there were a few good police officers out there, I didn't want them to end up dead, like the detective. I wouldn't be able to bear something like that on my conscience.

The terrible events of that day only strengthened my resolve that my dad couldn't be involved. At least not directly. If the reverend harmed him, I could never forgive myself.

And then I realized with a start what I was doing. That sick man had gotten inside my head. He had managed to turn me into one of his girls, obedient, scared, and forever trapped inside this evil house. There was no doubt in my mind that once I turned eighteen, I would join those corpses in the basement.

If I managed to live that long.
No way.

Once I finished my chores and knew I would have a few

moments to myself, I rushed to the room and grabbed my phone. Grace wasn't there, which was a relief. It was now or never. I wasn't wasting any more time. I shook myself, desperate to banish the reverend's presence in my mind.

I couldn't stay in this house with these murderers and child molesters.

I logged into the game, praying like hell that Hillie would be there, waiting for me.

I felt like sobbing out of pure joy when I saw a green dot next to her photo.

I opened a chat and started typing like crazy. I couldn't allow anyone to find me doing this. It would be too suspicious.

"Tell Dad to come and get me."

"What?" she replied.

"The reverend has a gun. He's already killed three people. Please help—"

I broke off typing as the door swung open.

Mrs. Bradford stood there, looking horrified to see me in the middle of the room, my phone in hand.

She immediately snatched it from me. "What are you doing?" she demanded.

Thankfully, I had just about managed to disconnect the chat. I looked to the floor, like a true repentant, like I'd been caught doing something I shouldn't have.

"So this is how you waste your time designated for study?" she yelled at me. "Playing video games?"

"I'm sorry, Mrs. Bradford."

"Don't you dare try that on me, girl. You are lazing away your time while there is so much work to be done," she snapped.

"Sorry, Mrs. Bradford," I parroted.

She raised her hand as though to slap me but just about stopped herself. "You have your Bible studies; go," she commanded.

Nodding, I grabbed my books and rushed out of the room. I didn't bother to ask for my phone back.

Hillie had got my message. That was all that mattered to me. All I had to do now was keep my head down again, not ruffle any feathers, and wait for Dad to come and get me.

I knew I could keep on the right side of the Bradfords. Just about. But how hard would it be to stay alive until Dad turned up? I didn't dare answer that.

I worked all day without breaks or complaints. I studied and did all my homework in record time, all the while being on my best behavior, hoping that would make them leave me alone.

But then the reverend appeared just as I was feeding the chickens. I turned around, and he was there, staring at me. He startled me, sneaking up on me like that, and I almost dropped the bucket with the grains in it, but caught it in time. I spilled some to the ground all the same, and the chickens rushed to peck around my feet.

I hated how jumpy I was around him, but it couldn't be helped. He'd killed a person right in front of me. I would never be able to forget the look in his eyes when he did it. It exhilarated him that he'd ended someone's life. That he had that kind of power. Not to mention he'd chosen to kill two young women so as to keep his dirty, disgusting secrets.

"You fit in our blessed family quite nicely," he observed.

I stayed silent, keeping my head down, hoping he would say what he wanted and then leave me alone.

But no. To make matters even worse, Mrs. Bradford came striding out of the house. Her expression was full of anger and jealousy. I knew she was preparing some fresh new hell for me.

"I'll have some additional chores for you tonight," he told me in his usual commanding manner.

His words sent chills down my spine. Was that what he called his homemade child pornography, *additional chores?*

Please, Dad, hurry, I prayed.

I simply nodded. Refusing him wasn't an option, especially since I knew he constantly carried that gun now, ever since killing the detective. He was completely unhinged; everything else was just a facade.

"Come with me," he commanded.

I immediately put the bucket down, falling into step behind him.

It was curious that Mrs. Bradford wasn't on the porch anymore. *Where did she go?*

We entered the kitchen. Patricia was washing dishes, and her eyes immediately filled with tears when she saw the reverend.

He didn't even spare her a glance, nor did we stop there. The reverend was looking for his wife.

We found Mrs. Bradford in the living room with Grace, fussing over some fabrics. By the conversation we interrupted, it was apparent she was choosing a fresh pattern to sew new couch cushions. No one needed to be a genius to know why she had the sudden urge to do that. The couch was spotless, but the part of it that had been stained by the detective's blood was paler than the rest from all the bleach.

It was a silent, but undeniable reminder of what had

happened. And it was clear Mrs. Bradford didn't want any kind of reminders around her.

As though changing the fabric on a few cushions could stop me, or anybody else for that matter, from remembering what happened in that room.

Mrs. Bradford looked at her husband questioningly as we walked in.

"Samantha will be the one doing the midnight chores for me tonight," he informed her.

My heart was beating so hard that it was strange to me how nobody else could hear it. I knew what he wanted from me. I knew what was expected.

I felt like crying. I felt like running away. I felt like falling to the floor in despair.

I didn't move a muscle.

Grace looked at me. Although it was obvious she felt sorry for me, at the same time she seemed relieved she wouldn't be the one going to that room tonight. Of course, I didn't hold that against her.

Mrs. Bradford looked shocked, but masked it quickly, without expressing her displeasure, simply nodding in agreement. Although she was jealous of me, she would still come to my room in the middle of the night to take me to that disgusting room, to take me to him.

The reverend turned to me. "You are dismissed."

On my way out of the living room, I realized I would have to figure out my own escape even if it came to a physical confrontation with the reverend. I was terrified of that, yet at the same time, I knew that the element of surprise was on my side. Especially now when they thought they had managed to tame me, to break me. My dad's training would be my secret weapon.

One way or another, I was leaving before I was forced to go to that room, to that man, as though I were an offering, a victim of his foul desires.

I would rather burn the entire house down with all of us inside.

33

JESSE

I was about to leave for work when Hillie came rushing to the farm.

"What are you doing here?" I asked, confused and slightly alarmed, knowing she was supposed to be at school.

"Sam reached out to me," she said and then stopped, trying to catch her breath.

Did she run all the way from school?

I waited on tenterhooks for her to continue. "And?"

She took her phone out, opening a bunch of screenshots. "We chatted inside the game so there wouldn't be any traces of it, but I made screenshots just to be safe."

I started reading in a rush. The reverend was a murderer. He'd killed three people. Get Dad. That was the gist of it. I had to read the words a couple of times simply to make sure I wasn't hallucinating.

Oh my God. It was exactly as I feared. Sam was in mortal danger. My gut feeling hadn't failed me, not even in this situation.

The fury inside me was already taking over, but I managed to choke out, "Thank you for showing them to me. Can you send them to my phone?"

Hillie nodded.

A few moments later my phone pinged, indicating I'd received the screenshots from her.

I entered the house and went to the gun cabinet. It was time to storm that farm and get my daughter back. It was what I was supposed to do from the start, but I'd foolishly listened to others while my daughter suffered. I wasn't going to allow that monster to torment her a second longer.

It was now more than apparent he'd killed those two girls Tanya and Maria, the ones who were presumed missing. Also, Sam mentioned that he'd killed three people. Who was the third? Did it happen before or after he killed those poor girls? And most importantly, how did Sam know about it?

She knows because she's Sam, I answered my own question.

"Can I help?" Hillie asked.

I shook my head. "No, Hillie. Go to school. I promise I'll get Sam back."

Reluctantly, she left me alone to prepare for battle.

It was a relief that I knew exactly where Sam was so that I could take them by surprise, overpower that piece of shit, and save my daughter. Save all the girls on that farm.

The notion that they fostered a bunch of girls, masking their monstrosity with generosity and self-righteousness, really made me see red. I was sure that a man like the reverend believed in divine justice, which was perfect considering he was about to experience it on his own skin.

Choosing my weapons with care, I filled a duffel bag

with all the extra ammunition I might need before closing the gun cabinet and exiting the house. Once I put everything in the truck, I went to see Billy. I hoped he would come with me. Billy had been a sniper during the war, so having him watch my six was always a good thing.

"Jesse? What happened?" he demanded the instant he saw me.

In my rush, I completely forgot I still had my favorite gun in my hand.

It was my favorite because it was a gift from Katarina. I even carried it with me when I was away. It was my lucky charm that always brought me back home to her from war. The irony that I'd also almost blown my own head off with it wasn't lost on me. But I banished all that because none of it mattered right now. Getting Sam back home safely was the priority.

"Sam managed to talk to Hillie," I said, showing him the screenshots. "I need to go and get her, and I want you to come with me."

Billy cursed, reading the messages.

"Exactly. Let's go save those girls."

Billy shook his head. "Call the police and show them what Hillie sent you. Let them handle this."

"Why would I call the police?" I said snidely. "Because they've been so helpful up until this point?"

"Because it's the right thing to do."

"I did the right thing many times, Billy. I begged them to send someone to make sure Sam was all right, and still they all turned their backs on me. So why would I trust that things would be different this time?"

They don't care. They never cared one bit about me or my daughter. To serve and protect, what a fucking joke.

Even the detective had disappointed me. Overton was supposed to call me the instant he saw Sam. I'd called him once he failed to check in, and he didn't answer. The bastard was clearly ducking my calls. I'd genuinely believed he wanted to help, but he was the same as his boss, the sheriff. In the end, it was all nothing but a bunch of bullshit.

"I only have myself to rely on, Billy." *And I believed with all my heart and soul, I could rely on you as well*, was implied.

"I'm not saying do nothing. I'm saying let's be smart about it."

"I'm going to get her, with or without you," I said, ready to leave, realizing I'd already wasted too much time with a person I considered my closest friend.

"Then go without me," Billy said firmly. "You're making a huge mistake, and I won't be a part of it."

"Are you really turning your back on me, on Sam, when we need you the most?" I asked, raising my voice.

"I'm doing this because I have your back. I'm capable of seeing the bigger picture, while you're too emotional."

"Sam's in danger."

"Yes, I understand. And I want her back, believe me. But you're not thinking straight. If you go in there guns blazing, someone will almost certainly get hurt."

"I intend on hurting someone," I said through gritted teeth. "Reverend Bradford."

"You can't guarantee he'll be the only casualty. Could you really live with the fact someone got hurt because of you? What if Sam got hurt?" he challenged.

I could see his point. It was just that I found that risk worth taking.

"You need to do the smart thing, Jesse," he insisted. "Please call the police."

"I'm leaving," I said. "Police be damned."

"I can't let you make such a colossal mistake."

"You can't stop me. I have to go and save my daughter."

"I'll call the cops on you," he threatened.

"You would do that to me?" I asked incredulously.

"To save Sam? In a heartbeat," he countered.

"You're not saving her. You're dooming her by keeping me here," I argued.

"That's not true. And I think deep down you know that too. That's why you came here in the first place," he pointed out. "We're not at war anymore, my friend. It's time to lay down our weapons and change tactics."

"I can't just do nothing," I said, somewhat defeated.

"Not do nothing, do everything, only in the right way, with the help of others," he corrected. "Professionals."

I nodded. "Fine. I'm going to trust you." I turned to leave once again.

"Where are you going?" Billy called after me.

"I'm going to see the sheriff, show the screenshots to him," I lied.

"Good choice," Billy said, holding out his hand to shake. "Call me if you need anything."

I won't. "I will."

I got into my truck and on impulse dialed Dr. Sheldon. After my altercation with Billy, I felt like a second opinion was in order.

"Is everything all right?" she asked.

"No," I replied honestly.

"What's happened?" she demanded.

"I received a text from Sam. She's in danger, she's begged me to come and save her, and that's exactly what I'm doing."

"I'm really sorry to hear that. Did you call the police?"

"No."

"Are you on your way there now?"

"Yes."

"Considering you're speaking with me now, clearly some part of you thinks that's a bad idea."

She sounds like Billy.

"Wrong. I tried turning to the police, and they refused to help me, and the CPS as well. Dealing with the legalities of it all takes too much time. So I'm calling because I need your help."

"My help?"

"Yes. And I'm not talking about the shrink part. I'm not conflicted about this. My mission is clear to me."

"So what do you need me for?"

"I want you to come with me. I want you to finish the mission if something happens to me." *If I die.*

"Oh," was all she said.

"Doc?" I prompted. "I need you to call the police to save Sam if I'm unable to."

"I don't like this plan, Jesse. I returned my uniform a long time ago."

"Once a soldier, always a soldier. Or are you telling me that you would turn your back on those in need?"

"You're trying to manipulate me."

"Is it working?"

"I don't know," she replied.

"Look, the detective who was supposed to help me failed to check in, and I'm worried about him, on top of everything else. I'm worried the reverend has done something to him because he came too close," I said, because now that I thought about it, maybe he was one of the three the reverend had killed. The three Sam had mentioned in her text.

"Okay, tell me where you want us to meet," she said.

"Come outside," I instructed. "I'm already here to pick you up."

34

SAMANTHA

I had to believe with all my heart that Hillie had managed to get my message to Dad by now and he was on his way to get me out of here. In the meantime, I had to find a way to help myself because this place was a barrel of gunpowder ready to explode. In fact, we were one spark away from going nuclear.

I wasn't sticking around for that.

I focused on how I could use Mrs. Bradford's medical report to my advantage. That was my golden ticket. I was sure the reverend didn't know his wife had gotten sterilized to prevent him from ever being a father. After seeing that secret room, I now understood there was some part of her that refused to allow *her* children to be subjected to the depravities of that man. However, at the same time, she had no problems subjecting the rest of us to it. That was precisely why she had to go down with him. Be punished for all the bad things she did, that she enabled over the years.

It crossed my mind I could blackmail her into helping me. But it was a matter of what she would fear more, being discovered by the reverend for helping me or his discovering that it was a deliberate act that meant she couldn't have children. The reverend would punish her either way, and I couldn't decide which direction she would sway considering she was completely unstable and thus unpredictable.

I guess I'll find out.

I decided to go and speak with her while she was in her sewing room, knowing that would ensure some privacy. Blackmailing her wasn't something I could attempt to do in front of the other girls.

Going upstairs that afternoon, I heard an argument between the Bradfords. I crept closer to their bedroom so I could listen in.

"You will go because I am ordering you to go," the reverend shouted. "I'm your husband, so you must obey me."

"Please don't make me go anymore," Mrs. Bradford said. "It's a sin to meddle in such things, not to mention a waste of money. We should let God bless us with a child if he deems us fit."

"How dare you imply I am not worthy to be a father," he growled. "You will have fertility treatments if I choose it."

In the next instant, Mrs. Bradford started whimpering, which I knew meant he was slapping her around.

"I decide what is sin, and what is not," he continued to rant, blaming her for their childlessness, accusing her of being a wicked, prideful, bad wife, all the usual crap he liked to spout.

"God linked me to such a disobedient wife, not as a punishment, but as a chance to prove my worthiness. And I will lead you to the path of righteousness even if I have to drag you there all bloody and bruised."

Oh my God, he is completely insane. Then again, I already knew that.

"Gareth, please stop," she begged. "I will never have children if you do this to me."

"Pain makes us stronger. Praise the Lord's name so you can see the light."

She started screaming, crying even more sharply. From the sound of it swishing through the air, I knew that he'd now gone for his belt.

I'd heard enough, so I returned to my room. Their being busy with their own toxic relationship gave me time to think about my next move.

I was now convinced that Mrs. Bradford would help me if I pressed her with that report because she would have no choice. The reverend would definitely kill her if he ever found out she'd done something like that behind his back.

Once the reverend finished beating his wife, he returned to his study to pray, or whatever he did after such savagery, and Mrs. Bradford stayed in the bedroom.

The rest of us acted as though it was just another Thursday, simply because it was. Sometime later, as we prepared lunch, Mrs. Bradford finally resurfaced. She had changed and fixed her hair; however, she couldn't hide the massive bruises on her face.

Usually, he'd beat her in a manner that wouldn't leave visible marks because we all had to look presentable for Sunday services. So the unmistakable message that her face conveyed now was a true testament to how unhinged he'd become.

Of course, we all pretended not to notice her red and swollen face as we worked.

She circled us like a shark, watching our every move, ready to strike. "Patricia, you call that wiping? You're just smearing all the dirt around."

Patricia was on her hands and knees, scrubbing the hallway floor, and stopped as Mrs. Bradford started yelling at her.

I gritted my teeth, watching the scene from the kitchen. The floors were spotless since we were forced to scrub them every day, but I knew that wasn't the point.

"It's disgusting what you're doing. You'll make everyone in this house sick. Is that what you want?" she asked.

Patricia started crying. The poor girl always had eyes filled with tears each time one of the Bradfords entered the room. I knew she blamed herself for the detective's death. She'd tried to save us all by telling the detective exactly what was happening in that secret room, but unfortunately her attempt at bravery had failed.

That was a lot of weight to be carried by a twelve-year-old girl.

"Start over, and scrub better, or I'll beat you," Mrs. Bradford threatened.

Patricia cried even harder but did what she was told.

My heart broke watching that sweet girl being subjected to that and so much worse.

Watching this scene, I started to doubt my plan. If I tried to blackmail Mrs. Bradford with the medical report, there was no telling how she would react. She could even try to kill me if she felt too threatened. She was insane, and people as desperate and unhinged as her should not be backed into a corner.

I needed a better plan. And since my options were pretty limited, the solution presented itself quite easily. I would widen this rift between my captors, and if I was lucky, they would destroy each other before they had a chance to destroy anyone else. *Or force me to go to that secret room tonight.*

THE OTHER FAMILY 241

Acting on this idea, I took the medical report about Mrs. Bradford's sterilization and put it someplace I knew for sure would catch the reverend's attention. Each afternoon he went to his study to write – his sermons, I guess – which was why I placed it on top of his papers.

I smiled to myself going back to my room. I'd lit the match and simply had to wait for the spark to cause an explosion. I just hoped I'd timed everything perfectly and that their fight and my dad's arrival would coincide.

Please, Dad, hurry.

It was on the tip of my tongue to warn Grace, but I didn't. It was better if nobody knew what I had done, at least for now.

"Do you know what you'll wear tonight?" Grace asked.

"Excuse me?"

"For your meeting with the reverend."

If there was a choice, I would wear military clothes and combat boots and would be armed to the teeth.

"I don't care about it because I've prayed to God it won't come to that," I said with a small smile.

To my surprise, Grace hugged me. "I'm sorry," she whispered before leaving the room.

I was sorry too. That those monsters had hurt her so badly. Hopefully, I would be able to correct that wrong, and soon.

35

SAMANTHA

As expected, all hell broke loose once the reverend found the medical report I'd left for him. Discovering his wife had acted against him brought him to such a state of rage that both Grace and I huddled by the door to listen in.

Will this work?

Although we were behind a locked door and in a different part of the house, we could hear them arguing as though we were in the room with them. They didn't go some-place private to fight this time: all pretenses at civility or decency had gone out the window once the reverend committed murder in front of us.

It was better that way, as far as I was concerned.

At first, Mrs. Bradford blamed one of us for planting that report; she claimed someone must have faked it so they would have an argument. But she must have known there was no point. Such evidence couldn't be faked, especially not in this house, when the only computer was heavily monitored and didn't have a printer connected.

Her weak attempt to explain herself with lies collapsed like a house of cards in a slight breeze.

"How could you betray me? For more than a decade you have been lying to me."

"Gareth, please let me explain—"

"You're worse than Judas. What did you get for your kiss of betrayal, you treacherous bitch?" he shouted.

"I wonder what this is about," Grace said.

I shushed her, wanting to hear more.

But for whatever reason, the arguing suddenly became muffled.

I frowned. *Is that it? Is it possible his rage has disappeared that quickly?*

The last thing I needed was for them to kiss and make up. I had to hear the rest of the conversation so I could prepare for whatever happened next. I took out my lockpick from my hiding place and started working on the lock.

"What are you doing?" Grace asked, horrified.

"I have to hear what's happening."

"Did you have something to do with it?" Grace guessed.

Without answering, I left the room and crept closer toward their room so I could hear them better.

"You've doomed us, Evangeline. How could you prevent me from having children?"

Is he crying? That seemed impossible, yet that was how he sounded.

"Answer me, woman!" he demanded.

So far it was all unraveling between them the way I wanted it to.

"It had to be done for medical reasons," she said. "I would die if I didn't do it."

If she'd started with that, she would have had a chance to

convince him. But she was panicking and grasping for straws, which I knew would be her undoing. The reverend could outargue anyone.

I couldn't ask for more.

"Stop lying to me, you wicked woman." I almost flinched as I heard him slap her. "You went behind my back. You had surgery. You chose to be *sterile!*"

"I didn't want to worry you," she cried.

He hit her again. This time, I heard her fall down to the ground.

"Tell me the truth, Evangeline, or so help me God, I will beat it out of your lying, barren mouth," he boomed.

"Yes, yes, I did it. Of course I did it. I went to the hospital, and I had that surgery," she confessed in a torrent of words.

My eyes went wide. I couldn't believe she'd told the truth.

"Why?" he demanded.

"Why?" she repeated. And there were traces of hysterical laughter in her voice. "Because the thought of having your children made me want to kill myself."

"Evangeline, how can you say that?" he gasped, and I thought he sounded confused, hurt even.

"Because it's the truth. The notion of having your child, a daughter, having such innocence in your presence was unbearable to me because I knew where that would lead."

"We agreed never to discuss it outside of that room," he replied.

His voice sounded strange, hollow. I couldn't quite decipher it. *Was it shame?*

"We're going to talk about it because certain things need to be said. You wanted the truth, so here it is. I didn't want my own daughters ending up in front of that camera, with you in bed, doing the same vile, perverted, disgusting things that you do to all the other girls in this house. So, Gareth, I had surgery, and I saved them from you."

Oh my God.

It was as bad as I feared. The reverend was a pedophile who had sex with – who raped – underage girls. Girls he'd sworn to take care of as a foster parent. And to make matters worse, he documented it all. And he did it with the blessing of his wife, even if that blessing was at first reluctant.

I wondered if I could find those photos. That would be the final nail in his coffin, I thought, if I had concrete proof of his devious, criminal behavior.

"And I know what you did to Tanya and Maria," Mrs. Bradford continued. "You killed them so they wouldn't tell the world exactly what kind of monster you really are."

The dam had definitely broken.

I listened, appalled, as Mrs. Bradford finished unleashing everything that was bottled up inside her in one powerful tsunami wave of hatred and resentment.

Then the reverend started shouting. It was purely the primal sound of an animal, an enraged, deranged animal. And next the mayhem started. I could hear him breaking stuff around the room as Mrs. Bradford screamed.

Instinct compelled me to take a couple of steps backward.

"I will kill you!" he shouted, in a voice that was so devoid of any kind of humanity it sent chills down my spine.

"No, stop, leave me alone!" I imagined Mrs. Bradford struggling against him, but I knew it was pointless. The reverend was much bigger and stronger than her.

I could hear him chasing her around the room.

It's just a matter of time before she reaches the door, I real-ized, deciding to retreat. The last thing I needed was to be discovered eavesdropping while he was in such a state. The reverend's fury should be solely directed at his wife. That was the plan, after all.

I found Grace still by the door when I returned to our room. Her eyes were beyond wide.

I wanted to say something to her, but the noises coming from the bedroom distracted me.

By the way he had started to grunt, it was apparent he was beating her with his belt.

"No matter how hard you beat me, I will never be sorry!" Mrs. Bradford yelled.

We watched, appalled, as she managed to run out of the room, with him chasing her around the house, beating her as he went. They ended up downstairs, but we could still hear them going at one another, Mrs. Bradford verbally slashing her husband while he was beating her with his belt and his fists.

He is going to kill her, came a terrifying thought.

"You don't deserve to be a father!" she screamed. "You wear the robe of a saint, but you're nothing but the devil."

"You're wrong, my dear wife," he shouted. "I am the alpha and omega, the beginning and the end, the first and the last."

Even I knew he was quoting a verse from the Bible. It was almost laughable, I thought, how he managed to delude himself he was God.

But then Grace and I both flinched and instinctively crouched, our hands over our ears, recoiling with shock.

"What was that?" she whispered, but we both knew the answer.

36

SAMANTHA

It was a gun. A gun had gone off.

My heart was beating like crazy. Although I dreaded knowing that the reverend had just killed his wife, I still hoped there was a chance it was the other way around. It would be poetic justice if one of his captors had managed to rise against him and end his life.

Could I dare to hope?

All that and more passed through my head as Grace and I waited breathlessly by the door. Waiting for any kind of sign, any kind of noise coming from downstairs.

Who shot who?

It felt like an eternity had passed when at last we heard something crashing in the kitchen. The killer must have broken something, realizing the gravity of the crime. Without a word, we both ran back to our beds, covering ourselves and pretending to sleep. It wasn't a conscious decision, it was done purely on instinct, no matter how ridiculous it was.

Grace screamed as someone burst into our room. As soon

as we dared put our heads out of the covers, we were faced with a gun pointing straight at us.

It was the reverend. I cursed under my breath. *Damn him to hell.*

Although he was dressed all in black, blood spatters were still visible all over him. He must have shot his wife from close range.

"Come with me," he commanded. "Now."

Grace looked at me, and I nodded ever so slightly. It was better to do what he wanted. We didn't have any other choice.

He took us to the kitchen. Mrs. Bradford was lying on the floor, which was turning dark, blackening red around her. He'd shot her in the chest, and there was a hideous wound where her heart was supposed to be. It was frightening to me how accurate his aim was.

Where did he learn how to shoot? I wondered as I watched the lifeless body of Mrs. Bradford. Her dead eyes stared at the ceiling.

The reverend waved in her general direction, without sparing her a glance. "Clean that up. Take that sinner to the basement; let her rot with the rest of the trash." Then he went to the living room and sat in his chair, still holding the gun in his right hand.

As we complied without a word, I blamed myself. Mrs. Bradford was dead because I'd revealed a secret she was keeping. I knew the risks. I knew he might snap and kill her, but I did it anyway. I didn't pull the trigger, but I definitely had blood on my hands.

It felt really confusing, being aware that my actions had such profound and permanent consequences. I was merely trying to survive, but I still felt guilt heaping up on me.

It wasn't easy dragging the body to the basement. Although Mrs. Bradford was a small woman, her body was very heavy in death. *Is that the weight of all her sins?* I thought.

I watched, both impressed and appalled, as Grace kicked Mrs. Bradford with gusto so that she fell down the stairs and landed next to the dead body of that detective.

Mrs. Bradford was horrible, and she got exactly what she deserved, I thought.

Even though it's all your fault? another part of my brain questioned.

The smell of rotten corpses down there was so pungent that I barely stopped myself from throwing up. I didn't want to be forced to wipe my own puke from the floor as well.

"You're finally understanding what it takes to survive in this house," Grace said, misunderstanding my expression.

I let her believe what suited her.

Once we'd dealt with the body, we returned to the kitchen to gather all the cleaning supplies.

The reverend rose from his seat in the living room and locked the basement door before he joined us in the kitchen. He informed us that he was going to his study to pray and reflect on what had happened. "I hope the Lord will show us the path to carry on after such a tragedy," he said with a strange expression on his face.

Apparently, he'd already forgotten that he was the one who'd killed his wife. He acted as though he were speaking with someone from his congregation, not a couple of eyewitnesses.

His kill count is going up by the day. I really didn't want to think about the fact he was capable of killing so easily because then I would be forced to think about who was next.

"Work in silence," he ordered. "I don't want to be disturbed."

We simply nodded and obeyed since *or else* was heavily implied in his command.

I fought nausea while we wiped the blood off the kitchen tiles and cleaned up the blood trail we'd created all the way to the basement. The rusty aroma of blood was all I could smell, and it even felt like I could taste it. We were aware that it was also expected of us to clean up any mess the reverend had created in the bedroom before he'd killed her.

As we silently worked, I thought of the younger girls. They were locked in their room, but I was sure they'd heard everything. I wished I could try to comfort them, but I didn't know how. That was why I did nothing, simply cleaned the floor as instructed.

And that bothered me deeply because, by doing nothing, I was proving Grace's point. Was she right? Had I become just like her, just like them despite my best efforts?

It took us a couple of hours to clean up all the mess, gather all the broken things, throw them in the trash, and then replace what we could, taking items from other rooms so that everything could pretend to be normal again.

I used my lockpick to open spare rooms so we could get a chair or extra blankets to replace the bloodied ones in the bedroom. My reasoning was that he wouldn't think twice about how we'd got those things from the locked rooms, but he would definitely be enraged if we left things as they were.

We both ignored that one specific room although I really had an urge to set it on fire.

In the end, we spoke with Chloe and Patricia through the locked door. I told them what had happened, without going into details, while Grace ordered them not to cry and told them they must act as though all was normal. Although it sounded harsh, it was necessary. We had to do everything in our power to survive.

However, once we returned to our room, I realized I couldn't keep silent any longer.

"Why don't you fight back, Grace?" I asked, getting into her face. "You've been here the longest, and I know they've done unspeakable things to you. I know what *he* did to you."

Grace shook her head, recoiling from me and averting her eyes.

"I know about the room," I insisted. "And still, you do what he wants like a good little girl." Part of me knew I was being cruel, but I was so angry it had to come out. And Grace was an easy target; she retreated so readily into the role of a victim.

But then she turned to face me, and her eyes flashed with fury. It startled me: I hadn't seen her like that before. I thought the Bradfords had managed to beat any kind of rebellion out of her a long time ago. Perhaps I was wrong.

"I do nothing," she seethed the words, "precisely because I have been here the longest. I've witnessed four murders so far, Samantha, and I'm afraid. I don't fight because I don't want to die. But I know I'll be next."

"Do you hear yourself? You know he's going to kill you, yet you still do nothing," I pointed out.

"That way, perhaps there is a chance..." she said meekly again.

"Better to go down fighting than settle for this, because this is no life, Grace. This is a death sentence," I insisted.

"And you show me every day what your idea of fighting means to all of us," Grace said snidely.

"What is that supposed to mean?"

"Ever since you came, things have gone from bad to worse," she said, and the accusation was clear in her voice.

I couldn't believe she was blaming me for all of this. "Excuse me? All I've done is try to get us out of here."

"Did you make sure that the reverend found out about Mrs. Bradford's operation?"

Something in her body language made me ask, "Did you already know about it?"

"Yes, Mrs. Bradford confessed to me a couple of years ago in a moment of weakness. She apologized for dooming me so she wouldn't have to doom her children."

I could only stare at her. She'd sat on such knowledge all this time and done nothing with it. They really had broken her spirit. In some screwed-up way, she'd deluded herself that she was part of the family. That was beyond tragic.

"You didn't answer my question. Did you do it?" Grace asked.

"Of course not," I lied.

I'd decided to play it safe. Although I sympathized with Grace and felt deeply sorry for her, I also knew I couldn't trust her, not completely. The last thing I needed was for Grace to use that information against me and rat me out to the reverend so she could become the new Mrs. Bradford.

I knew that sounded like a completely crazy idea, but then again this was a crazy house, so anything was possible. Besides, Grace looked desperate enough, like she would do anything to save herself.

"I have no idea how he found out about Mrs. Bradford's secret, but I'm glad he did," I concluded.

Grace didn't press me after that.

It was getting pretty late, but for some reason the reverend insisted on rounding us up in the living room. We stood in a semicircle in front of him, with our heads bowed. Grace was to my right, Chloe to my left. And Patricia, silently crying, was beside Chloe. As expected, she was taking Mrs. Bradford's death the hardest.

I noted how creepily, hungrily, the reverend stared at Grace. I realized to my horror that he was contemplating a similar idea to the one I'd had earlier about Grace replacing Mrs. Bradford.

Of course, I wasn't the only one who noticed. Grace went pale, bowing her head, trying to appear smaller than all of us.

When I saw her like that, so cowed and afraid, I hated him with my entire being. I wanted to jump on him, grab the gun from his hand, and shoot him in the head repeatedly until I was certain he was dead and wouldn't come back to haunt us.

"There will be a few changes in this house from now on," he started. "First of all, give me all your shoes, now," he commanded.

The girls took off their shoes and placed them next to the reverend's feet.

I stayed put; I was already barefoot. I detested such a fate wholeheartedly. However, I realized that even if I'd managed to regain my shoes somehow, I would still have lost them now. In some weird way, that made me feel better.

"Second, we will have more praying hours. I will root all evil from you so you don't end up wicked and twisted like Evangeline."

I wasn't surprised he was blaming his wife for the fact he'd killed her. He was a master at twisting reality to suit his own ends, after all.

"If any one of you disobeys me in any way or tries to run

away like those two Jezebels, I will shoot you in the back and leave you for the crows to feast on your flesh."

Crows? I thought.

He really was completely unhinged. With Mrs. Bradford gone, he could do whatever he pleased, and that was very bad for us. I truly had no words to describe the danger we lived in now.

Nonetheless, I wouldn't allow him to defeat me. I was certain I wasn't staying here to serve him in his deranged religious cult. My dad was on his way, and he was going to deal with this man once and for all.

I just hoped he would hurry up. I needed him to get here before I was forced to go to that room.

37

JESSE

While I waited for Dr. Sheldon to join me, I went through a mental checklist of all the guns, ammo and gear that I'd packed. I was pretty confident I had all the firepower I would need to get Sam back.

My 10mm pistol was on the seat beside me, and my shotgun was lying behind the seat. Both guns were fully loaded. I was taking no chances. If I had to act on the fly, I could. The rest of the equipment was in the duffel bag in the back.

I was taking every possible precaution. I hadn't lost my mind when Hillie came to me with that message from Sam, which was quite surprising for me, come to think of it, and I realized it must mean my therapy was actually working.

I had a plan despite looking as though I'd packed half my arsenal and was rushing blindly into the unknown. Of course, I would first scout the place, assess all the potential dangers. After choosing the entry point, I would get in and get Sam out. If the reverend got in my way, I would simply deal with him. Easy, efficient.

I would do whatever it took to save my daughter from that murderer and his wife.

I was aware I might have to be on the run from the law for the rest of my life if I killed that motherfucker. But that was a risk worth taking. Besides, I'd heard Mexico was really nice this time of year, most times of year, or so I'd heard.

My phone started ringing. It was Billy.

I had no intention of answering. He would figure out soon enough that I'd chosen a different path.

Will he try to stop me?

I was still pretty angry at Billy. I never expected he would betray me. He'd gotten soft in his old age, but I hadn't. And it was on me to right this wrong, considering I was to blame for the fact that we were in this situation in the first place. This was my chance to atone for my sins, to atone to Sam for almost leaving her all alone in this world.

I would never try to kill myself again, but I would kill for her, to protect her, any day of the week. I might lose my freedom entirely to protect her, I might take a bullet during my altercation with the reverend, maybe even from the police, and I'd made my peace with that as well. My life for my daughter's safety was a fair trade.

Perhaps that was why Billy couldn't understand my primal need to do everything in my power to save her, no matter what, because he'd never experienced such unconditional love, such a pure bond between a father and a daughter.

I immediately felt bad. I knew how much Billy and Emily had struggled to have children, and they never could. Besides, they always treated Sam like their own. At times, during my darkest moments, Billy was a better father to Sam than I was, which was to say parents, like love itself, came in different forms.

I texted Billy to tell him I was on my way to the farm. I made sure to mention I had help.

I checked the time. Dr. Sheldon was taking a long time to join me. Only a few minutes had passed since we'd ended the conversation, but I was so anxious to resume my journey that it felt like an eternity.

As though summoned by my thoughts, I watched as Dr. Sheldon left the building, she looked around, and I honked.

She jogged to the truck and opened the door. "I'm still not sure this is the right thing to do," she said as a form of greeting.

"It's the right thing to do," I insisted as I picked up the 10mm and put it in the glove compartment so she could have a seat, which she did.

She also eyed the shotgun behind the seat, but to her credit, she didn't ask about it.

I really appreciated that she had agreed to come with me. I said as much.

"What you shared didn't sit well with me, and that's why I felt the need to help," she said.

"Why?"

Dr. Sheldon sighed. "I've seen situations when parents had a strong instinct that their child was in danger and were prevented from doing anything because of hospitalization, a protection order, or custody issues. Five times in the last decade I've seen the results of not doing anything. The end result was always the same, a badly abused kid or a dead one. And I'm sick and tired of staying on the sidelines because of all the protocols that were put in place to protect but, ironically, in reality, only hinder us and prevent us from springing into action. I'm painfully aware that child protective services as a system is broken, and I know that pedophiles and traffickers, not to mention all kinds of other abusers, take full advantage of that."

As I processed everything she'd said, I realized I hadn't even considered that something of that sort might be going on. Sam had said she was in danger, and my mind went one way, when in reality it could be something else entirely. The reverend had killed three people, and I never stopped to think what his motive might be to do something like that.

Could it be...

Oh my God.

What kind of parent was I when I didn't even stop to consider all the dangers surrounding my daughter? As my mind swirled with unimaginable possibilities and awful images, I started to freak out. I squeezed the wheel tightly, hitting the gas. I had to get to Sam as soon as possible.

"Relax, Jesse, take a deep breath. You're not a bad parent for not thinking about all the predators in this world."

"How did you know that's what I was thinking about?"

"Because I'm good at my job," she deadpanned.

Despite myself, I smiled. "It's true. That's where my mind went. It's ironic that I tried to prepare Sam for all kinds of potential dangers that could fall upon us in the future, and I never considered including existing ones."

"That's understandable. Women are more prone to experiencing that kind of danger, so we're more aware of it."

"That's no excuse," I grumbled.

"I'm sorry I mentioned anything. I ramble when I'm nervous."

I glanced at her before refocusing on the road. "I'm glad

you feel so strongly about it. It means I made the right decision."

"I'm glad you think that way, and I can't wait to meet Sam. She sounds like a remarkable young woman."

"She is."

As we talked about Sam, part of me wondered if Dr Sheldon had changed the subject so I would stop spiraling, because once again I was perfectly calm and focused on the mission ahead. *Damn, she is really good at her job.*

"Do you have a plan?" she asked at some point.

"Reach the farm; then rescue my daughter by any means necessary."

She pursed her lips. "Okay, I like it. It's concise and easy to follow."

"Glad you agree."

"Do you mind if I extend it a little?" she asked.

"What do you mean?"

"Well, based on the guns surrounding us, and while assuming you have more in the back—"

"A lot more," I agreed.

"A lot more," she repeated. "So I'm just guessing here, but it's safe to say your plan revolves around busting inside all guns blazing?"

"It's an effective way of getting what I want," I pointed out.

"True, but how about we try a different tactic before resorting to force?"

"What do you have in mind?"

"Talking," she said slowly as though fearing that was a foreign word to me.

I made a face. "I have nothing to say to that man. He's a

murderer, and there's no telling what Sam's had to endure while living in a house with him."

"I was suggesting I should go and speak with him. Maybe I can get your daughter out on some false pretense."

I shook my head. "I don't want you anywhere near him. Because Sam isn't the only girl he's holding hostage. There are three more girls living there, and we have to help them all."

"I see," she said. "Then we go with your plan."

38

SAMANTHA

Ever since the reverend shot his wife, he'd been pacing around erratically with that gun. It was a complete one-eighty in behavior. When I first met him, he was stoic, calm, always in control, but totally unpredictable at times, which was scary, while now he was erratic, unhinged, and completely unpredictable, which was totally terrifying.

Then he produced my phone from somewhere – I thought Mrs. Bradford had hidden it someplace – and gave it to me.

"We don't want your daddy to be worried about you," he commented.

I accepted it immediately. If he was dumb enough to give it to me, then so be it.

He demanded we continue with our daily chores as though everything were normal.

I noted the other girls were freaked out by this recent turn of events. More so than me. Of course I was afraid. How could I not be? But I didn't allow my fear to paralyze me.

After a while, he rounded us up in the living room and

gave a long speech about what had happened to his wife. He was convinced in his delusions that God had used him as an instrument for justice to punish her for disobeying her husband and lying to him.

He expressed deep concern for the state of our souls, and he prayed to God it wasn't too late for him to save us. To turn all that was wrong into right.

He thanked God for using him to punish his wife.

It was on the tip of my tongue to ask if he planned on punishing himself as well. After all, he was the one abusing the girls, photographing them, filming them while they were at their most vulnerable. I said nothing, of course. I wouldn't be able to reason with a dangerous lunatic who seemingly believed everything he was preaching.

After threatening that he would kill us without hesitation because he had that right, a right that was given to him by God, he sent us to our rooms, locking us in.

Every once in a while, we could hear him shouting. It sounded like he was arguing with Mrs. Bradford. Which was all complete nonsense, of course, but I didn't care. As long as he had other amusements, I was left alone to pace the small room and come up with my next course of action.

We couldn't stay in this house. It was just a matter of time before he believed that he'd received a command from God to kill us all.

And I couldn't even imagine how he would react on Sunday when he would have to explain why his wife was missing from the service and why his always perfect-looking foster daughters were bruised and obviously scared.

"Samantha, please don't make it worse," Grace pleaded in a small voice.

I stopped mid-step to look at her; then I approached her

bed and sat down. "I'm trying to make it better. You're aware we can't stay here, right?"

"What other choice do we have? He has a gun."

I was about to reply when we heard our door being unlocked, and then the reverend, half mad, stormed into our room.

Chloe and Patricia were right behind him, and both girls were crying uncontrollably.

"You're coming with me," he commanded.

We both stared in shock.

Growling, clearly impatient, he grabbed Grace by the arm and started dragging her out of the room. She struggled; he had grabbed her too tightly.

"Come with us, or I'll shoot her," he told me.

I did what I was told. And to my utmost shock, Grace stopped fighting altogether as soon as she saw the gun up close. She had that glazed look on her face, the same one she had each time Mrs. Bradford came to take her away. That frightened me more than anything else.

In the hallway, we all started walking toward the other part of the house. I instantly knew what that meant. He wanted all of us inside his secret room.

Oh my God. Every part of my being told me to run away, to try to save myself. The rest forced me to remain calm and think, which wasn't easy. The feeling of panic was too great; it screamed inside my head.

"Since the lady of the house betrayed me and paid the price for that with her life, you will take over all her wifely duties," the reverend informed Grace. "Starting right now."

She simply nodded, looking completely submissive, but also terrified.

"We will all go to my playroom together, and then I will

have some alone time with my new wife, Mrs. Grace Bradford," he told the group as though he were speaking about something normal, something fun and celebratory, not about abuse or rape.

Chloe and Patricia cried even harder.

I was horrified at the prospect of it all. I was running out of time, and I didn't know what to do. I cursed myself for not stealing one of the knives from the kitchen because now I saw that I had the perfect opportunity to stab him in the back. And I would gladly do it, without a shred of remorse or hesitation.

As we reached the secret room, the reverend put the gun away so he could get the key and unlock the door.

At that moment something changed within Grace. Some kind of switch got pulled, and she started to struggle once again. "No, I won't do it," she said while trying to get out of his hold.

"What are you doing?" he asked, shocked by her behavior. "Stop that, right away," he ordered, but she wasn't listening. If anything, she struggled even harder to get away from him. He had to use both hands now to subdue her.

I saw this as my opportunity. While he was distracted by the newly awakened, defiant Grace, I pushed the younger girls behind me, ran full speed that short distance toward them, then jumped with all my power onto his back.

He stumbled a little, but recovered quickly. He was freakishly strong.

Seeing how I'd attempted to come to her rescue, Grace started fighting harder. I felt like cheering for her newfound strength and courage, but sadly I had more pressing and immediate issues.

I used the move Dad and Billy had taught me to try to

strangle the reverend with my arms around his neck. It was a very efficient move; then again, when I practiced it, my target wasn't moving around so erratically and with such strength.

I'll have to share that oversight with my dad if I survive this.

When I survive this, I corrected.

The reverend was stumbling around, slamming into things, trying to dislodge me, all the while stubbornly clinging to Grace. I wasn't complaining. While he was focused on her, he couldn't deal solely with me. With his focus divided, he was prone to making mistakes.

"I will never do those things again!" Grace screamed.

"I will kill you all for disobeying me, you vile creatures," he ranted.

I noted that he was starting to get out of breath. If I could just outlast him, I knew I would be able to eventually put him to sleep. Or even choke him to death. I wasn't picky.

And then I saw him releasing his hold on Grace with his right hand, and I knew what that meant. As he fumbled around his waist, trying to get the gun, I focused on choking him with all my might. I wasn't about to allow him to use that weapon.

Following my lead, Grace bit him hard on his arm.

He shouted in pain, and as the gun dropped from his grip, it went off.

39

JESSE

As we drove, Billy rang and apologized for threatening to call the police on me. I decided not to hold it against him, especially since he now offered help. I told him to stay put. I didn't expect too much resistance from the reverend. Nothing I'd heard so far suggested he had any kind of military training.

Billy also said he'd finally gotten in touch with his cousin James, who lived in the area. Apparently, his cousin had one of those pay-as-you-go phones and hadn't renewed it when it ran out of minutes until last night. It turned out that James thought Bradford was creepy, and he'd always stayed clear of him and his congregation, which only made me more suspicious of this so-called reverend.

It specifically stayed with me how James described the congregation who followed the reverend as behaving with a strange kind of worship and devotion. He clearly enjoyed the power and status of being a cult leader rather than a mere pastor.

No wonder he managed to delude himself that the rules didn't apply to him, that he could do whatever he wanted.

After my call with Billy, I told Dr. Sheldon everything I'd just learned about Reverend Gareth Bradford.

Dr. Sheldon said that if it was true, it was troubling on a few different levels. I took it that she thought he would be extremely dangerous.

"Do you think I should expect trouble from him?" I asked.

"I don't have enough information. However, I suspect a person like that can easily snap if things don't go his way. If his perception of reality started to unravel for whatever reason."

"Good to know." I picked up speed, knowing I needed to hurry.

Dr. Sheldon was silent for a few minutes as she checked Google Maps. "I think this is close enough," she finally said.

I parked at the side of the road and got out. Dr. Sheldon picked the perfect spot. We were close enough to the farmhouse, but out of their sightline, especially since there was a big tree with broadening branches blocking the view that I could use to camouflage the truck.

We really were in the middle of nowhere. Now I understood why Sam hadn't tried to escape. She had nowhere to run to.

"What are we going to do now, wait for full dark?" she asked.

It was already twilight, and the sun was nearly almost gone. "I don't want to wait," I replied.

We still had enough light to see by, so I grabbed my binoculars and looked toward the farm. There was nobody milling about apart from a few scrawny chickens. There were no children playing in the yard. The place had a deserted feeling to it.

A pretty basic wire fence ran around the edge of the property. It was high, but I wasn't concerned about it. I had my wire cutters in the truck. That wasn't what caught my attention, though.

"Check it out." I pointed, then offered the binoculars to Dr. Sheldon.

"Cameras," she said as she spotted them immediately.

"Yup."

The damn cameras were installed all around the property. Some were pointed on the outside to monitor who was coming and going, but the curious part was that the rest looked inwards, as though to monitor what was going on inside the property.

That son of a bitch had isolated all these kids in the middle of nowhere and built a prison to house them so he could do whatever he wanted. The very thought of it filled me with fury.

"I have to say this coincides with my theory that Reverend Bradford," she said, articulating his name with distaste, "suffers from a narcissistic disorder, to say the least."

"Can narcissists turn serial killers?" I wondered.

"It happens."

Rummaging through my duffel bag, I grabbed a bullet-proof vest to put on underneath my shirt. "Do you have any advice on how to handle him?"

"A bullet through his head would handle him nicely," she deadpanned.

"Luckily, I'm very proficient in that kind of handling," I countered in the same manner.

It took me by surprise that Dr. Sheldon shared my view

that it would be better for humanity if the reverend died today. Then again, she was an ex-soldier. We saw things and experienced things that made us see how sometimes the death of an individual was the only solution to a vast number of problems.

In this case, the reverend's death could free a bunch of innocent girls from their prison. It was as simple as that.

As I continued to gear up, I handed her a gun and a few extra clips just to be on the safe side.

"Are you sure you don't want me to come with you? I could watch your six," she offered.

"No, wait for me here. Besides, I think it's better if he thinks I came alone."

Dr. Sheldon nodded. "I can see how that plan can have its merits. I just wish we could stay in touch in some way."

"I'll call you if I need backup," I reassured her.

"You'd better."

"If I don't return with Sam in about fifteen minutes, and you don't hear from me, go get help."

I needed time to get to Sam and get her out. Then I needed to have a head start because we would have to flee the scene of the crime before the sheriff came to deal with that piece-of-shit reverend. If he was still breathing once I finished with him, I hedged.

"Are you sure this sheriff will come if I call?" she asked, clearly having second thoughts. "I know you two don't get along."

"He'll come if you call him," I reassured her. "I'm off."

"Please be careful," she advised, checking her gun with confidence, making sure it was loaded and ready to be used. I liked that on a woman.

I nodded.

Since I'd memorized where all the cameras were installed, I had no problem staying clear of them. I cut a piece of fence, luckily it wasn't electrified, so I could get in, then crawled through a bush until I hid in a cornfield. Very slowly, not to disturb the foliage too much, I neared the house. I couldn't hear a single sound coming from it. There was no TV on, no one talking or walking about. It was very strange.

If I didn't know better, I would think the place was empty. But a family van was parked in the garage, so it was safe to assume they were all inside, being freakishly quiet. That was deeply troubling because Sam was a pretty noisy teen. She was known to hum songs even while eating.

My gut feeling told me she was inside, so I circled the house, getting to know my surroundings. My training and war experience helped me to avoid all the motion-sensitive lights, uncovered windows, and cameras. I noticed a few major gaps in the defense system. It was apparent an amateur had installed it. That would work in my favor.

I found a few potential entry points. Besides the obvious, a back door leading to a kitchen, there was a second-story window I could climb to without being detected. There were basement windows as well; however, they were on the small side, so it would be a tight squeeze. Besides, breaking a glass window, especially since I couldn't know for sure how deep the basement was, would create a lot of noise.

I opted to climb through the second-story window. Although it was risky because I wasn't familiar with the layout of the house, I determined it was still better than going in from downstairs.

It was easy to climb up. I looked through the window

and saw an almost empty room. That was a relief. There was a table near the window that I would use to get inside.

So far, so good.

All of a sudden, I heard a man yelling. "What are you doing? Stop that, right away."

Without question, I knew that was the reverend's voice – but it wasn't aimed at me. I crept closer, looking at how to open the window without having to break it. I didn't want to alert the bastard that I was near.

In the next instant, it became apparent that some kind of struggle was occurring inside the house. At some point, I thought I heard Sam shouting. But I didn't allow panic to overpower me. To save her, I needed to do what I did best, and that was kill.

A strange kind of professional coolness washed over me, and for a split second, I felt like I was back in the war zone. I was back in that house searching for survivors, finding nothing but death instead.

My heart started beating like crazy. *No, not now.*

I repeated the mantra Dr. Sheldon had taught me that pushed me back to the here and now. I clung to that detachment, but didn't allow it to overpower me. I planned on using it without allowing it to consume me.

And then I was jolted from my concentration by the sound of a gun going off.

I knew I'd run out of time. I had to act now. There was no time for subtleties.

Sam needed me.

I immediately sprang into action. Lifting my boot, I was tempted to break the glass with one powerful kick, but then I reconsidered it. I couldn't announce my presence like that. Especially if a loaded gun was in play. I had to approach this scenario from a safe distance, that was the only way I could assess the situation and save Sam, which meant I needed another plan and fast.

I jumped down to the ground and started running. I reached one of the back side windows and decided to use it as an entry point after making sure the room was empty. Using the butt of the gun, I broke the window. In the next second, I was going through it, jumping to the floor. I made some noise, true, but not as much as I would have upstairs. With any luck, the reverend and the others wouldn't hear me coming.

Once again, I started running, trying to find the stairs. I had no idea what would be waiting for me up there, but I was prepared for anything. Of course, I would do my best to not allow any innocent people, the girls who lived with Sam in the house, to get hurt.

Hold on. I'm coming, Sam.

40

SAMANTHA

When the gun went off, Grace jumped away, then froze in place. And she wasn't the only one. We all took a collective pause to make sure the bullet didn't hit any of us girls. It didn't, which was a relief.

I hoped with all my heart the reverend would end up as the one who was bleeding. Unfortunately, he wasn't.

And then the moment passed, and the reverend doubled his efforts to push me off him.

Grace stopped helping me, and the younger girls watched the fight from a safe distance without interacting.

I was left completely alone to fend for myself. *Why are they just standing there?* They should help me, I thought, because we could only overpower him together. Only together could we win; only together could we save ourselves.

My grip around his neck was solid. But the reverend was fighting back with all the strength and determination he had, and he was so enraged by our mutiny that that energy was fueling his madness too. It was becoming harder and harder to hang on, especially considering I didn't have Grace to help me out anymore.

The only good thing in a pool of bad was that thanks to me holding him in a chokehold, he couldn't quite crouch down and get his gun back.

"I will kill you all for this disobedience," he threatened. "Do you know who I am? Do you know how much power I wield?"

I almost wanted to laugh at his absurd words, but I was losing strength, and I knew it was only a matter of time before he would throw me off like I was some rag doll. I had to do something, and fast, to truly overpower him.

"Don't just stand there," I yelled to no one in particular. "Do something!"

And at that point, the reverend turned sharply and pushed himself backward.

The sheer force of it made me knock my head against a cabinet. I discovered at that moment that the expression "she saw stars" wasn't merely a phrase. I was rendered completely disoriented.

The reverend tried to pry me loose, grabbing at my arms, trying to break them apart.

Shaking my head, desperate to shake the pain away, I forced myself to make a counterattack. Unfortunately, I was too slow. He yanked me hard by the arm, and I lost my grip, slipping down off his back.

I cursed.

He turned toward me, his eyes flashing with hate, his nostrils flaring with frustration. He didn't care I was only a fifteen-year-old girl. He wanted me dead.

I took a step backward, but there was nowhere to run. In one swift move, he pushed me against the wall, knocking the breath out of me, pinning me there with his body as he wrapped his hands around my neck and started to squeeze. He was determined to choke me to death.

Panic rose in me, and I struggled with all my strength. I dug my nails into his hands, trying to pry them away, but he was just too strong. As each second passed, the less oxygen I had, and the more I panicked, forgetting all the training I'd had with Dad.

I'm going to die! I screamed inside my head.

"I knew you would be a troublemaker the instant I saw you, and I was right," he yelled at me.

I tried to say something, tell him I was glad I was a thorn in his side, but I couldn't form the words because of all the pressure against my neck.

"I will so enjoy doing this," he growled into my face, his eyes bulging with deadly menace. "It's just a shame I didn't get a chance to play with you first."

There was so much I wanted to throw in his face. But I couldn't. I had to preserve the precious oxygen I was fast running out of.

"Go to hell," I mouthed since that was the best I could do.

I could see on his face that he'd managed to understand that. As a result, he gritted his teeth and squeezed even harder.

Stars danced in front of my eyes. I was no expert, but I was pretty sure that meant I was running out of time. My life was ebbing away from me.

I tried fighting, but even that became too hard for me. My arms felt heavy. Since prying his hands away proved fruitless, I abandoned the effort. If I could grab something and whack him in the head, I knew the pain would distract him long enough for me to get away.

And then I remembered the most basic thing. I managed to just barely raise my knee, but it was enough. I hit him hard and fast in the nuts, and he hissed in agony. The pressure of his hands around my neck loosened long enough so I could take a breath and scream.

My eyes landed on Grace. "Grab the gun," I pleaded. "Shoot him!"

Then he slapped me hard before he resumed choking the ever-loving life out of me. It hurt so much that I felt like sobbing.

Grace made a tentative step forward.

The reverend turned his gaze to glare at her. "Grace, don't you dare move, or I'll kill you too."

He will kill all of us either way, I wanted to say but couldn't.

His words stopped Grace in her tracks. She looked between me and the reverend, her expression ambivalent.

I'll be long dead before she gathers the nerve to act against that man, I thought with irritation.

But thankfully, my plea managed to wake someone else up.

I noticed a flash of movement as Chloe ran off but quickly returned.

I could see from the corner of my eyes that she held something. Was it a weapon? Was there a second gun in this place? Did she intend on poking him with a knitting needle?

"Are you planning on killing all of us?" Chloe asked, her voice wavering but determined.

I realized she was holding a phone. My phone. That

cheered me up no end. I hoped she had the police on the line.

"I'll do what needs to be done to eradicate evil from this household," he growled.

"You're the evil one," Patricia snapped at him.

"Can you repeat that?" Chloe asked him. "I want to make sure everyone can hear you."

"What are you talking about?" the reverend asked, turning his head to look at her.

"I'm live streaming on Facebook," Chloe explained almost cheerfully. "I hope you're all seeing this man trying to kill Samantha Cotton," she added. "Please, we need help."

The reverend's stance immediately changed as he realized he had a much broader audience. This turn of events clearly rattled him, and although he didn't want to stop choking me, his grip definitely wasn't as strong or committed as it was before.

I gave it my absolute all to pry his hands away while his attention was divided, while he was riddled with uncertainty about how to spin this situation to his favor.

"You're bluffing," he said. "You would never do something like that to me."

"Wave," Chloe urged. "This is going live."

The reverend finally realized that Chloe wasn't joking around, that this threat was real.

"Stop filming immediately," he ordered, a distinct note of panic in his voice.

Chloe didn't move a muscle. "It's time everyone learned what kind of monster you are. Reverend Gareth Bradford killed two girls who lived in this house."

"Stop speaking right this instant, I command you," he boomed.

"Tanya and Maria. He killed Detective Overton, who came to help us, and today he killed his wife, Evangeline Bradford, another monster," Chloe continued.

"I didn't kill anyone. I am the instrument of God," he said, in a vain attempt to defend himself.

I was painfully aware that I was about to grow too weak to do anything anymore. I was about to run out of air. But Chloe's actions gave me hope that there was a chance we could survive this, even as I continued to fight him off.

"Grace, take the phone away from Chloe," he commanded. "And get that gun from the floor for me, now."

Chloe looked at Grace with uncertainty, but she didn't stop filming.

My vision started to get blurry again, and pretty soon it would be game over for me. *I don't want to die. Please help me,* I prayed, not really sure to whom.

And then Grace started moving, and she picked up the gun from the floor.

"That's a good girl; now give it to me; then I can deal with Chloe," the reverend ordered, holding out a hand while continuing to press hard against my neck with the other.

With him having only one hand on my neck, I could breathe again, just barely.

Grace held the gun with both hands, pointing it at him.

"Shoot him," I tried to say. *Don't hesitate; just do it.*

He started to laugh. "Are you going to shoot me, Grace? Do you think any of this matters? Do you think you will accomplish anything?"

"We matter, and we will stop you," Grace replied.

That only made him laugh harder. "Stop fooling around, Grace. I know you won't turn against me."

"And why is that?" Chloe asked instead of Grace.

Grace appeared to be in a trance. She wasn't even blinking while she held the reverend at gunpoint. Her stance was full of confidence, her hands unwavering. I was impressed.

"Because I know the truth. She likes it," he taunted. "She likes to be with me, that's why she always returns to me, night after night. She is my Eve, my favorite temptress."

Grace paled, and I felt a surge of compassion for her.

He chuckled again. "That's why she will never shoot me. Because I own her. Do you hear me, Grace? You belong to me."

We didn't get a chance to hear what Grace had to say, if anything, because all of a sudden, the sound of shattering glass startled all of us.

41

JESSE

As I rushed up the stairs, all I thought about was Sam.

When I reached them, it took me a second to take the whole scene in. A man I recognized from my research online was strangling my daughter, who was trying to fight him off while three other girls stood around them. The smallest girl was crying, a slightly older one was seemingly filming everything, and a third one held the reverend at gunpoint. *That's probably the gun that went off.*

I also noted the absence of Mrs. Bradford, and that kept me on high alert, not wanting her to jump out at me with a knife to defend her husband.

I trained my gun on the asshole and stepped forward. "If you don't let my daughter go by the time I count to one, I will blow your fucking head off," I said calmly, because that was no threat, it was a fucking promise.

"Mr. Cotton, do you always walk into someone else's house uninvited?" the reverend replied almost conversationally.

"I was invited, and I said let her go," I barked out. "Don't make me repeat myself."

"I was just educating her, but I understand now where her lack of manners comes from." The reverend grabbed Sam, then pushed her in front of him.

Sam barely reached his shoulders, yet he still tried to hide behind her. *Pathetic leech.* His grip was around her neck and on her left shoulder. She gasped for air. That made me see red.

"Maybe it's time I educate you to pick on someone your own size."

"It wouldn't be a fair fight. You're holding a gun."

I had to admit that this to-and-fro was getting on my nerves. "That's right. And this young lady beside me is holding a gun on you as well, which means get your filthy hands off my daughter," I snapped, losing patience.

"Grace is not important," he said dismissively. "However, will you risk shooting your daughter just to get to me?"

"I never miss." I dared to look at Sam for a split second. Although banged up, she was on high alert, which was good.

"Then I'll even the odds. Grace, give that gun to me," he said.

The girl looked at the reverend as though not completely understanding his words. The gun started to tremble in her hands, and the lack of expression on her face really started to bother me. It smelled of trouble.

I had to take care of this situation before she snapped out of that stupor and gave him the gun or, worse, reacted to something and started shooting. I couldn't allow that, not while my daughter was in the crossfire.

I had to admit that the reverend wasn't a complete idiot. He knew the shield in front of him was smaller than him, which was why he somewhat crouched and moved around, trying to make himself a harder target to hit. At the same time, I noted that he wasn't in complete alignment with Sam.

My daughter moved ever so slightly, just the way I'd taught her, so that now part of his left side was exposed.

I gave a signal to Sam that something was about to go down, so she could be ready to react. I knew I was about to startle the other girls; nevertheless, that was a risk I had to take.

Without wasting any more time, I shot the son of a bitch in the foot.

The reverend screamed in pain.

Sam pulled from him, spun around, and kicked him in the ribs, since his grip on her had already loosened, and then she rolled away, rushing toward me.

The other girls screamed as the reverend dropped to the ground, writhing in pain and bleeding heavily from his foot.

My aim had been perfect. I'd wanted to incapacitate him, and I did. I was also proud of my self-control that I hadn't put a bullet into his skull, *yet*.

"Dad," Sam breathed, her voice all scratchy. Painful-looking bruises were already forming on her neck.

I held her tightly in my arms while still taking aim on that asshole. "You okay?" I asked her.

"I am now."

I nodded because all of a sudden I was so angry it was hard to breathe let alone talk. I wanted to empty the entire clip into that man's skull. Then again, he was no man. A real man would never behave in this manner.

"What are you screaming about, you dim-witted cows? Give me that gun or shoot the bastard. Look what he did to me," he rambled, staring at the girl he'd called Grace, yet screaming at all of them.

Now that Sam was safely nestled beside me, my top priority was to take the gun away from that girl. It was a huge liability.

"You're down on the ground and bleeding, and still you think you're the one in command," I noted with a shake of my head. Dr. Sheldon was right; this man definitely had a diagnosis.

The reverend's eyes flashed with anger, annoyance, and something else. Madness, perhaps.

"You got your daughter back; now leave," he told me.

"Our score is not settled." *Not by a long shot.*

He sat up and leaned against the wall. "I won't say a thing to the police if you just leave us be. Go now, and let me live with my daughters."

"We can't leave these girls with that monster, Dad," Sam pleaded with me.

"Of course not," I reassured her. Something like that had never even crossed my mind.

"He's pure evil. There are four dead bodies in the basement," Sam informed me.

"Four? You said three to Hillie," I said.

"It's true, he's killed four people," the girl with the phone agreed. "He killed two girls who tried to run away. He couldn't let them go because he'd forced them to do pornography."

My blood froze in my veins.

"And then he killed the detective," the girl with the phone continued.

So I was right; the detective hadn't blown me off; he'd gotten himself killed. Now I felt bad for thinking ill of him at first. He had been a good man, trying to do a good thing, and it had cost him his life. *I will avenge you, my man.*

"And today he killed his wife, and he wants Grace to take her place," she concluded.

"Lies, all lies," the reverend countered feverishly. "These girls are all wicked. God sent them to me to return them to the path of righteousness."

I was thoroughly disgusted by these revelations, and I needed a moment to process it all. The situation in this house was far worse than I could ever have imagined. This man was a sexual abuser of children, and then to cover up his crimes, he killed anyone who threatened to expose the truth.

I really wanted to blow his brains out then and there. I could picture myself pulling the trigger so we would all be done with him, justice served.

Then again, that wasn't the kind of man I wanted to be anymore. That wasn't the example I wanted to give to Sam. I was done killing, and the reverend needed to pay for everything he'd done to these girls. He needed to pay for taking so many lives.

"You deserve to die for everything you've done," I said eventually. "But I believe it's a far greater punishment to let you live and go to jail for the rest of your disgusting life, you poor excuse of a man."

The reverend started laughing. "Jail? I'll never go to jail. I'm a man of God. I'm a pillar of the community, and nobody will believe you over me. Nobody will believe such lies from some ill-behaved, vindictive girls and some crackpot survivalist. I'm the victim here."

"And what about the dead bodies?" the other girl questioned.

"You all did that," the reverend said.

By the look on his face, one would think he believed that. He was completely insane. It was genuinely frightening being confronted by someone like that.

"We have everything recorded, you asshole," the girl with the phone pointed out.

"Which I didn't give my consent for," he countered.

Sam looked at me. "Is he right?"

The reverend now turned to look at Grace. "Grace, give that gun to me. This little mutiny is over."

Grace started walking toward him, very slowly and tentatively, as though some invisible thread was pulling her forward against her will.

I couldn't believe that she would listen to him after everything. Was his power over her that strong, that complete? I dreaded the answer.

"Grace, please don't give him the gun," Sam pleaded. "Think of what you're doing."

"Please, Grace, don't let him win," the other girl cried out too, while the third simply cried.

I could see that it was obvious Grace wasn't listening. She only had eyes and ears for the reverend.

I knew this girl was traumatized, abused, hurt, but I had to stop this one way or the other. Although it pained me greatly, I took aim to shoot. My plan was to shoot his hand before he could reach for the gun. However, I could already see that she would block me a bit and that my angle would be wrong, which meant I would be forced to shoot at the gun itself.

"That's a good little girl," the reverend practically taunted while Grace walked closer to him. He was absolutely gloating.

"Don't be his slave, Grace; fight back," Sam tried again.

"Your words mean nothing," the reverend snapped. "Grace belongs to me, and she always will."

My finger started to itch. *Maybe I should put a bullet into his head to stop him from talking ever again. Save us all from all this misery.*

And then it was too late. Grace stood over the reverend.

Without a word, wearing that same blank expression on her face since I arrived, Grace made a move as though to give the reverend the gun.

Instead of doing that, she fired. The bullet went straight to the reverend's head, taking half of his face in the process, and he slumped back to the ground.

She had killed him.

42

SAMANTHA

There was a lot to process since the moment Dad arrived. I knew I was saved the instant I saw him.

While the reverend was strangling me, all I wanted was for Dad to shoot him so we could all be done with him. But then he didn't. And I understood why. It was to offer these girls and me proper closure. It was to show us there was justice in this world after all.

Unfortunately, everything changed in an instant once again when Grace shot the reverend. She simply approached and pulled the trigger. And just like that, with a flick of her finger, the monster was dead.

That is her form of closure, I suppose.

There was a collective moment of silence as this new reality, a reality without the reverend living and breathing, started to sink in.

"Is he really dead?" Patricia asked, breaking the silence.

"Yes, he is. He won't be able to hurt us ever again," Chloe replied.

The two girls started hugging and crying.

Grace dropped the gun. When it hit the floor, she snapped out of her state and looked about like she was emerging from a dream.

I'd never seen her like this before. I couldn't quite describe the change, but she seemed lighter somehow.

The two girls invited her with a gesture, and she went to them, sharing a long group hug. It didn't matter that she had blood on her. Because that blood belonged to the man they all hated from the bottom of their hearts.

I hugged my dad tightly, relieved and happy this nightmare was finally over.

Eventually, the girls let go of one another, and Grace looked startled as though noticing my father for the first time.

"Should we call the police?" I offered.

"We will," Grace replied. "But you can't stay here and wait for them. You need to leave."

"We're not going anywhere without you." I was adamant.

"We can't just leave," Grace explained. "We need to tell the world what's happened. But you have to go. Last week, I overheard the reverend telling someone in the sheriff's department to arrest your dad on the spot if he ever came near this house."

"So the bastard did have connections in the sheriff's department," my dad grumbled.

Grace nodded. "So go now, or they'll arrest us all."

"All the more reason why we should stick around and argue about it," I insisted.

A minute ago, Grace was like a zombie or a girl possessed, but now she was her usual infuriating self. I instantly felt bad for having such a thought and banished it.

Dad took charge. "I think I have a solution. Let's get out

of this house first and continue our conversation on the porch."

We all started to leave when Grace stopped us. "Just one more thing."

I looked at her questioningly as she approached the reverend. Then she spat on him. The other girls followed suit, me included.

That felt good.

"Now we can leave," Grace declared.

I liked this new version of Grace. Probably the real version of Grace. And for her to emerge, only one very bad man had to die.

"So what's the plan?" I asked Dad once we were outside. Being able to breathe fresh air after being stuck in that house for too long felt divine. It felt even better knowing I would never have to return to it again.

"I have a friend waiting at the foot of the drive."

"Is it Billy?" I asked.

Dad shook his head. "Let me call her," he said, dialing.

Her?

As he spoke over the phone, my mind was still buzzing with all this new information. Dad came to save me. The reverend was dead. Mrs. Bradford was dead. *I'm free. Finally.* We were all free. Sort of. We still had this big mess to clean up, which meant we were not quite out of the woods yet.

"What will happen to us now?" Patricia asked.

I wished I could tell her a nice family would adopt her. That she would live in a nice house with a big yard, and a cute dog, and be happy for the rest of her life. She deserved that after enduring all this pain and suffering. We all did.

Unfortunately, I already knew that life didn't work that way.

"She's on the way," Dad informed me, and true enough, we saw the truck approaching us. My dad's truck.

The arrival of this newcomer saved us from having to answer Patricia. The truck stopped in front of us, and a woman got out. My dad introduced her as Dr. Sheldon. I noticed immediately that she was very pretty.

"How can I help?" she asked.

"We need a plan of action," my dad explained. "My options right now are to stay and possibly end up in jail, or leave, but I don't want to leave without these girls."

"And I'm not letting you leave without me," I said, feeling the need to point that out. I wasn't going to allow anything or anyone to separate us again. He was my family, and family had to stick together, no matter what.

Although my father was imperfect and flawed, I felt like he was actually trying for the first time to get better, and that meant everything to me. Not to mention he was always there for me. And that was why I wanted to go with him. I couldn't trust the system to make a good decision, not after this fiasco. The system was broken, and those people definitely didn't have my best interests at heart. I'd experienced that as a fact. That was why it was on me to decide.

"And where is the reverend?" Dr. Sheldon wanted to know.

"Dead upstairs," Grace and I said at the same time.

"Good," Dr. Sheldon replied.

I think I like her.

"You can both leave," Grace offered to me. "I'll stay with the girls to clean up this mess."

"No, you need to come with us too," I insisted. "I don't

want to leave you here at the mercy of the system again. You'd be better off without relying on the government."

"I don't want to be forced to run for the rest of my life," Grace pointed out. "I'm tired, Samantha. I'm almost eighteen, and I want to be free."

"What about us?" Chloe asked with great sorrow in her eyes.

"I'm not leaving you. I'll find a way to take care of you. We're sticking together," Grace promised.

Can you really make that promise? were the words on the tip of my tongue. "Grace, you can't do it all by yourself. Let me and my dad help."

"Samantha, this is my choice. Please let me make it."

Perhaps she was right. For way too long she'd been forced to live in a certain way, behave in a certain way. For way too long she'd been forced to do despicable things, without having a voice, and without free will. If this was what she wanted, then so be it.

"Okay, but that still doesn't solve the problem of all those dead bodies inside the house," I said, pointing out the obvious.

"I see this is a real conundrum," Dr. Sheldon replied.

"Any suggestions?" my dad asked her.

"I believe Grace is right. You and Sam need to leave. You've suffered enough, and it's not worth risking jail time over that monster."

I couldn't agree more.

"And I'll stay with the girls. I'll make sure they're well taken care of and nothing bad happens to them ever again," Dr. Sheldon promised. "You have my word."

"I shot the reverend," Grace said meekly. "Will they try me as an adult? Will I go to jail?"

"You won't go to jail," I insisted. "You protected yourself; you protected all of us."

"That's right," Dr. Sheldon agreed. "You did what you had to do, and I'll hire a lawyer to prove that if it comes to it."

Grace looked somewhat reassured.

"Are you sure you can handle it all by yourself?" my dad asked Dr. Sheldon.

"Yes, go," she said, and her voice brooked no argument. "You must promise me that you won't stop working on yourself. You're a good dad, but you can't stop with what we were doing. Your healing isn't complete."

"I promise," my dad replied without a thought.

I finally put the pieces together. This was the therapist he'd talked to me about. "I won't let him stop either," I added.

"Perfect," Dr. Sheldon replied. "And I'll try to keep you out of this."

"Don't bother. There's a video that's probably circling the web already with everything that happened today broadcast on it," I said, making a face.

I wasn't looking forward to living with something like that for the rest of my life. It was common knowledge that what ended up on the internet stayed there forever. *I will seriously kill myself if I become a meme!*

"Oh, right, this is yours," Chloe said, giving me my phone back.

"Thanks, and thank you for doing what you did. It saved my life." It was true: I would be dead if it weren't for Chloe. She'd bought us time until my dad arrived. Then again, I was sure we would have been able to save ourselves without him, I thought as I looked at Grace.

"There's a video?" Dr. Sheldon asked.

"I'll explain everything later," Grace reassured her.

Dr. Sheldon handed the truck keys to my dad.

"Thank you for everything," he said to her.

I turned to look at Grace, Chloe, and Patricia. "I don't know what to say. For whatever strange reason, I don't want to leave you," I confessed.

"Samantha, Sam," Grace corrected herself, "thank you for everything, and for what it's worth, I'm sorry I told the reverend you might try to run. I was scared for you. You and your dad saved us."

There were tears in all our eyes as we hugged each other.

I clung to those girls, feeling connected to them for the first time. They weren't my real sisters, I didn't even like them that much at times, but in this moment right now, I knew I loved them and that I would always be there for them.

43

JESSE

It was all over now. The war was over.

Sam was once again with me, as she should be, which meant all was right in my world.

I parked the truck at the side of the road so we could look at the house and see what was happening. I didn't feel comfortable leaving without making sure the police would actually do their job.

We got out and sat on the hood. My daughter was lost in thought, and usually I would let her be, but I asked, "You want to talk about it?"

Sam took a deep breath and got me up to speed with all that had happened since she'd arrived at that damn farm.

It filled me with fury listening to how she'd tried to resist and fight back against their restrictions, all the while enduring all kinds of punishments. And then she got to the really scary part, the part about a secret room with its bed and its camera, and a basement where dead bodies were stuffed in a corner. I felt like I should say something to her, but didn't know what. I wished I could ask Dr. Sheldon, but it was about time I learned these things on my own.

Eventually, we saw the police cars accompanied by an ambulance driving toward the house. It was pretty dark outside by then, which worked in our favor. They really didn't have to bother with the ambulance. Hearses would have been more practical.

Of course, it didn't take long for the news vans to gather at the entrance of the farm and start reporting.

"Glad we dodged that bullet," I commented, feeling grateful nobody would get a chance to shove a camera into my face.

Sam said nothing.

"Are you feeling guilty you're not there with them?" I guessed.

"Maybe," she confessed. "It was just so horrible, Dad. And the worst part was that I didn't do anything about it."

"What do you mean you didn't do anything? You got me here; you inspired the other girls to fight," I pointed out, not liking her frame of mind at the moment.

At the same time, knowing the reverend was the reason my daughter was now feeling like this, thinking like this, made me see red. If I could resurrect that bastard to kill him all over again, slowly and painfully this time around, I would.

"You put up one hell of a fight," I added.

She touched the bruises around her neck and winced. And then she smiled. "I really pushed all his buttons."

I was very proud of her. "I wished you didn't have to go through it alone. I tried to get to you, but they wouldn't let me."

"I know, Dad. We both did our best."

We stayed silent for a bit. "I had hoped I would be able to accomplish something when I saw that detective arriving," Sam said eventually.

"Detective Overton, I met him," I offered. "I convinced him to pay you a visit, to make sure all was well."

"I figured that was the case when he mentioned fire elemental," Sam replied.

"That was the only thing that came to mind at the moment."

"It worked," she said with a nod.

"In the end, I only managed to get him killed," I said with a frown. I felt horribly guilty about that. If only I knew then what I know now, I would never have sent him on that mission. We could have come up with a better plan.

"Dad, that wasn't your fault. The reverend killed him because one of the girls broke their silence and told him about the two dead girls and the secret room, and she begged to be taken away." Sam shivered at the memory of it.

I hugged her. I believed that physical connection managed to calm both of us down, at least a little.

So the reverend panicked and killed the detective. "Why did he kill his wife?" I asked.

Sam looked away. "That was my fault. I discovered something about Mrs. Bradford that she'd kept as a secret, so I made sure the reverend discovered it too. He got so mad about it that he killed her."

"That's not your fault, Sam. You didn't kill her. You were smart, getting your enemies to fight among themselves," I insisted. "You weakened them."

"I guess," she said meekly.

It all made sense to me now. All the pieces fit. *Well, almost.*

"How did the reverend know who I was?" I asked. "He called me a survivalist."

"I also have a feeling he knew more than he should have," Sam provided.

That didn't sound right to me. And I was sure something like that was illegal. *Is there a chance he targeted Sam and me on purpose?*

It was obvious he had a lot of influential friends, including in the sheriff's department. A man like him, with his vile tastes, who was to say he didn't make a deal with someone from CPS to get him what he wanted?

I planned on discovering the truth and uncovering all his corrupt, despicable helpers too. Anyone involved in this horror show should be severely punished. Bringing them all down and destroying them for good was my new mission in life. That, and helping Sam heal.

"I can't believe that in the end, Grace was the one who killed him," she said after a short pause. "Good for her."

"Good for her," I agreed.

Sometimes the only way to overcome your nightmares is to slay the monster plaguing you in the first place.

"Do you think they'll be all right?"

I understood what she was asking me. "With time," I replied honestly. "And some proper help."

"I wish I could do more for them," she said with a sigh. "It feels cowardly to leave them like this, to deal with all that mess."

I hugged her. Katarina and I raised her well, to always take care of others. Unfortunately, at times that entailed feeling like this. Like she'd failed, like she'd not done enough.

"Sam, my little soldier, I'm very proud of you for surviving such a terrible ordeal. You helped the other girls survive as well, and more importantly, you showed them the strength that lies within them, and that is no small thing considering the circumstances," I pointed out. "And I know your mother is very proud of you as well. We couldn't have asked for a better daughter," I said, while my eyes grew all watery, misty.

I told the absolute truth. Katarina would be proud. She would also get after me for putting our daughter in danger in the first place, but that was a different matter.

Then again, every cloud has a silver lining. These girls would still be living in oppression, abused every day if Sam hadn't come and messed with the Bradfords' plans.

"Thank you for coming for me," Sam said, and I noted tears in her voice as well.

"Of course I came, always," I replied without thought.

"Yeah, but now you're at risk of losing everything," she said glumly.

"Sam, you're my everything, so I haven't lost a thing."

"What about our house? Our lives back home, our friends?"

"None of that matters to me. As I said, you're the only thing that matters. I'll never stop trying to be a better dad to you because I know I haven't always been." And I had plenty to make up for. "I'll never try to hurt myself again, and I'll never leave you alone again either," I vowed. That was my biggest regret, one I would spend the rest of my life trying to atone for.

We hugged again. And I held my daughter tightly, letting her feel all my love.

As we had our little heart-to-heart moment, on the farm things were unraveling the way they should. The girls were questioned, crime scenes were established, and the press was kept at bay. As she'd promised, Dr. Sheldon remained with the girls the whole time.

"We'd better leave before the manhunt begins," I said.

They would know one girl was missing by now, and they would immediately assume she had something to do with everything that had happened. Cops were known to be limited like that.

Although Sam had mentioned there was a video of the whole showdown, thanks to the girl with her phone, it would take a while to untangle this whole mess, and I really didn't want us waiting around for that to happen.

"Where are we going?" Sam asked as we got into the truck.

Luckily, we had our emergency bags already packed in the back, where I always kept them in case we needed to bug out. There were enough clothes, cash, and canned goods to sustain us for weeks. Still, I wasn't planning on keeping us in the wild that long, or at all. I wanted Sam to sleep in a safe bed as soon as possible.

"Wyoming border, I have some friends there, with a big piece of land," I replied. I knew they would hide us and help us to stay off-grid for as long as we wanted.

"Are they survivalists like us?" Sam guessed.

I nodded. "At times like this, you can only trust family and friends, nobody else."

44

SAMANTHA

A few months had passed since Dad rescued me from the reverend, although he liked to say I rescued myself.

As promised, Dad took us to his friends who lived close to the Wyoming border. Logan and Maya Grey were cattle farmers, and their ranch felt like it was the size of a small European country. The couple and all their children welcomed us like we were family. They settled us in one of their workers' cabins, which was really nice and cozy.

Dad and I helped around the ranch, and it helped take my mind off everything I had endured to get to this place. I had nightmares still, but knowing Dad was beside me, protecting me, helped a lot. There were days I missed home and my friends, but I reminded myself that home was where my family was, and friends were one video call away, so all was well.

Dad started fixing cars and other equipment on the ranch, and word got around, so now he was making a pretty decent living. We could live someplace else if we wanted to, but we liked the ranch, and we wanted to stay off-grid. We didn't want to deal with the police, the prosecutors, judges, social workers, and all the other government people who had failed us time and time again.

I was relieved when it became public knowledge that the reverend was forcing his foster daughters to pose for photographs and videos of them dressing and undressing for his pedophile ring. However, he'd never caught on camera the actual acts of him raping them, and I knew Grace, Chloe, and Patricia were grateful that was the case.

Although I felt sorry that the girls had to be re-traumatized in such a way, I thought it was important for everyone to know the truth. I worried that some would try to portray him as some kind of saint and defend him to the end. Luckily, that didn't happen. What irked me the most was the fact they called Mrs. Bradford a victim, not another criminal, but there was nothing I could do about it, at least not while we were still in hiding.

I wished with all my heart that they were both now in hell, experiencing everything they did to the girls, tenfold.

Dad asked me if I had been one of the reverend's victims. It wasn't an easy conversation for either of us. I told him everything that man did to me. Although he never got a chance to take me to that secret room, dress me up, or abuse me, he did plenty of other stuff; he wounded me. And I knew I would have to carry those scars for the rest of my life.

Some of the reverend's friends and congregation members were arrested when detectives went over the house and investigated the reverend's office. The police managed to bust that vile pedophile ring, making the world a safer place, at least a little bit. We found out from Dr. Sheldon that the reverend had a file about me and my dad. It looked as though he might have actually targeted me.

I wasn't surprised when it was discovered the sheriff was one of the reverend's circle of abusers.

Dad took the news harder than I did. "I should have known. I begged for help, and he wouldn't budge. Now I know why. He was covering his ass. He was a sick fuck like the other guy."

A few people from CPS were also arrested and charged. Surprisingly, the social worker who was assigned to my case was clean. She'd genuinely believed she was doing a good thing. I saw her on TV crying her eyes out, blaming herself. And I was glad. She should feel guilty and blame herself for not doing her freaking job properly. Maybe in the future she would do better and actually help some boy or girl by sending them to a safe and loving environment, and then checking in on them to make sure they felt safe and loved.

It was also discovered why the reverend killed Tanya and Maria. It was exactly as we suspected all along. They planned on running away and sharing their story with the authorities – so he was afraid of being exposed. It was never proven, but I sincerely believed Mrs. Bradford had helped him. Tanya's diary was found among the reverend's things, and in it she'd written about all the details of the abuse she'd suffered. It broke my heart to learn of the things she and the other girls had to endure.

Grace, Chloe, and Patricia told the world how the reverend killed Detective Overton to protect his secrets. And how he killed his wife in a fit of rage. My little blackmail stunt never came to light. Grace was never charged for killing the reverend. It was self-defense, period. Everything turned out for the best. Thankfully.

Of course, there were stories about me too. They called me the ringleader who encouraged the other girls to mutiny against the Bradfords, which eventually resulted in the reverend's demise when Grace killed him with his own gun.

Although that wasn't what happened, I had to admit, if only to myself, that I kind of liked that version of events. Perhaps it could inspire others to never accept the fate that was forced on them. That it was better to fight than live in oppression.

The police searched for me and my dad, but not for too long. We were called persons of interest, but we had no intentions of answering that call. At one point they even presumed I'd died in all that chaos because the video Chloe made stopped moments before my dad shot the reverend in the leg. Apparently, my phone battery had died, but Chloe simply pretended to keep filming to mess with the reverend's head.

I really loved that girl.

I was relieved that all the girls were safe and sound and together. Dr. Sheldon kept her word and managed to get Grace a job. And since she had turned eighteen, and this was such a public case, she was allowed to take care of Chloe and Patricia and become their legal guardian.

They all lived with Dr. Sheldon, who helped them get past all the traumas they'd endured. I knew my dad sent them money each week, and I was glad. I wanted to see them to make sure they were really safe, but I didn't know if that was allowed.

Once Dad deemed it safe enough, we drove to the nearest town to get supplies. I was really looking forward to it. Although life on the ranch was never dull, I was itching for some civilization. Besides, I could use some new clothes even if they came from a thrift shop.

Although this was my first time in this small town, I

didn't feel like a complete outsider. All the people were friendly. People back home had treated us like pariahs, yet here it seemed that the residents had no problems with the Greys being survivalists.

After we bought everything we needed, Dad decided to stop at a diner. As the waitress delivered our orders, my eyes landed on the TV. I groaned. It was just our luck that a program about the infamous Bradford Farm murders was airing.

Dad followed my gaze. "Want me to ask them to change the channel?"

I shook my head. Although part of me was worried someone might recognize us, I was curious to hear what they had to say. We stayed informed, but I always liked to hear more. Dad called it my morbid curiosity.

It was clear that the story about a reverend who molested young girls who were supposed to be in his care and who had killed a bunch of people on his farm was refusing to go away. Each day new things were discovered, and more people were brought on air to speak out about Reverend and Mrs. Bradford. It appeared the whole country had a macabre fascination with the Bradfords and their house of horrors.

Today one of the reverend's childhood friends was being interviewed. I watched for a few minutes.

"Do you think we can ever go home and resume our lives on our farm?" I asked.

Dad stopped eating to look at me. "I don't know, kiddo."

"Do you miss it?" I asked.

"I miss the memories I created with your mom there. Then again, besides Billy and Emily, I don't miss that place," he said honestly.

I nodded, understanding. We were still in touch with

Billy and Emily, and they'd even promised to come and visit soon.

"How about you?" he asked. "Do you miss it?"

"Sometimes. At the same time, I really don't feel ready to deal with the police, the CPS, and all that lot," I confessed.

"Then it's decided. We'll stay on the ranch for a while."

That was fine by me.

I glanced at the TV. "Oh, Dad?"

"Yes?"

"Could you ask them to change the channel after all?"

I'd had enough of the Bradfords for a lifetime. It was time to concentrate on better things in life.

THANK YOU FOR READING

Did you enjoy reading *The Other Family*? Please consider leaving a review on Amazon. Your review will help other readers to discover the novel.

ABOUT THE AUTHOR

Theo Baxter has followed in the footsteps of his brother, best-selling suspense author Cole Baxter. He enjoys the twists and turns that readers encounter in his stories.

ALSO BY THEO BAXTER

Psychological Thrillers

The Widow's Secret

The Stepfather

Vanished

It's Your Turn Now

The Scorned Wife

Not My Mother

The Lake House

The Honey Trap

If Only You Knew

The Dream Home

Lie to Me

The Other Family

Theo Baxter Psychological Thriller Box Set

The Detective Marcy Kendrick Thriller Series

Skin Deep - Book #1

Blood Line - Book #2

Made in United States
Cleveland, OH
06 March 2025

14936026R00187